Puffin Books
Editor: Kaye Webb
Warrior Scarlet

'If the thing is worth a fight, fight for it and do not hear the Grandfather too clearly. There are ways – ways round, and ways through, and ways over. If you have not two hands for a bow, then learn to use a throw-spear with such skill that your enemies, and your brothers, forget that it is not from choice.'

So Talore One-Hand the Hunter advises Drem, who has plunged into the depth of unhappiness because his Grandfather said he could never take his place among the warriors of the tribe. Drem had only one good arm, and for this reason, said Grandfather, he would have to go and keep sheep with the Half People. But Drem, inspired by Talore's words, renews his lifelong ambition to prove himself a man and a warrior. He goes to the Boys' House and patiently embarks on the long, tough training for manhood, in spite of his handicap. The prize is the right to wear the warrior's scarlet – but to win the prize and to prove oneself a man it was necessary to kill a wolf single-handed. With fierce determination Drem stubbornly defeats obstacle after obstacle, from the taunts of his companions to his fight with another New Spear before the King himself – but physical ability was not the only thing necessary for him, for the black time came when he missed his wolf and was sent to the sheep, after all.

How, even then, Drem triumphs at last, and beyond his wildest dreams, makes an absorbing and moving tale, told by one of the foremost authors for young people writing today.

Rosemary Sutcliff

Warrior
Scarlet

Illustrated by Charles Keeping

Puffin Books
in association with Oxford University Press

Puffin Books, Penguin Books Ltd, Harmondsworth, Middlesex, England
Penguin Books, 625 Madison Avenue, New York, New York 10022, U.S.A.
Penguin Books Australia Ltd, Ringwood, Victoria, Australia
Penguin Books Canada Ltd, 41 Steelcase Road West, Markham,
Ontario, Canada
Penguin Books (N.Z.) Ltd, 182–190 Wairau Road, Auckland 10,
New Zealand

First published by Oxford University Press 1958
Published in Puffin Books 1976

Copyright © Oxford University Press, 1958

Made and printed in Great Britain by
Cox & Wyman Ltd, London, Reading and Fakenham
Set in Monotype Bembo

Historical Note

'The Bronze Age.' The words have the ring of strong magic about them, conjuring up harp music and the clash of weapons, the thunder of ponies' hooves and chariot wheels along the green ridgeways of the Downs, the rattle of the loom-weights where the women are weaving by the house-place door, the wind-torn, smoky flames of a chieftain's funeral pyre. It is a description that could stand, without much alteration, for Homeric Greece; and that, I think, is the secret of the magic. The time of which Homer sang was the Heroic Age of Greece, and the Bronze Age is ours. Far rougher and more primitive than the Greek, of course, but a Heroic Age, all the same, though the heroes are forgotten.

But this story is not about Kings or heroes or battles (not even a Heroic Age could be all heroes and fighting) and there are no chariots in it, because when I came to write it down, I found that although the Golden People had ponies, it was the next wave of invaders who brought chariot warfare into Britain. It is the story of a boy called Drem, who lived with his Tribe on what is now the South Downs, nine hundred years before the birth of Christ. His land and his people were not cut off from the rest of the world; the Baltic amber and blue Egyptian beads that the archaeologists find today in Bronze Age grave mounds show that clearly enough. But probably he never heard much of what went on in the world beyond his own hunting runs; a world in which Troy had fallen three hundred years ago, and Egypt was already past its greatest days, and a hollow among the hills by the ford of a rather muddy river had still more than a hundred years to wait before wild Latin herdsmen pitched their tents there and founded Rome.

Contents

1   Scarlet on the Loom

The old shepherd sitting with his face turned seaward and his broad-bladed spear across his knees, seemed as much a part of the downs as did the wind-stunted whitethorn trees along the bank behind him: a little man, dark and knotted and tough as a furze root, with fine wrinkles round his eyes, under their jut of badger-grey brows, that told of a lifetime of looking into the distance in sun and wind and rain. He was naked save for a sheepskin belted around his waist, and on the bare brown skin of his sides and shoulders showed the puckered silvery lines of more than one wolf-scar. Two great herd dogs lay beside him; one old and wise and grey-muzzled like himself, one young and gangling; and a boy of about nine summers old squatted at his feet, playing with the ears of the young one.

The boy also was half naked, but his kilt was of rough woollen stuff dyed with the red-brown crotal dye, and in all other ways he was as different from the old man as though they came from different worlds; the skin of his broad, hot-tempered face – of his whole body – freckle-dusted and fair, his hair the colour of polished copper, and his eyes grey with golden flecks in them; eyes that would seem when he was excited or angry to be all gold.

The boy stopped playing with the dog's ears, and laid his arm across his updrawn knees and his chin on his arm, gazing southward where the chalk fell in long, slow turf slopes and ridges, between willow and hazel choked combes, into the forest and the Marsh Country far below, and the Marshes spread away and away to the shining bar of the Great Water on the edge of the world. Below him the turf of the steep combe-side was laced with criss-cross sheep-tracks, and the faint formless cropping sounds of the flock at the bottom came up to him along the ground. Far off and lower down on the other side of the combe, he could see the tiny figures of Flann and his dogs, on watch also over the sheep. Flann whistled to one of the dogs, and the sound came clear across the combe, a tiny, shining arrow-point of sound in the great quietness. A little warm wind came up from the south, trailing the cloud shadows after it across the Marshes and up the slow-gathering slopes of the Chalk, thyme-scented and sea-scented and swaying the heads of the blue scabious flowers all one way. The shadow of a hawk swept across the turf below him, and the sun was hot on his head: the day was good.

Drem – the boy's name was Drem – heaved a small sigh of contentment. He liked it up here on the High Chalk with Doli and the others of the shepherd kind. Several times this summer and last, since his legs grew long enough for the journey, he had come up, and spent a night, or two nights, with the sheep. It was good. This time, he had been with Doli two nights already, sleeping in the shepherd's bothie by the dew-pond, and now he supposed it was time to be going home, because he had never been more than two nights away from home before; his mother was one to worry, and when she worried her hand was hard.

'It is good, up here,' he said by and by.

'Aye, it is good up here – when the sun shines and the wind blows soft without snow in it, and a man need not be away after a straying ewe, knee-deep in snow, and the wolves crying,' Doli said.

Drem screwed his head over his shoulder to grin at the old man. 'You need some of your own sheep medicine. Tell me more about the wolves. Tell me how you came by that long scar on your ribs.'

The old man shook his head, his gaze on the flock in the combe bottom. 'I have told you that story, aye, and more than once.'

'Tell it again.'

'Nay, it is hot, and I am in no mood to tell over again stories that I have told before.' Doli brought his gaze up out of the combe, and let it rest on the boy's face. Nothing else about him moved. He never moved without need. 'I have told you all that there is to tell about wolves and fights with wolves, and it is not good to talk of such things even in the summer. I have told you all the stories and the dreams that are of my people, save for those which may not be told. I have told you about Corn King, and Earth Mother; and I have told you how Tah-Nu, the Father of my people, in a land where the sun casts no shadows, dreamed a dream of the north, and how he hollowed out the trunk of a great tree and put into it his woman and his child and his hunting dog and a basket of barley seed, and paddled after the dream across the Great Water, and how he came to this land after many days, and sprang ashore and found that he had grown a shadow. Surely I am a great teller of stories, but even

I must have rest. Maybe when you come again I shall have found in my head another story.'

Drem wriggled round, sticking a leg out sideways on the slope, to come face to face with the old man. He said, partly in the tone of a question, partly as one repeating a thing said before, 'And there was no one in the land before Tah-Nu, and no one after him except his children and his children's children, and his children's children's children, until we came?'

'Nay. Tah-Nu was the first, but there were others after him, before you came,' Doli said. 'There came giants as red-gold as you are, with great spears of bronze against which our flint spears were but brown-tufted rushes. So they set us to tend their herds, and sometimes they took our women to tend their fires and bear their sons; and in a while and a while and a while we became, in some sort, one people. *Then* you came, as it might be yesterday, and treated the children of the giants as they had treated us. Now we are all the Half People, Tah-Nu's children and the children of the giants alike, and we come at your call. But we who have yet the old blood strong in us, we the Little Dark People, we have the long memories, and we remember while we tend your sheep that once, when the long grave-mounds yonder against the sky were new, Tah-Nu's children were the lords of the land.'

Drem nodded. 'Does it ache in your belly, when you remember that?' If you asked a thing like that of most of Doli's kind, they would only look at you sideways beneath their brows, and make you an answer that slid out from under your question like an eel from under a stone. But Doli was different.

The old shepherd shrugged, his gaze level enough on Drem's face; yet his answer slid a little, all the same. 'The wind from the east is a cold wind, and blood runs from a spear-thrust, and if a man be too long without food he will die. And all these things are bad; yet he would be a fool who spent his life grieving for such things.'

Drem waited, looking into Doli's face; but nothing more came, and the old man's face was shut as he gazed out over his sheep once more. It seemed that the time had come to be on his way again.

He gave a parting pull to the young dog's ears, drew his legs under him, and stood up. 'Now I go, if you will tell me no more stories.'

Doli looked up at him, mocking a little under his brows. 'It is a long trail back to the village, and a sad thing it would be if the evening stew was all of it eaten before you came.'

'As to that, my mother will keep something for me in the pot,' Drem said, with the assurance of the Lordly Ones of the world, for whom something is always kept in the pot. 'Nevertheless, I go now. Maybe I will come again before barley harvest. But if I do not, then surely I will come up and help with the droving when the time comes to bring the flock down at Samhain.'

'Come when you will. You have a way with the sheep; and it is in my heart that you would make none so ill a shepherd.'

Drem cocked up his head and laughed, rocking on his heels. 'Nay, I leave that to Tah-Nu's children. I shall be a warrior, after the way of my kind. Yet when I am a man I shall come up with my kind also, when the time comes to keep the Wolf Guard in the winter nights.'

'I will tell it to the Wolf-people, that they may grow afraid.' Doli said.

Drem flushed, still laughing. 'You laugh at me, and that is not good! But I will come back before barley harvest.'

He swung on a hard brown heel, and set off at a trot, following the curved bank of the great enclosure where the sheep were driven for shelter at night; and a short way beyond, on the crest of the hill, passed the turf-built bothie by the dew-

pond, where Hunno, the brother of Flann, was swabbing a raw place on a sheep's back with elder-water to keep off the flies. He did not stop to talk to Hunno, who was a surly little man with small round eyes like jet beads, but went on at a steady wolf-trot, heading for home.

Presently he struck the green Ridgeway that ran from the world's edge to the world's edge along the High Chalk, and followed it for a while, until another track came up from the seaward Marshes and crossed it; and then he turned inland. The sun was westering as he came dipping down into the steep combe that sheltered the home steading; and all the great, rounded, whale-backed masses of the downs were pooled and feathered with coolness, the shadows of a stunted white-thorn tree reaching across half a hillside, every rise and hollow of the land that did not show at all when the sun was high casting its own long, liquid shadow across the gold. The family cattle-ground in the head of the combe was already in shade, but farther down, where the combe broadened, the turf roofs of the steading – drying up now in the summer heat – glowed tawny as a hound's coat in the sun-light, and the smoke from the house-place fire was blue as the fluttering haze of flower-heads in the flax plot as he trotted by.

He entered the steading garth by way of a weak place he knew of in the thorn hedge, instead of going round to the gateway that faced towards the corn-land down the combe, and made his way between the byre and the shelter where the two-ox plough was kept. Drustic must be out hunting, since there was no sign of him about the farm-land, and would scarcely be home by dusk; but his mother and the Grandfather would be there, and Blai. As he reached the back wall of the house-place and saw the familiar strip of warm darkness where the roof turf had been rolled back to let in more air and light, the idea suddenly woke in him that it would be fun to get in that way and drop on them like an earwig out of the thatch when they did not know that he was anywhere near.

The roof of the house-place came down to within elbow height of the ground all round, and the pitch was not very steep, but the sun-dried turf was slippery, and so it was not as easy to climb up as it looked. He managed it, however, working his way up with infinite care until he could reach the edge of the opening, and after that it was easy. He drew himself up a little farther, then shifted his grip and slipped through between the rafters that showed in the gap, found a one-hand hold inside, and next instant, all without a sound – for few people could move more silently than Drem when he chose – was lying full length along the edge of the loft floor.

The half-loft in the crown of the roof was full of warm, crowding shadows through which the bar of fading sunlight from the gap in the roof fell like a golden sword. There was a warm smell of must and dust, and the sharper, aromatic tang of the dried herbs hanging in bundles from the rafters, and the animal smell of the skin rugs laid aside there until the winter. Spare farm tools were stacked deep under the eaves, and the raw, grey-brown bundles of wool from the last clip, and the

wicker kists in which the household kept their clothes and gear. Harness hung among the herbs, and a smoked bear ham; and there, too, were the two-handled crocks full of honey that kept the household in sweetness from one bee harvest to the next.

At the open side, almost in the smoke of the hearth fire that wreathed past on its way to the smoke hole, hung two shields: Drustic's shield that had been their father's, and the great bull's-hide buckler with the bronze bosses that was the Grandfather's and would be Drem's one day.

But at the moment Drem had no interest to spare for the loft. Lying flat on his stomach and shielded from sight by the great roof-tree and the Grandfather's buckler, he was peering down over the edge into the main body of the house-place below. It was fun to see without being seen. Out of the fireglow and the fading sword of dusty gold, the great living-hut ran away on every side into brown shadows with a bloom of wood smoke on them, but where the light fell strongest near the doorway, his mother was working at her loom; a big upright loom, the warp threads held taut by a row of triangular clay weights at the bottom. He could hear the small rhythmical sounds as she passed the weaving-rod to and fro and combed up the woof between each row.

The warm, fatty smell of the evening stew came up to him from the bronze pot over the fire, and brought the warm water to his mouth, for he had not eaten since the morning bowl of stirabout with the shepherd kind. The Grandfather was sitting beside the fire as usual, on the folded skin of the bear that he had killed when the world was young; a man like a huge old brooding grey eagle that had once been golden.

On the other side of the hearth, the Women's side, Blai squatted on her heels, turning barley cakes with small, flinching hands in the hot ash. She was exactly beneath Drem, so that he thought how easy it would be to spit on her, like spitting on the back of a hare as it sunned itself on a far-down ledge of the old flint quarry north of the summer sheep-run. Blai was not his sister; her coming belonged to the time that he could only just remember, when a bronze-smith had come by from the Isles of the West, and his woman with him – a wild, dark creature with hair and eyes like the night. She had been sick already, and in the night she had died and left a new babe bleating in the fern against the wall. The bronze-smith  had not seemed much interested, and two days later he had gone off along the track that led inland, leaving the babe behind him. 'What should I want with the creature?' he had said. 'Maybe I will come back one day.' But he never had come back. And now Blai was rising seven years old, black as her mother had been, in a house where everyone else was red-gold like flame, and somehow never quite belonging to them. Blai believed that one day the bronze-smith would come back: 'One day, one day my father will come for me!' seemed to be her talisman against all ills, the faith that she clung to as something of her own. But of course he never would come back; everybody knew that except Blai. Blai was stupid.

Drem decided not to spit on her after all, because that would betray his presence in the loft, and turned his attention back to his mother. The cloth on the loom had grown a little since he saw it last, though not much, because there was so much else to do; a piece of fine chequered wool, blue and violet and flaming red. There was red wool on his mother's weaving-rod now, the true burning Warrior Scarlet that was the very colour of courage itself. No woman might wear that colour, nor might the Half People who came and went at the Tribe's call. It was for the Men's side. One day, when he had passed through the Boy's House, and slain his wolf single-handed, and become a man and a warrior of the Tribe, with his Grandfather's shield to carry, his mother would weave scarlet on the loom for him.

The Grandfather raised his great grey-gold head from watching bygone battles in the fire, and turned to gaze on the woman at the loom. 'It grows slowly, that piece of cloth,' he said, in a voice that came mumbling and rattling up from the depth of his great frame. 'When it is finished, let you use it to re-line my good beaver-skin cloak. The old lining is worn to shreds.'

Drem's mother looked over her shoulder, showing a tired face in which the beautiful bones stood out so sharply that it looked as though you could cut you hand on it. 'I had thought to use this piece for Drustic; he also needs a new cloak, for his old one does not keep out the wind and the rain.'

'Drustic is young, and the wind blows less cold for him. He can wait. Let you set up the loom for him next time.'

'Next time and next time and next time,' Drem's mother said quietly. 'Sometimes I wish that I had been born to the Men's side; sometimes I grow weary of the spinning and the weaving and the grinding corn.'

The Grandfather spat into the fire. 'By right there should be three son's wives to weave and grind for me!'

'Then there should be three sons for them to weave for also,' Drem's mother said with a spurt of tired and angry laughter, thrusting back a bright wisp of hair that had strayed as her hair was always straying from the blue linen net in which it was gathered, and looked round again. 'Or would you have them all widows?'

Drem knew his mother in this mood; it came when she was very tired; and he began to feel that it would not be a good idea to play his earwig-out-of-the-thatch trick, after all.

The Grandfather drew his brows together, and glared. 'Aiee! A hard thing it is that I grow old, and of all my three sons there is not one left, and that the wife of my youngest son should taunt me with it! A hard thing it is that I should have but one grandson to carry my spear after me; I who have been among the greatest warriors of the Tribe.'

('The Old One grows forgetful,' Drem thought. 'He has lived so long with old battles that his mind grows dim; and he has forgotten Drustic.')

His mother turned again from her weaving, with a fierceness that struck him even at that moment as odd. 'Two grandsons there are at the hearth fire! Have you forgotten?'

It was then that the Grandfather said the thing that altered the whole world for Drem, so that it could never return to being quite the same as before.

'Nay then, I have not forgotten. I grow old but I can still count the tally of my ten fingers. Two grandsons there are at the hearth fire; but a grandson at the hearth fire is not a grandson among the spear-warriors of the Tribe. Is it likely, think you, that the young one will ever win his way into the Men's side, with a spear-arm that he cannot use?'

There was a sudden silence. Drem's mother had turned back to her loom, but she was not weaving. The Grandfather sat and glowered. And in the warm shadows of the loft above them, the small boy lay on his stomach, staring down at them with dilated eyes, and feeling all at once cold and sick. Only Blai went on turning barley cakes among the hot ashes, her small wan face telling as little as usual of what she thought or felt.

Then Drem's mother said, 'Talore the Hunter is one of the great ones of the Men's side to this day.'

'Talore the Hunter was a man and a warrior before ever he lost a hand to the cattle raiders,' the Grandfather said, deep and grumbling, and he eyed her with a kind of disgusted triumph. 'Na na, it is in my mind that the boy must go to the Half People when the time comes. He is often enough away with Doli and the sheep as it is; maybe he will make a shepherd.' He spat again. 'Lord of the Sun! That I should have a grandson herding sheep! I, who have been such a warrior as men speak of round the fire for a hundred winters!'

'If the child fails, then he must go to the Half People,' Drem's mother said, and her voice sounded tight in her throat. 'But it may be that he will not fail. He is your own grandson, and not lightly turned from the things he sets his mind to.'

'So. But it is not his mind alone that must be set.' The Grandfather flared his nostrils in a derisive snort. 'Say then that he comes through his years in the Boy's House and slays his wolf at the end of them, and the time comes for him to receive his weapons; there must be two warriors, let you remember, and one of them not kin to him, to bring each New Spear before the Clan. And who shall I find, think you – or Drustic if I have gone beyond the Sunset – to stand for a one-armed champion?'

'It is six summers before that question need be answered – and must I then answer it this evening?' Drem's mother cried. 'If he fails, then let him go to the Half People as I say, and let you be thankful that there is Drustic to carry your spear after you!' She gave a swift exclamation and turned from the loom towards the open pottery lamp that hung from the roof-tree just below Drem's hiding-place. 'The light fades, and if I am to finish this stripe before Drustic is home to be fed, I must have the lamp.'

Quick as a lizard, Drem darted back into the shadows.

'Surely there is a rat in the roof. I heard it scamper.' He heard her voice, dry and hard, behind him as he slid out through the opening in the roof. He dropped silently to the ground, driven by an odd panic fear of anyone knowing that he had overheard what passed in the house-place, because somehow – he could not have said why – that would make it quite unbearable.

The little stilt-legged hut where the seed corn was stored seemed to offer refuge and he dived under it and crouched there, breathing hard as though he had been running.

The sun was gone, but a golden after-glow was spread behind the Chalk, and there was still light to see by. And crouching there among the timbers that upheld the floor, he looked at his right arm, as though he had never seen it before: his spear arm that he could not use, the Grandfather had said. It was thinner than his left, and somehow brittle looking, as though it might snap like a dry stick. He felt it exploringly with his left hand. It was queer, like something that did not quite belong to him. He had always known, of course – when he thought about it at all – that he could not use that arm, but it hadn't seemed important. He held things in his teeth and he held things between his knees, and he managed well enough without it. Certainly he had never for a moment thought of it coming between him and his Warrior Scarlet.

But he thought now, crouching under the floor of the corn store and staring straight before him with eyes that did not see the golden after-glow fading behind the Chalk. Never to take his proud place among the Men's side with the others of his kind; to lose the world he knew, and go out into the world of the Half People, the Dark People, the Flint People, whose homes, half underground, were the little green hummocks in the hidden combes of the Chalk; who came and went at the Tribesmen's call, though they never owned the Tribesmen as their masters; to be cut off, all his life, from his own kind . . . He was only nine years old, he could not yet understand all that it would mean; but he understood enough – more than enough. He crouched there for a long time, whispering over and over to himself, 'I *will* be a warrior of the Tribe. Let you say what you like, Old Man! I will show you – I will *show* you' – lashing up anger within himself, for a shield against fear.

When he went back to the house-place it was almost dark. Drustic had returned from the hunting trail, and the newly paunched carcass of a roe hind was hanging from the birch tree beside the door, out of reach of the dogs who were fighting over the offal, the white of her under-belly faintly luminous in the dusk, where the blood had not fouled it. He went in through the fore porch, where the ponies were stabled in winter. The apron of skins over the inner doorway was drawn back, and the tawny glow of the lamp and the low fire came to meet him on the threshold as he checked, blinking. The evening meal was over, and the Grandfather, it seemed, had returned to his watching of old battles in the fire. Drustic, with a half-made bow-stave across his knee and a glue-pot beside him, was busy on the great hunting bow that he was building for himself, while on the Women's side of the hearth their mother sat spinning. She looked up as Drem appeared. 'Cubbling! Here is a time to be coming home! When it drew to sunset I said, "He will not come now until tomorrow."'

'I would have been home by sunset, but – I stopped on the way. There were things to look at and I stopped on the way,'

Drem said. But he could not meet his mother's eyes. Keeping his head down, he went to squat beside Drustic, holding out his hand. 'I will hold it steady while you put on the binding.'

But Drustic hated anyone else to meddle in a thing that he was making. He looked up slowly – all his movements were slow and deliberate – and said quite kindly, 'Na, I can manage well enough. Let you learn to shaft a spear; that is the thing for you to do.'

Drem snatched his hand back as though it had been stung. You needed two hands for a bow, but you could learn to use a spear with one. That was another thing that he had not really thought about.

And at the same moment, his mother called to him. 'See, there is some stew left. Let you come round here and take your bowl. You are not a man already, that you should eat on the Men's side of the hearth.'

Drem came at her call, and took the black pottery bowl of stewed mutton that she held out to him, and squatted down in the fern. As he did so, he caught sight of Blai squatting far back in the shadows, picking the furze prickles and bits of dirt from a lapful of raw wool, and watching him as she worked. And he realized that Blai also had heard what the Grandfather had said. So he turned his shoulder on her, hunching it in a way that was meant to show her that she mattered so little that he had not noticed that she was there at all.

And somehow in doing that – he overset the bowl.

It was such a small thing, a thing that might have happened to anyone. But to Drem, coming so close on the heels of what had gone before, it was overwhelming. The words that the Grandfather had said, Drustic's refusal to let him help with the bow – they were things that came from outside; and a thing that came from outside could be in some sort shut out; it could be defied and snarled against. But this was different; this came from inside himself; there was no defence against it, and it let in all the rest.

Dismay and something that was almost terror swept over him as the warm stew splashed across his knee and into the fern. The Grandfather grunted; a grunt that said as plainly as words could do, 'See now, did I not say so?' And his mother caught up the bowl, crying in exasperation and something under the exasperation that was as though he had hurt her, 'Oh, you clumsy one! You grow more clumsy every day! Can you never look what you are about?'

Black misery rushed up into Drem's breast, so that it was as though his heart were bursting because there was more misery in it than it could hold. He raised a white, desperate face to his mother's, and shook his head. Then he scrambled to his feet and bolted for the doorway.

'Where are you going? – Come back, cub!' his mother called after him; and he called back mumbling that he was not hungry, that he would come again in a while, and stumbled out through the fore porch into the summer night.

The gateway of the steading was closed, as always after dark, by an uprooted thorn bush, and he went out through the weak place that had let him in earlier that evening before the blow fell that changed the world, and making his way round the steading hedge, started down the chalk-cut driftway between the lower corn-plots and the half-wild fruit trees that were his mother's care.

He had no clear idea what he was doing or where he was going, or why. Blindly, instinctively, he turned to the wilderness, like any small desperately hurt animal seeking solitude from its own kind and the dark and a hole to crawl into.

2 Talore the Hunter

Lower down, the combe ran out into a broadening valley that swung northward, opening into a vast half moon of rolling chalk hills above the forest and the marshlands far below. Drem followed the valley down, because down was easier than up, but he did not think of which way he was going; he simply went. Down and down, by swirling slopes and plunging headlands of turf, by bare chalk and tangled furze and through the whitethorn bushes of the lower slopes, until at last the great trees of the Wild came climbing up to meet him.

The Great Wild, mist haunted, spirit haunted, rolling away into the unknown; the wilderness of forest and marsh that was the place of wolf and bear and wild pig, the place of the Fear that walked among the trees, so men said, after dark; where only the hunters went at night, taking their lives in their spear hands and trusting their souls to the charms and talismans of amber and bear's teeth and dried garlic flowers that they wore about them.

At first it was quite easy travelling, for anyone used, as Drem was, to wandering about in the dark. The hazel and elder and wayfaring trees of the forest verge grew well apart, and there was little undergrowth; but as time went by, the trees crowded closer and closer; oak and ash, alder in the damper places, holly everywhere, great thickets of it, mingled with black masses of yew, matted together with a dense undergrowth of thorn and brambles. And wherever the trees fell back a little, the bracken grew head high to the small boy who thrust his way on, deeper and deeper into the fastness, driven by the misery and the furious bewilderment within him like a small wild thing driven by the hounds.

Utterly lost in his own desolation, Drem never noticed how the forest darkened and crowded in on him, until suddenly a piece of rotten tree-trunk gave under his foot, and he all but went through into an ants' nest; and that woke him up, so that as he gathered himself together again, he was suddenly aware of his surroundings. He had never been into the forest at night before; never so far as this, even in day-time, and he did not know where he was. And, swift-footed fear overcoming his longing for refuge, he had enough sense left to tell him that it was not good to be so far into the forest alone at night, and that he must get back to the woodshore. He knew the direction to take without even having to think; the north side of any tree, especially any oak tree, smelled quite different from the south, and he had only to head south to strike the Chalk again at last.

So he turned his face southward, and set off. But he was desperately tired, and he dreaded going home, because going home would mean facing the thing that he had run away from; and his dread somehow made it harder to find the way.

The trees that should have begun to thin out crowded thicker and thicker about him as he went, and there was no way through the tangled thickets of bramble and holly, so that he must cast about for the narrow game-tracks worn by the feet of the deer, that never led in the right direction. It seemed that he would never win free of the choking tangle, and he was too tired, too wretched to care very much. Only – only it seemed that a change was coming over the forest.

Or maybe it was that he was awake and aware of the forest now as he had not been before; awake to the darkness and the crowding trees that were suddenly – not quite what trees should be, not quite what they were in the day-time; to the furry hush that was full of voices, the whispering, rustling, stealthy voices of the forest, that were not the voices of the day-time, either. There were little nameless rustlings through the undergrowth, the soft swish of wings through the branches overhead; in the distance a small animal screamed, and Drem knew that somewhere a fox had made its kill. Surely the whole forest was disturbed tonight. But those were not the sounds that raised the hair on the back of his neck. Once he thought he heard the breathing of a big animal close at hand, and as he checked, his own breath caught in his throat; something brushed through the undergrowth towards him, and there was a sudden silver pattering like rain among the leaves – but it was not raining. He pushed on again, more quickly now, carelessly, stumbling often among the underbrush; and when he stopped once more, to listen and make sure of his direction, suddenly the breathing was there again; a faint, slow panting, just behind him. He whirled about, his hand on the knife in his belt, but there was nothing there. Nothing but the furry darkness. And far off through the trees, he thought that something laughed. His heart was racing now, sickeningly, right up in his throat; he struggled on again, blindly. Mustn't stop any more; it was when you

stopped that you heard things. But even as he blundered on, above the brushing and crackling that he made, above the drubbing of his heart, he heard that soft, stealthy panting, as though the Thing prowled at his heels. But it was not only at his heels now, it was all around him, in front as well as behind, and the forest itself, the whole forest was like some great hunting cat crouched to spring. 'Don't run!' said the hunter that was born and bred in him and that knew the ways of the wild through a hundred generations. *'Don't run!'* But terror had him in its power, and he was running, with no more sense of direction than a mouse with a stoat behind it.

Brambles tore his skin, fallen branches tripped him, low-hanging boughs slashed across his face as he crashed through the undergrowth that seemed to lay hold of him with wicked, clawing hands. This was what the hunters spoke of under their breaths around the fire. This was the Fear that walked the forest, the Terror of the Soul. He had never felt it before, but the hunter within him knew it; the Fear that prowled soft-footed beyond the cave mouth and the firelight.

Panting, sweating, sobbing, he crashed through a screen of alder scrub on the edge of a little clearing, and next instant had pitched forward and was rolling over down a slope rustling with last year's leaves. He reached the bottom with what breath he had had left all knocked out of him, and found himself almost under a great hollow bole of roots and uptorn earth where a huge oak tree had come down in some past winter gale. It seemed to offer shelter, the shelter that even a very small cave gives from the Fear that prowls outside; and with a shuddering gasp, Drem crawled in as far as he could over the deep, rustling softness of drifted oak leaves, and crouched down, pressed against the roughness of the torn roots.

For a long while he crouched there with drubbing heart, still shivering and sweating, while the Fear snuffled about the opening of his refuge. But little by little the Fear faded and went farther away. Strength and steadfastness seemed to come out to him from the torn roots of the great tree that had been a forest king in its day; his heart quietened and his breath came slower. And gradually his terror and his misery alike grew dim. He did not know that he was falling asleep like a small, exhausted animal . . .

He woke with a crash, and the taste of terror in his throat. There was hot breath panting in his face, and something was snuffing at his shoulder.

For a moment he lay quite still, everything in him seeming to curl in on itself and turn to ice, knowing that the thing could only be a wolf, and that if he made the slightest movement it would be at his throat before ever he could whip the knife from his belt. Then a voice said softly, 'Sa, what have we here, then? Off, Swift-foot! Back now, Fand!' And his eyes flew open to see a man – or something in the shape of a man – bending over him, head and shoulders blotted dark against the white light of moon-rise; and the thing that had been snuffing at his shoulder drew back with a whine.

There was a swift exclamation, and a hand flashed down on him as he flattened back against the earthy root-tangle behind him; and like a wild thing cornered, with nothing in him but a blind instinct to fight for life, he snapped at it, his teeth meeting in a finger. He was shaken off, and in the same instant, as it seemed, the hand was on his shoulder, and he was jerked bodily out from under the tree roots and set on his feet, still kicking and struggling and trying to bite, in the full moonlight. The hand held him at arm's length in a grip that he could not break though he twisted and squirmed like an otter cub; but the man's voice when he spoke again was not harsh, despite his bitten finger. There was even something of laughter in it.

'Softly, softly now! There is no need for such a snarling and snapping!' Then, as Drem, reassured by something in the voice ceased his struggling: 'Why, it is old Cathlan's grandson!'

Drem stood quite still now, and looked at the man, while three great hounds sat down around them with lolling tongues and eyes shining in the moonlight. The man was slight and dark – dark for one of the Golden People – and had faintly the smell of fox about him; and even in his stillness, as he stood holding Drem at arm's length, was the swift, leashed power of a wild thing. He was naked save for a fox's pelt twisted about his loins; and the moon caught the blade of the long hunting-knife thrust into his girdle, and the coils of a great snake of beaten copper that coiled again and again about his left forearm, the head lying level with his elbow, the tail curled downward into a hook that served him instead of a left hand.

'So it is you who walks the forest tonight, making all the Wild uneasy,' said Talore the Hunter.

Drem nodded.

'A small cub, surely a very small cub, to be sleeping out in the forest.'

Drem said fiercely, 'I have seen nine summers, and I sleep in the forest because I choose.'

'Surely that is as good a reason as any other,' said the man, with the laughter deepening in his tone. 'But now, I think, the time comes to be going home.'

There was a silence among the crowding trees. Then Drem said, 'Let me be. I will go back in a while and a while.'

'Na, not in a while and a while,' Talore said, and he looked down at Drem in the moonlight, with eyes that missed nothing of the small, desperate figure before him. 'This part of the forest is no place for small cubs, alone. Therefore we go together, you and I; and we go now.'

He released Drem's shoulder, and stooping with the lithe and lazy swiftness that was in all his movements, caught up from among the brown leaves and white-flowering dead-nettle at his feet his hunting-spear, and a newly flayed badger pelt, which he flung across his shoulder. 'Come,' he said, and with an almost soundless whistle to his hounds, turned to the steep slope behind him.

And rebellious and resentful, bewildered by the swiftness with which the unknown terror whose hand he bit had become Talore the Hunter, and by the man's mastery over him, which was different from anything he had experienced before, Drem came. The Fear was gone from the forest, and the chill fresh-ness of the dawn was in his face as, with the three hounds, he followed at the shadow-silent heels of the hunter, threading the mazy deer-paths that seemed to have turned themselves about to lead in the right direction after all. He felt spent and empty as though he had cried until he had no more tears to cry with; and nothing of last night seemed quite real; it was all dark and confused and had the sick taste of nightmare that remains in the back of one's mind after one wakes. He wished he could talk about it to Talore. Talore with his copper snake would under-stand as no one else in Drem's world could. It would be good to tell Talore. But he knew that if the hunter was to stop in his tracks, and turn, and say 'Cub, what Thing was it that you ran from, into the forest?' the words would never come. So there was no good thinking about it.

The light was growing all around them, wherever the trees fell back a little; moonlight and dawn-light watered together; and as they came down to a narrow brook a willow wren was singing among the alders. They followed upstream a little way, and suddenly Drem knew where he was. He knew this brook, he knew the ancient willow bending far out over the water, where the brook broke up into a chain of pools. Just up yonder through the trees was the track, the ancient track under the scarp of the downs that echoed the Ridgeway along the High Chalk far above. Even as he realized it, they came out on the edge of a clearing, and Talore checked among a tangle of elder bushes with a swift gesture that halted boy and hounds alike.

Ahead of them in the clearing the light was so strong that already the foxgloves were touched with colour; and the low ground-mist of the summer morning lay like gossamer in the hollows among the fern. And peering, breath in check, through the low-hanging elder branches, Drem saw that on the far side of the clearing a herd of roe deer were grazing, their fawns all together at a little distance. One big hind was grazing a little apart from the rest, between them and the elder scrub; and Drem judged that she was well within spear throw, knowing that in the hands of a skilled hunter a light throw-spear could kill at forty or fifty paces. One of the hounds was standing against his leg, and he felt the tremors running through the brute's body, though no whimper of excitement broke from him, or from the other two. They had come on the herd up-wind, and so there was nothing to carry the smell of danger to the deer, and they grazed on undisturbed. Every moment Drem expected to see Talore throw and make his kill; but the moments passed, and when he stole a sideways glance at Talore, the hunter was watching the herd through the white curds of the elder blossom, with a keen, quiet pleasure narrowing his dark eyes, and the throw-spear still at rest in his hand.

A few moments later, he gave a soft whistle. A curious, low note at sound of which the nearest hind raised her head and looked towards the elder tangle, then began, obviously not in the least startled, to drift back to the main herd. One or two others looked up and began to drift also, a hind barked to her fawn, and in a few moments the last of the deer had melted into the trees and the morning mist.

Drem looked again at Talore, puzzled, and spoke for the first time since they had set out on the home trail. 'You could have killed her – the one this side of the herd.'

'So. Very easily.' Talore had been on the point of moving again, but he checked, looking down at the boy.

'Then – why not?'

'I have killed once already tonight and have no need to kill again,' Talore said. 'There is meat enough in my house-place, and a deer-skin fetches but a small price from the traders.' And then, seeing Drem still puzzled, 'Never kill what you cannot use. If you kill for skins, kill for all the skins you need; if for food, fill your belly and the bellies of hound and woman and child at your hearth and set store by, that they may be full another time. But to kill for the sake of killing is the way of the weasel and the fox, and the hunter who kills so angers the Forest Gods. Let you remember that when you are a man and hunt with the Men's side!'

Drem had not meant to say it, a moment before he would not have thought that he could say it, but the words seemed to burst out past the silence in his throat in a small, hoarse rush that had nothing to do with his will. 'Most like, when I am a man, I shall not hunt with the Men's side.'

There was a pause, and a little wind riffled through the elder branches, fetching down a shower of petals. Then Talore said, 'Who with, then?'

'The Half People.'

'And who says so?'

'The Old One, Cathlan my Grandfather.'

Talore stood leaning on his spear and frowned down at Drem with a suddenly quickened interest. 'Let you tell me why.'

Drem scowled at him, the old misery aching in his throat, and did not answer; and after a moment Talore flicked the tail of his

B   33 copper snake at the arm which the boy carried trailing like a bird with a broken wing. 'Because of that?'

Drem nodded.

'So. Men call me Talore One-Hand as often as Talore the Hunter, yet no man has ever questioned my right to the scarlet.'

'Sabra my mother said that – something of that. But you were a warrior and a – a great one of the Clan before ever you lost a hand to the cattle raiders.'

Talore smiled, his swift, dark smile that raised his lip over the strong dog teeth at the corners of his mouth. 'The Grandfather again.'

And again Drem nodded, and again Talore leaned on his spear and looked down at him. 'Listen, cub,' he said at last. 'If the thing is worth a fight, fight for it and do not hear the Grandfather too clearly. There are ways – ways round, and ways through, and ways over. If you have not two hands for a bow, then learn to use a throw-spear with such skill that your enemies, and your brothers, forget that it is not from choice.'

Drem looked at him in wonder. How could Talore – even Talore – know about Drustic's bow? And then he realized that Talore did not know about *that* bow, but that for him also there had been a bow that he could not draw, and a spear that must take its place. There were things to think about, here. But first there was something more; a question to be asked. Drem looked at the ground while he asked it, because he could not bear to look into Talore's face. 'If I did – all those things, and learned to kill a buck at – at sixty paces with a spear; and slew my wolf at the Wolf Slaying – a – a greater, fiercer wolf than most, would there – might it be that someone among the warriors would stand for me with the Grandfather, when the time comes for me to go before the Tribe, after all?'

The silence that followed seemed to him so long that he began to give up his new hope. Then Talore said, 'When the time comes that your mother weaves scarlet on the loom for you, let you remember this dawn in the forest, and bid the Grandfather send word to me.'

Just for a moment, he could not believe it. Then he looked up, slowly, his eyes suddenly all golden. '*You?*'

'Who else has so good a right, small brother?' Talore said.

They looked at each other for a moment, steadily; a look that was the sealing of a bond. Then Talore straightened, shifting his hold on his spear. 'Come now, it is near daylight, and they will be half mad for you at the home steading. You will know your way, now?'

Drem nodded.

'So. Then our ways part here. Good hunting, cub.'

And in a little, while the hunter melted in among the trees, going on up the streamside towards the village, Drem struck up through the fringes of the forest on to the swelling flanks of the Chalk.

It was almost broad daylight, the moon pale as a bubble in the shining sky; and the red plough oxen were stirring and stamping in their stalls, when Drem came up the chalk-cut driftway to the gate of the home steading. The thorn tree was drawn aside and the gateway open, and he walked through and across the garth to the house-place, suddenly so weary that he could hardly drag one leg after the other. He heard Drustic's voice as he came to the door, 'Na, he is not with Doli. The Gods alone know where he is or what has come to him!' and saw his brother standing over the Grandfather, who sat hunched in his cloak beside the fire that looked as though it had been kept up all night. He caught the Grandfather's rumbling answer. 'The child is bad; always I have said that the child is bad. He has no respect for *me* his Grandfather! If the Sun Lord so wills it, he will come back when he is hungry enough.'

And then they saw him, both it seemed in the same moment, and also in the same moment old Kea, the mother of all Drustic's hounds, got up with waving tail, yawning her pleasure, and came to greet him. But Drustic reached him first, in a couple of strides, and caught him by the scruff of the neck and jerked him forward into the fireglow beside the hearth, demanding, 'Son of blackness, where have you been?'

Drem stood and rubbed his neck and glared. 'It was a very bright night. I went to catch a fish, but they were all shy.'

The Grandfather snorted, a snort that might mean unbelief or only derision; and Drustic said, 'And so, because you chance to feel like catching a fish, our mother must seek you all night through the woodshore, and I must trail up along the High Chalk lest you had gone back to Doli and the sheep!' As he spoke he took down a whip of tanned ox hide that he used for the hounds, and stood drawing the dark leash again and again through his hands. 'You know what happens to a puppy of the dog pack when he runs off in such a way?'

Drem faced him squarely. He had known that this must happen, and he was ready for it. 'You thrash him.'

Drustic glanced for an instant, questioningly, at the Grandfather, the lord of the house; but the Grandfather spat into the fire, hunching his blanket farther round his shoulders. 'Na na, I am too old to be troubled with the training of puppies. The thing is for you to do – and see that you do not hold your hand.'

'I shall not hold my hand,' Drustic said roughly. He was clearly very angry, his young, ruddy face dark with his anger. He reached out and fetched Drem a buffet on the side of the head that sent him sprawling across the wood pile by the fire. Drem crouched there, his head ringing from the blow; and waited with shut teeth. He knew that by the end he would be yelping like a puppy, but he would not yelp before he must. He sensed that his brother's arm had swung up, and waited for the sting of the descending lash across his shoulders.

But it never came. Instead, something small and fierce out of the shadows flung itself on Drustic and bit him, as last night Drem had bitten Talore the Hunter.

Drustic yelped with surprise and pain, and shook his attacker off and cuffed her aside, then raised his whip again. But as he did so, Drem heard his mother's voice from the doorway, crying with a rush of thankfulness, 'Ah! You have found him!' And then, 'No, Drustic. No!'

Everything was very confused and confusing, but it seemed to Drem that he might be going to escape a beating after all. He got up from where he had been crouching, as his mother came swiftly in, her heavy hair falling loose and her kirtle torn and mired. 'Cubbling, where have you been? You were with Doli then?'

Drustic was standing, solid and still angry and beginning to be bewildered, sucking his bitten thumb, while Blai crouched snarling silently, and holding her head, among the hounds where his cuff had sent her. He spat blood into the fire. 'Nay, you were wrong, my mother; he has but now come in, so bold as the King himself in his high Dun, to tell me he went to catch a fish.' Then, rounding once more on Drem. 'Get down again. I have not finished with you yet.'

'No, Drustic,' their mother said again. 'You shall not beat him – not this time.'

The Grandfather raised his great grey-gold head and looked at them with eyes that went golden when he was angry or glad, just as Drem's did, but it was anger now. 'Woman, this is for the Men's side. Leave it for the Men's side's handling, and tend to your distaff!'

Drem's mother paid no heed to the old man. '*Not this time!*' she said again.

'But why not?' Drustic demanded, his brows puckered with bewilderment. 'Am I not to train the cub at all? *Why not?*'

'Because I say not, I who gave both of you life!' their mother said; and she caught the whip from Drustic and flung it into the far shadows. Then she turned to Drem, with her hands held out, and the crooning softness in her voice that came there all too seldom. 'Baba, cubbling, why did you run off like that? I would have given you more stew – the bowl was not broken –'

Her eyes were searching his face. He thought she guessed that it had not been a rat in the roof; guessed why he had gone; and that was why she would not let Drustic beat him. But she could not be sure, and while she was not sure she could not speak of it to him. He did not want her to speak of it to him. So he stepped back, and stood with his feet apart and his head up, while Drustic shrugged and went to pick up his whip and hang it in its accustomed place. 'I did not want any more stew. I wished to catch a fish. I went down to the river, into the forest to catch one; but the fish were all shy.'

'But what did you do by yourself, all alone the long night in the forest? You are torn to pieces, and your kilt in shreds. Aiee, baba, you look as though you were new come from battle – and you must be so hungry.'

'I am hungry,' Drem agreed, 'and the brambles are sharp in the forest. I crawled into a hole under an oak tree and slept.' He had not forgotten the Great Fear, but he shut his mind to it. 'And later I met Talore the Hunter in the forest, and we walked together, and talked, in the way of men!'

His mother was already taking a barley bannock out of the bannock basket that hung from the edge of the loft. 'Eat now, and you shall have better in a little.' Then, as she gave the bannock into his hand, 'Talore the Hunter? And what could there be for you and Talore the Hunter to talk of?'

That was one of the things about Drem's mother; often she

wanted to know too much. He stuck his chest out, swaggering a little, with his mouth already full of bannock. 'Did I not say that it was man's talk?' Then he looked over his shoulder at his angry brother. 'I am tired of trapping fish. Let you give me one of your old throw-spears – the one with the three nicks in the blade that you never use now.'

3   First Kill

Barley harvest came, but Drem did not go up to Doli and the sheep again. Wheat harvest followed, and they threshed, and then winnowed the grain with an old grey goose wing, and saved the best for seed, and parched the rest to prevent it sprouting, before it went into the skin-lined store pits in the chalk. Samhain came, the feast of in-gathering when the year turns to the dark; the flocks were driven down from the high pastures for branding, and there was all the excitement of the great cattle round-up and the red business of the winter slaughtering. And Drem did not go up, as he had promised, to help with the droving. That way was closed to him; he could not go to Doli and the shepherd kind again . . .

Winter came, and the wolves howled closer and closer in the darkness, while Tribesmen and Half People alike kept the Wolf Guard over the lambing pens. Spring came, and Drustic ploughed the family corn plots with the two red plough oxen, followed by a wheeling, crying cloud of gulls, the shadows of wings mingling with the shadows of the drifting clouds along the shoulder of the downs. Seed-time came, and with all the other children of the Outland farms and the village away down the valley, Drem was busy all day long at the bird scaring. And so almost a year went by.

On an evening about the time of sheep shearing, Drem went down the valley towards the village and the house-place of Talore the Hunter, with a message from his mother for Wenna about a sitting of mallard eggs. He had been to Talore's house-place more than once since that summer dawn in the forest. Talore had three sons, all grown men, even the youngest of them who had gained his scarlet last Beltane, but they were kind to Drem in an off-hand way, tossing him a word in passing as though tossing a scrap of meat to a well-intentioned puppy. Fat Wenna, the wife of the eldest son, who looked after the household, was kind to him too, when she was not too taken up with the stew or the wet girl-child squalling in the rushes. And there was always the hope that Talore would be there.

He was hoping that now, as he came dropping down from the Chalk at a steady wolf trot, with his throw-spear over his shoulder. It was a wild day, the wind driving a racing tumble of cloud low across the downs, and the stray gleams of sunshine scudding before the rain; and the long tongue of the woods that thrust up from the valley was roaring like a forge fire as he came down through the head of it with the rain in his face. Rain trailed across the crest of the Hill of Gathering, above the village, blurring the outline of the round gravemound of the long forgotten warrior who slept there with his copper sword beside him; and the cluster of turf-roofed huts and house-places about the Chieftain's steading seemed to huddle under the bluff hill shoulder with the head-down dejection of ponies sheltering under a bank. But ever after in Drem's memory that was to be a shining day – one of the cluster of shining days that a man may hold in the hollow of one hand when he is old and looks back.

The steading of Talore the Hunter had fewer out-sheds than most, for though he and his sons farmed a little, their wealth was not in herds or corn-land but in dressed skins, and their own skill and cunning on the hunting trail, with spear and bow and dead-fall trap. Æsk, the eldest son, was squatting by the doorway now, cleaning a raw beaver skin with a bronze scraper, while a couple of great hounds beside him snapped up the scrapings; and when Drem had stopped to give him the day's greeting, he said with a jerk of his head behind him. 'Something fine to see in there.'

'Is it the puppies – Fand's puppies?' Instantly Drem was alight with eagerness.

'Maybe. Go in and look.'

More than two moons ago, when winter was quickening into spring, Talore had taken Fand, the wisest and most beautiful of his hounds, and rubbed her brindled hide with certain herbs to take away the Man smell, and tied her to an alder tree by the forest pool where the wolves came to drink. The hunters and shepherds did that sometimes, for a hound bitch mated with a wolf had fine cubs, and brought strong new blood into the dog pack. And in the morning there had been the pad marks of a he-wolf all about her, and the wolf smell on her hide, and they had known that presently there would be strong puppies born to Fand the Beautiful.

Drem swooped through the low doorway into a warm, smoky gloom laced with firelight, pitched his throw-spear in the direction of the place where it was the custom to stack weapons on entering a house, and not even noticing Wenna setting curd cakes to dry by the fire, made for the place against the wall, fenced off with hurdles and piled with russet fern, from which came small unmistakable squeaks and rustlings. Talore had shifted back one of the hurdles, and was squatting on one knee in the opening, giving little bits of meat to Fand, who half lay, half sat, her eyes luminous in the gloom, surrounded by small things that Drem could not really see in the crowding shadows, save as a wriggling and a squirming among the dried bracken fronds.

Talore turned on his knee and looked up at the boy with a swift, dark flash of shared pleasure that made nothing of the difference in years and status between them. 'I heard your voice. See now, the cubs are come.'

Drem, who had checked his headlong arrival, squatted down beside the hunter, his own eyes very bright under his wild, rain-wet flame of hair.

Fand dropped her muzzle and sniffed at one of the tiny rat-like creatures against her flank, with a kind of proud bewilderment. She had had many litters in her time, but just at first she always seemed a little puzzled by the puppies.

'Ah, my beautiful, that was bravely done!' Talore said, with a leaping gentleness in his voice, as he gave her the last piece of meat, and turned his hand to caress the warm hollow under her chin.

There were five of the whelps, Drem could see now; blind, helpless, squirming, yet already thrusting among each other for first place against their mother's flank and the chief share of the warm milk that meant life.

Talore slipped his hand under one of the puppies, and scooped it up. Fand licked his wrist as he did so, but when Drem tried to pick up one of the tiny creatures she rumbled warningly in her throat, the rumble rising to a sing-song snarl; and he drew his hand back empty, saying, 'But you know me, I am Drem. Do you think that I would harm your cubs?'

Talore smiled, and the dog teeth showed white at the corners of his mouth. 'In a little, ah, before their eyes open, she will let you take them even from under her. Now her temper is shaken and unsure; it is no more than that.' He returned the puppy, and took up another, whose coat was brindled black and amber. 'Aye, they are fine cubs. But this one, it is in my heart, will be the finest of the litter.' And while Fand watched with only a faint warning growl, he set the puppy on Drem's knee.

With strange things happening inside him, Drem slipped his hand under its small chest and sat it up, its fore paws dangling over his wrist. It was as rat-like as its brothers, its still damp hide soft as a mouse's skin, its stomach pinkish and almost naked, palpitating with very new life against his palm. And on its breast and throat there shone already a blaze like a small silver flame. The creature whimpered, its soft muzzle thrusting and fumbling against Drem's hand, seeking for the warm milk that it had lost. And Drem, looking down at it, saw it with the eyes of love, so that his whole heart went out to it, his whole soul caught up in longing. It was not just because it was a puppy, he had held many puppies before now, in his world that lived by its hounds and herd dogs; and of them all, it was to this one that his heart cried out, 'Brother, we are for each other, you and I!' This one, with the white flame on its breast.

Ah, but what was the use? If it had been a weakling, the outcast of the litter, maybe Talore would have given it to him instead of drowning it; but it would be the finest of them all, Talore had said so, and he could see the truth of that for himself. And there were always hunters throughout the Clan who would pay any price that Talore liked to ask for one of Fand's puppies, for Fand's puppies always had her wisdom and her beauty.

Now the puppy was nuzzling harder and more urgently under his hand. Talore said, 'He is hungry. It is time that he goes back to his mother,' and picked him up and set him again among his brothers, laughing as he thrust his way back to his mother's flank.

'Come,' said Talore, rising. 'Better that we leave her to herself now.'

So Drem got up, with one last, longing look at the tiny rat-like thing squirming among its litter brothers, and presently, quite forgetting to give Wenna the message about the sitting of mallard eggs, went his way, out into the gusty greyness of the evening, leaving his small fierce heart behind him.

In the days that followed, he seized on every excuse to go

down to the village, until at last the time was almost come for the cubs to leave their mother. By that time Fand was growing tired of her family and had returned to her usual place at Talore's heels; and the low hurdles of their pen were the only thing that kept them from exploring all over the house-place at all times of the day and night and probably ending by being trodden on by Wenna or killed in a fit of exasperation by one of the other hunting dogs.

On a summer evening, a grey evening as the other had been, but full of the soft, regretful stillness of mizzle rain instead of the wet turmoil of wind, Drem, who for several days had not been able to escape from the work on the farm, met Talore on his way home from visiting his traps, and came trotting back among the hounds at his heels. And now, the hurdle shifted back, he was squatting on his heels in the fern, with the cubs all about him. The rain dripped from the eaves, and the flames fluttered under the pot in which Wenna was seething deer meat in milk; the wet girl-child chirrupped and bubbled to herself on a deerskin beside the hearth, and the puppies squealed and whickered together. Fand pushed past Drem and snuffed among her cubs, thrusting them this way and that with her broad muzzle; but she no longer lay down among them, for her time for feeding them was done, and she was tired of being nipped and crawled over.

They were twice the size that they had been when first he saw them; they had become woolly and venturesome and had long since ceased to look like rats. He looked up at Talore, who had come across the hut to join him, after hanging up his kill. 'Does Fand not feed them any more?'

'Nay, the time for that is over; they eat meal stirabout and meat now.'

Something seemed to twist in Drem's stomach, and he put out his hand to the cub with the white throat, and bowled it on to its back, feeling the nip of its little sharp teeth in his thumb. 'Ah – ee! Fierce wolf-dog! You would bite, would you?' He rolled it from side to side while it squirmed with delight; and still playing with the puppy, so that he need not look up, he asked in a carefully levelled voice, 'Then – their new masters will be taking them soon?'

'Any day now,' said Talore.

Drem swallowed. 'You will – have chosen who they go to?'

'Surely. The little red one I keep myself, and the mealy grey. This one, Belu from above the ford will trade me a length of cloth for – poor Wenna cannot clothe four men with her weaving – and this one goes to Gwythno of the Singing Spear.'

That left only the cub with the silver blaze, now muzzling into the hollow of Drem's neck, for without quite knowing that he did so, he had caught it up and was holding it against his breast.

'And that one' – said Talore, and let the end of the sentence fall, watching the small, braced, tell-tale figure crouched among the fern, with the puppy held fiercely, protectively, against his breast.

Drem looked up, and met Talore's dark, narrowed gaze upon him, and waited, with a sudden intensity of waiting that hurt him somewhere beneath his breast-bone. He heard the drip of the summer rain from the eaves, and Wenna crooning to the girl-child as she turned barley cakes among the hot ash. The puppy whimpered protestingly at being held so close, its little body warmly alive against his, its breath like the breath of all puppies, smelling of garlic. Soon its warmth and liveness would be under someone else's hand, it would learn to come to someone else's call, and hunt with a master who was not Drem . . . And still the rain fell, drip-drip-drip from the eaves, very loud.

'Do you want him so badly, then?' Talore said.

Drem lifted bright, grave eyes to his face and nodded. He could not speak.

'Then it is in my mind that I will sell him to you,' Talore said, 'at a price'.

It seemed to Drem that the rain was louder than ever. '*Drip-drip-drip*' marking off the silence with little dark arrow-heads of sound. Price? What price could he give for the cub? He was not Belu to have fine cloth to trade. His eyes searched Talore's face, looking for the meaning behind it.

'What is the price?' he asked at last, and his voice sounded husky in his own ears.

Talore smiled. 'I grow weary of mutton and of deer meat. The price is a bird for the pot – but it must be brought down with the throw-spear.'

Drem frowned at him a moment in bewilderment, knowing that Talore could bring down wild fowl for himself at any time he chose, and had besides, three sons to hunt for him. And then he understood. It was proof of his own skill with the throw-spear that was really the price of the cub.

Well, it was a year since he had first set himself to master the throw-spear; he had some skill, he knew. Suddenly he grinned, flinging up his head like a pony, in a way that always showed when he was ready for battle; and the dripping of the rain under the eaves went back to its proper place. 'I will pay the price,' he said, 'I will pay it tomorrow, Talore.'

Drem did not say anything in the home house-place about what he was going to do; he could not speak of it to anyone until it was done. He slept fitfully that night, waking often,

until the first faint paling of the sky where the roof turf was
rolled back warned him that it was time to be on his way.
Then he pushed back the deerskin covering and got silently to
his feet, feeling to make sure that his knife was safely in his belt.
There were a few bad moments while he felt for his own spear
among the others in the rack, and got it out, but he managed it
without the blade clattering against its neighbours, and with a
sigh of relief turned to the entrance. Old Kea raised her head
beside the fire to watch him, but made no outcry, for the hounds
were well used to night-time comings and goings; and since it
was summer time there was no stirring and stamping of ponies
in the fore porch to betray his passing that way.

Yesterday's rain had gone over, and there was a new-washed
cleanness in the air, a smell of wet, refreshed earth. The curlews
were already calling over the High Chalk, but at this time of
year they called almost all through the short nights; and there
would be plenty of time to reach his chosen hunting ground
before dawn.

He had left the last of the corn plots behind him, and was
turning down to the little brook that had its spring in a deep
hollow under the grazing ground, when his ear picked up the
pad of running feet behind him – very small, swift feet on the
downland turf – and he had scarcely time to swing round
before a flying shadow came down the slope and Blai was beside
him, panting with the speed she had made.

Drem was angry. 'What do you come after me for?' he
demanded. 'Go home, Blai.'

'I saw you go,' Blai said in the little clear voice that had
somehow the note of a bird call in it and never seemed to
belong to the same person as her narrow, shut-up face, 'and I
thought maybe – if it was a hunting, you would need food for
the day.'

Food; yes, he had not thought about food. Well, it was for

the Women's side to think of such things. 'What have you got?' he demanded.

'Only a barley cake. That was all I could steal without waking them. But it is a big one.'

'It will serve,' said Drem handsomely, and tucking his throw-spear under his arm, took the hard, crusty bannock that she thrust into his hand. 'Go home now, Blai, and do not you be telling anyone that I have gone hunting.'

'I will not, then.' Blai hesitated on one foot, half going, half staying. 'Drem – let you take me too!'

Drem said with harsh reason, 'You! What use would you be?'

'I would do anything – I would be your hound – '

But Drem was already turning away. 'Na, I do not need a hound today. And' – suddenly he could not hold it back – 'soon I may have a hound of my own to hunt with me!'

Behind him as he went, he heard her cry out in a little defiant voice, 'One day – one day my father will come back for me – ' But she was crying it out to herself, not really to Drem.

Drem crossed the brook – it was so narrow still that it did not even need a stepping stone – and went on to his day's hunting, leaving her standing there.

A faint bar of amber light was broadening in the east as he came down through the oak and hazel and whitethorn scrub of the lower slopes, eating the bannock as he went so as to have it out of the way, and headed for the marshes. A great, slow, full-bodied river, winding south from the forest uplands far inland, found a pass in the hills just there, and went winding and looping out to join the Great Water. Many streams rising in the lower flanks of the Chalk ran down into it, and in several places across it beavers had built their dams – generation after generation of beavers that had been there, Drem supposed, as long as the river had been there, and would stay while the river stayed. And the choked river had flowed out over its banks, spreading far and wide; and so came the Marsh. Sometimes after the winter rains the water spread far up into the forest, making a lake that was a day's trail, two days' trail, from end to end, and all the pass through the Chalk was a winding arm of water out of which the alders and sallows raised their arms to the sky. But in the summer it was mostly land of a sort, sour and sodden and very green: reed beds and alder brakes and dense covers of thorn and sallow, and thickly matted fleeces of yellow iris, all laced with winding, silver riverways and spreading, shallow lakes alive with the wild fowl that came inland at the breeding season and did not go back to the coast until autumn came again.

No one lived in the Marshes that lay inland of the Chalk, for at night mists rose from them and evil spirits prowled abroad in the mists to give men the sickness that filled their bones with shivering fire; and even at high noon in summer time there was always a dank smell of things wet and rotting, for the cleansing wash of the tides that came up and went down again twice in every day over the sea marshes could not reach so far through the Chalk. But the hunters went there after the wild fowl and the beaver.

So Drem headed for the Marsh now, and in a clump of sallows on the edge of one of the many spreading sheets of water, settled himself to wait.

He was shivering with mingled cold and excitement and a breathless sense of the importance of that day's hunting. Away eastward the bar of amber light was brightening to gold, and the gold was catching echoes from the water that lay everywhere, and all around him was a stirring as the Marsh woke into life. Light and colour were coming back into the world; and suddenly something dark, almost like a rat, darted from among the pale roots of the rushes close to Drem, hesitated, half doubled back, and then scuttled across to the next clump. When the water-rail moved, other things would soon be stirring. Very soon now, Drem thought, any moment now, and drew his knee farther under him. His hand cramped on the spear shaft, and he opened it, feeling it wet and sticky with the long tightness of his grip; and went over feverishly in his mind everything he had ever been told, everything he had ever found out for himself about the throw-spear; and licked his lower lip, and waited again.

He was so twanging taut that when, without an instant's warning, a mallard drake beat up from the rushes not three spears' lengths away to his right, he was thrown completely off his balance. Next instant he had recovered himself, and sent the light throw-spear, thrumming as it flew, after the quarry. It missed so narrowly that it carried away the tip of a wing feather, and for one instant he thought he had made his hit, before the spear plunged back into the rushes and the mallard darted off, raising its wild alarm call to the morning skies. And suddenly with a great bursting upward, the Marsh was alive with startled and indignant wings.

In a while, the morning fell quiet again, and he could hear teal and widgeon, curlew and sandpiper crying and calling in the distance; but all around him the Marsh was silent; empty under a shining and empty sky.

Drem hit the stem of the nearest sallow with a passionate fist; but that only hurt his knuckles and did nothing to mend what had happened. He was almost crying with fury as he slid out of his cover and searched among the reeds for his throw-spear. It took him a few moments to find it, because he was blind with rage and disappointment; but he found it at last, and settled again to wait. But the wild fowl did not return though he heard them calling in the distance; and at last, with the sun well up and the level light streaming across the Marshes, he knew that it would be no use waiting any longer.

He left his hiding-place, slipping along in the lea of the sallow bushes. Maybe he would be able to flush something and knock it down before it got out of range. But though he hunted far and wide as the shadows shortened, he never got within spear-throw of a bird; and something was growing in him that was frightened and a little desperate. There would be other days; Talore would not sell the cub away from him at once, because he failed on the first day of all. But last night he had said, 'I will pay the price tomorrow.' And somehow for him there was only this one day; that was the bargain. Somehow, in his mind, the thing was mixed up with his Warrior Scarlet; he must earn the price of the cub today, he must keep his bargain perfectly and completely, and give proof of his skill with a throw-spear *today*, if his mother was ever to weave scarlet on the loom for him.

It must have been noon or later, when, as he came crouching down the fringe of a long straggle of alder trees, he heard the rhythmical creaking sound, half eery, half musical, of a swan in flight, and turning, saw the great bird flying low towards him

across the level of jewel-green turf between two spreading
sheets of water. The sun was on its feathers, and its shadow flew
beneath it like a dark echo along the ground; a bird of snow
and a bird of shadow ... Drem saw the proud spread of
shining wings, beating with slow, almost lazy power and
beauty, as it flew with outstretched neck; he heard louder and
louder the half musical throb of the wing beats; and the great
swan stole on his sight. It seemed rushing towards him,
blotting out the world with the white spread of its wings. He
was caught up in a piercing vision of white, fierce beauty that
was like thunder and lightning and an east wind, like a sun-
burst. He was scarcely aware of rising to his feet as the great
bird swept towards him, climbing into the sunlight, scarcely
aware of his spear-arm swinging up and back in its own perfect
curve of movement ...

The spear went thrumming on its way. It took the swan in
the breast, and the great bird pitched in the air, half turning
over its own length, and dropped.

Drem started from cover of the alder trees and ran towards it.
The swan was still alive, and threshing where it had fallen, with
a dreadful, broken struggling. Drem ran in among the flailing
wings that could have broken his leg even now, if a blow had
landed square, and finished the work with the knife from his
belt. The struggling ceased with a last quiver.

The swan – a big cob – lay dead, its neck outstretched as in
flight; and Drem pulled out the spear which was still embedded
in it. There was blood on the white feathers. Blood on snow,
Drem thought, standing over it; blood on his own hand, too;
and the living, flashing beauty was gone. Desolation as piercing
as the moment of vision had been stabbed through him. How
could a little spear that he had thrown almost without knowing
it, blot out in an instant all the power and the swiftness and the
shining?

But the desolation passed as the vision had done, and he was left with the fierce hot pride of his first real kill. He stabbed his knife into the turf to clean it, and thrust it back into his belt; then stood to think what he must do next.

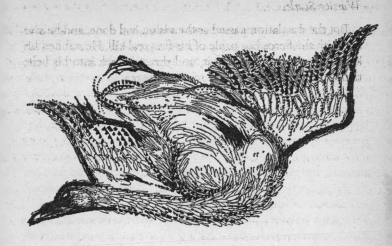

4   The Price of Whitethroat

The first thing he realized was that he could not possibly get his kill back to Talore alone. He had seen himself proudly walking into the steading with a teal or a widgeon hanging from his hand; how much more proudly with a swan on his shoulder, the huge white wings drooping all about him! But those wings must be as far from tip to tip as the height of a man. And when he tried, he found that he could not even get the swan on to his shoulder without help, let alone carry it all the way back. The only thing to do was to hide it, and go and tell Talore.

He got hold of the bird, and began to drag it back towards the alder trees. It took him some time to do, because instinctively he was trying not to spoil it. It was his kill, and still beautiful, though with a moveless beauty now; and he wanted it to keep the beauty until Talore saw it. Little by little, the great wings fanned out on the grass, he got it back: in at last among the tangle of alders and the thick-growing rushes and wild iris. Dragging it deep into the tangle, he folded the great wings close so that it might take up as little space as possible, and dragged up handfuls of brown, flowering rushes and cool, sword-shaped iris leaves and spread them over it in a thick layer until there was no gleam of white to betray it to the magpies and the ravens. Then he got up, picked up his spear and cleaned it as he had cleaned his dagger, by stabbing it into the turf, and taking a last careful look round him to be sure of knowing the place again, set off for the village and the steading of Talore the Hunter.

He had wandered long distances to and fro in search of his kill, but turned back often on his trail, so that he was not so far out into the Marsh as he had expected. But even so, the way up through the midge-infested hazel woods and along the flank of the Chalk was a long, hard one, and his bare, briar-scratched legs were beginning to be very weary when he came within sight – and smell – of the village.

It was the time of the wild garlic harvest, when the women and girls went down the stream sides and through the cool, dark places of the forest fringe, searching for the rank-smelling star-white flowers, and gathering the plants into big rush baskets; and for days the village and every outlying steading reeked of the white flowers spread out on the south sides of the low turf roofs to dry. Yesterday it had been no good trying to dry the flowers, but today the sun shone hot, and the swallows were flying high for fine weather, darting and swerving against the blue of the sky, and every roof had its patch of wilting white stars; the pungent waft of them came to meet Drem as he climbed up between the village corn plots towards the steading of Talore the Hunter.

Talore was not there, nor any of his sons. Only fat, good-natured Wenna sat on her heels in the house-place doorway, grinding corn for the next day in the big stone quern; and she cried out at sight of him, '*Now* what thing have you been doing? Tch tch, you're hurt – there is blood on your fore-head —'

Drem had not known that; it must have come off his hand when he pushed back his hair. 'Na, I am not hurt,' he said. 'I have been hunting, and I have killed. Now I would speak with Talore.'

'He is away down the valley about a heifer calf,' said Talore's son's wife, smiling at him across the quern, now that she knew he was not hurt. 'Do you want to go in and look at the cubs? Gwythno came for his today, and Belu also, but there are still three cubs left.'

Drem shook his head. That was a thing that he was saving.

'Are you hungry, then?' Wenna asked.

Drem thought about this a little. In the intensity of his thinking about other things, he had forgotten about being hungry, but now he realized that having eaten nothing but Blai's bannock all day, he was as empty as last year's snail shell. 'I am hungry,' he agreed.

'Bide you —' Wenna rose, and disappeared into the house-place, leaving him alone with the girl-child, who lay in a soft deerskin, sucking the bead of red coral that hung round her neck, and gazed at him out of solemn, sloe-black eyes. Drem stared back at the girl-child, then poked it gingerly in the middle with one toe, to see what would happen, prepared to retreat and swear he hadn't been near it if it screamed. But it kicked inside the deerskin, and made pleased noises. So he poked it once more, then abandoned it rather hurriedly as Wenna came back.

'Here – take this, then,' she said, and gave him a wheaten

cake smeared with dark honey, and squatted down again to her grinding.

Drem sat down with his back against the rowan-wood door-post in the sunshine, and ate his wheaten cake, licking the golden dribble of sweetness round the edges, and watched Wenna scoop the grain from her basket into the hole in the upper stone of the quern, and the coarse creamy meal that came up between the two stones as she rubbed, on to the spread skin under the quern. Every now and then she stopped rubbing, and scooped up the meal into a crock beside her. Drem did not offer to help; it was woman's work, and he was of the Men's side, a hunter, and had made his first big kill.

The shadows were lengthening though it would not be evening for a long while yet, and Wenna had finished her grinding, and gone in again, carrying the baby with her on her hip, and Drem was alone before the house-place door, when at last Talore came home, driving a small, dispirited brown heifer calf on the end of a rope.

Drem scrambled up and went to meet him as he came up between the store shed and the woodstack, with the calf lurching from side to side on the end of the rope, and the three hounds loping at his heels.

'Well?' Talore said questioningly when he saw him, leaning back to check a sudden rush by the calf.

'I have come for the cub,' Drem said. 'I can pay the price.'

Talore's dark brows went up. 'Where is it then? In the pot already?'

'I could not bring it with me. It is too big.'

'Have you killed a wild ox with your throw-spear?' Talore's voice deepened, as it always did with laughter; and the dog teeth showed at the corners of his mouth. 'It was a bird I said, remember.'

'It is a swan!' Drem's pride came rushing up into his throat. 'A cob swan – big, big as a cloud!'

'So? That is a kill indeed!'

They were all heading for the byre by now, and the calf had set up a dismal bawling. Drem nodded urgently. 'Down in the Marsh, it is. I could not carry it, so I hid it and came back. I thought maybe – we could go for it – now.' His voice trailed away a little, as it dawned on him that perhaps that was rather a lot to ask at the day's end.

Talore glanced down at him, at the same time putting out a leg to fend the calf from a determined sideways rush in the wrong direction. He was tired, and wanted nothing but to sit down and stretch out his legs and polish his spears while he waited for Wenna to make ready the evening meal. But looking at Drem's proudly eager face with the doubt already beginning to shadow it, he said, 'Let you help me to stall the calf, and then we will go down together and fetch this kill.'

They stalled the calf in the warm-shadowed byre, and left it to Wenna's tending; and, in a little, were heading down again toward the Marsh, Talore loping ahead with the long, light stride of the hunter, the hounds and Drem close at his heels.

The blue summer dusk had deepened into the dark, and the white owl who lived in the shed of the Chieftain's great herd bull was hawking to and fro like a silver shadow across the corn land, when they came up again towards the huddle of the village under the Hill of Gathering. Talore walked ahead as before, and Drem and the hounds padded at his heels; but now the hunter carried Drem's swan on his shoulder, the great wings drooping wide behind him – pale, paler than the soft wings of the hunting owl in the darkness, or the white, wilting stars of the garlic spread on the hut roofs to dry.

The skin apron over the house-place doorway was drawn back, and a stain of light came to meet them, thick and golden like honey trickling from a tipped jar. Inside, the sons had returned from their hunting and were gathered about the hearth, where the fire sank low, for the evening meal was long past, burnishing their weapons, while Wenna stitched at a piece of yellow cloth by the light of a mutton-fat lamp hanging from the roof tree.

There was another man sitting by the fire, his back to the doorway, a big, broad-shouldered man who turned as they crossed the threshold, revealing the heavy, reddish face of Morvidd, the Chieftain's brother. And behind him in the shadows squatted a boy of about Drem's age, nursing his father's spear – a boy with a quarrelsome and unhappy face; but Drem, who had run with him in the same pack all his life, did not of course see that. He only knew that Luga the son of Morvidd was apt to be at the root of any trouble that broke out among their own kind.

'So. You are here at last,' the man said, rather loudly, while the two boys cocked their heads at each other.

Talore checked just within the doorway and returned the greeting more courteously. 'And you, Morvidd the Chieftain's brother, you also are here, and welcome. I had not thought you would be back from your trading until the moon was on the wane.'

'I am but this evening returned to my house-place; and one told me that Fand has whelped and the whelps are ready to leave their dam. Therefore I am come to make my choice of one of them.'

Talore stood smiling a little, the great swan on his shoulder, its wings falling wide behind him. 'Others have made their choice already. There is none of the cubs left without a master.'

Æsk, the eldest son, looked up from the spear he was burnishing, and said swiftly. 'I told him that, my father, but he would wait for you none the less.'

Morvidd's face had turned a deeper red as it always did when he was crossed, so that his eyes looked like little bright splinters of glass in the redness of it; and he began to bluster. 'Did I not say to you, last Fall-of-the-leaf, that I would give you a fine copper cooking pot that had never known the fire, for the best cub in Fand's next litter?'

It seemed to Drem that everything stopped, between breath and breath, and there was a sudden cold emptiness inside him. He saw the grin of triumph on the face of the boy Luga. Then Talore said, 'Did I not say to you last Fall-of-the-leaf that I do not promise unborn cubs to any man?' And everything went on again, and the grin faded on Luga's face.

Morvidd forced a laugh, and an air of joviality; clearly he wanted one of the cubs very badly. 'Nay then, we will leave that part of it. I come now, and there are three cubs yet in the litter. I've a mind to the one with the white blaze on its breast – the best cub of the three, without doubt; and I'll give you the cook pot for him – a good big cook pot – and a length of fine bleached linen cloth thrown in. What do you say to that?'

'I say that above all the litter, that one is already sold,' Talore said.

'Who to, then? Who to?'

'To the boy here.'

Morvidd stared for a moment, then flung up his head with a roar of laughter. 'And since when does Talore sell his hound cubs to children for a handful of wild raspberries? Ah, but of course if that is the way of the thing it is easily undone. I see the thing is more than half a jest!'

Talore slipped the swan from his shoulder and flung it down beside the hearth. 'Nay, it is not a jest, the bargain was fairly made and the boy has paid the price – the agreed price – and the thing is finished.'

The great swan lay there, spread-winged in the firelight and the lamplight; one of the hounds sniffed at it and was cuffed aside by the second son. Morvidd finished his laugh rather abruptly, and stared down at the swan and then at Drem and then back at Talore, angry again, and the more angry because he was puzzled. 'This – *this*?' He reached out a foot and prodded the great bird contemptuously in a way that made the rage rise in Drem's throat – his swan, his beautiful kill, the price of the hound of his heart, to be treated so! 'Surely it is not a hand but a head that you lack, Talore! What sort of price, beside a fine copper cook pot, is a dead swan for a hound puppy? Tell me that!'

Drem clenched his sound hand into a fist; and then above him, Talore said with that leaping gentleness of his, 'This swan is a better price than if it were as many copper cook pots as there are fingers on my one hand.'

The two men stood facing each other beside the fire, the one big and red-gold and blustering, swaying a little on his heels,

the other slight and dark, and still as a forest pool; while the rest of the big firelit hut looked on, the boy Luga watching his father out of the shadows, expectantly.

Then Morvidd said, 'And that is your last word as to the thing?'

'That is my last word.'

'Then you're mad!' Morvidd let out a kind of baffled roar. 'You're a fool, Talore One-hand! To shake your head at a fine copper —'

Talore cut across his blustering, with the same gentleness. 'That you have said before. Nay then, Morvidd the Chieftain's brother, there is a thing that you forget, in all this. It is I who choose what master Fand's cubs shall go to, and what master Fand's cubs shall not go to; I, and no other. And I choose only masters who to my mind are worthy of them.'

For a moment Drem thought that Morvidd was going to burst like an old skin bottle filled too full, then he seemed to collapse as though the bottle had been partly emptied. He blinked, and swallowed loudly, then gathered himself together and strode to the doorway. On the threshold he turned, some of his bluster coming back to him, and shouted: 'Then here is *my* last word. There are better cubs easily come by for a smaller price; and do not you be trying to sell a cub to *me* when Fand litters again and maybe no man needs another hound!'

'I will not, assuredly, I will not,' Talore said, looking after the big angry man as he flung away into the night; and the familiar note of laughter was deepening in his voice.

The boy Luga made after his father, turning also on the threshold with a long, lowering look that took in everybody in the house-place but rested longest upon Drem, before he too was gone.

'He was very angry,' Drem said, when the sound of footsteps had died away.

'He will forget,' Talore said. 'He blusters – like a west wind he blusters; but a west wind blows itself out in a while.'

But Drem had a feeling that however quickly Morvidd's fury blustered itself out, it would be a long time before Luga forgave having seen his father worsted and made to seem foolish.

Ah, but what did that matter? The thing was over; and Drem drew a long breath, and turned his gaze again to the swan lying spread-winged in the firelight. They were all looking at the swan now, while Wenna set aside her stitching, and rose to set out the deer meat which she had been keeping hot for the lord of the house in a pot among the embers. 'Gwythno was here at noon, and Belu from the ford a while before. I gave them the puppies as you bade me ... I would have liked a copper cook pot, but I suppose we can do without.'

'Nay then,' said Talore, laughing. 'We are none so poor that we must trade a puppy for a cook pot. If your heart is set on such a thing, then go and speak with Kian the Smith, and tell him he shall have two dressed wolfskins from me, for making it.'

Talore's sons were all round Drem now, laughing. 'That was a great hunting,' they said. 'Little brother, that was a fine kill – see, it is all but as big as himself!' And the eldest son caught him a friendly buffet between the shoulders that landed like the blow of a bear's paw and all but sent him sprawling into the fire.

Triumph rushed up into Drem's throat, all the fiercer and more sweet for what had gone before. Just for one dreadful moment following on Morvidd's words, he had seen his swan, his beautiful kill, as so small a price for the cub that it was not really a price at all. Just a big dead bird, beginning to be tattered and unlovely. But then Talore had said that it was worth as many copper cooking pots as there were fingers on his one hand, and the white rumpled feathers on which the bright blood had turned brown were shining with pride and beauty again.

'It is a fair price,' said Talore, seeing where he looked. 'Let you take the cub now.'

Drem nodded, for the moment beyond speech, and crossed to the hurdled-off place where Fand stood with her muzzle down and her tail slowly swinging, among the yippings and whimperings that came from the piled fern.

His heart was beating right up in his throat with the joy of the moment as he pulled the low hurdle aside and reached down among the small, sleepy forms in the bracken, and grasped the one with the silver blaze by the scruff of the neck and lifted him out from between his brothers. Fand made no protest, and indeed seemed scarcely interested. He held the puppy up, swinging a little from its loose scruff; he laughed as it tried from arm's length away to lick his nose, and knew that the perfect moment, the best moment of all had come.

'I have bought my hound!' he said to the world at large. 'I have paid the price for him, and he is mine! I shall call him Whitethroat!'

'So, that is a good name,' Talore said. 'And now it is time to be going home.'

Drem looked up from the puppy. 'I shall need to leave my spear here until tomorrow,' he said, 'so that I can carry the cub.'

'Assuredly,' Talore nodded. 'His legs are but two moons old, and the way will be over long for them; yet first make him follow you a little. It is so that he will understand that he is your hound to follow at your heel.'

Drem looked at the hunter doubtfully a moment, then squatted down and set the puppy on its legs. 'Will he come, do you think?'

'Call him, and see.'

Drem got up and took a step backward, 'Hi! Whitethroat, come!' The puppy continued to sit on its haunches. It was too small as yet to prick its ears, but it fluttered them, gazing up at Drem with the air of one trying to understand what he would have it do. Drem drew another step towards the doorway. 'Come! We go home now, brother.' The puppy whimpered and made a small thrusting motion towards him. Aware that everyone in the house-place was watching them, Drem took yet another backward step. He was almost at the threshold now. 'Whitethroat – here!' His throat ached with urgency, and the words came hoarse. He whistled a two-note call that he had never thought of before, but that seemed to come to him now as the proper call between him and Whitethroat. The small, brindled, half-wolf cub got up, sneezed, shook itself and waddled towards him, its stomach brushing the ferny ground. Once it hesitated, and looked back at Fand its mother with an air of uncertainty, and then padded forward again. And Drem knew that he had been wrong in thinking that the moment when he picked it out from the litter was the best moment of all.

He was across the threshold now, looking back over his shoulder as he went; and the cub gave a bounce and quickened to a rolling trot. They went down between the out-sheds together, the hunter leading, the hound at his heels, as it should be; as it would be in all their lives together. But at the edge of Talore's steading, Drem stopped in answer to a protesting whimper, and scooped up the puppy and settled it against his shoulder, in the crook of his sound arm.

So Drem walked home up the sweeping flanks of the Chalk, through the still summer darkness, with his hunting dog asleep, warm and live and unexpectedly heavy, in the crook of his arm; and a kind of chant of triumph singing itself over and over again within him. 'I have bought my hound! I bought him with a great white swan – a swan like a sun-burst, that I slew with my throw-spear! I have bought my hound, and he is mine! He was sired by a wolf, out where the wolves pass at the Spring Running; and he will be the swiftest and the bravest hound that ever ran with the Clan, and he is mine! Mine is the cub to me because I paid the price for him – I, Drem the Hunter; I bought him with my kill!'

It had been a long day and a hard one, and it had given him his hound and his first big kill, and the proof of his own skill with a throw-spear that brought him just so much nearer to his Warrior Scarlet. It had been a good day.

But he had been right in thinking that it would be a long time – a very long time – before Luga the son of Morvidd forgave, or forgot.

5 The Dagger and the Fire

At most places the brook ran deep sunk between steep alder-fringed banks; but at the loop just below the ancient trackway, the current had formed a low spit which was a favourite bathing place with the boys of the Clan. It was a good place, in the blue and green noon-tides of summer when the high sun splashed through the alder leaves and fell in freckles of gold on the dark water, and the shadows might be lit at any moment by the irridescent flash of a dragon fly. Summer was over now, and the water turning cold, so that you splashed in and out again, shouting, and tumbled over each other in sham fight on the bank to get warm, while you dried off and got your kirtle on again; but it was still a good place, on a fine autumn evening, with the westering sunlight slanting in spears of tawny bright-ness through the alders and the nut leaves, and the shadows blue as woodsmoke.

There were some boys down there now; Luga the son of Morvidd, and fat, good-natured Maelgan, and little dark Erp of the Half People, who could swim like an otter under water, and two or three more, with the usual pack of dogs. Drem sat a little farther up the bank than the rest, re-tying the ankle thongs of his raw-hide shoes, a thing which always took him rather longer than it took the others, because of having to do it one handed. And beside him, nose on paws, and superb bush-tail curving away into the tangle of the past summer's willow-herb, lay the great, brindled, black and amber hound whom more than a year ago he had picked, small and woolly and half asleep, from among his litter brothers in Talore's house-place, and whistled to follow him.

Drem made the thong fast, and half drew his legs under him,

beginning to think about going home to supper. He wondered what there would be; stew of some sort, he hoped,
for as usual he was hungry. And if Blai, who had gone down
the brookside with a withy basket, came back in time,
maybe his mother would have made some of the sweet, dark,
pippy mess that she brewed with blackberries and honey to
spread on barley cakes; but more likely that would be
tomorrow.

For the moment they had fallen quiet, and in the quiet, a
flash of living blue lit across Drem's eyes, as a kingfisher
swooped down to a low-hanging branch of the great willow,
upstream.

Luga picked up a flint from the grass beside him – there
were always a few along the spit, rolled down from the made-
place where the cattle came to drink – and flung it. It missed
its mark and skittered over the top of the branch into the water
beyond with a sound like a fish leaping, and the kingfisher
darted off with a gutteral anger-call.

Drem hooted derisively, and Luga scowled. 'I was not trying
to hit it.'

'Yes you were,' Drem said.

'I was not, then.'

'You can never see anything alive and – and *liking* being
alive without wanting to throw something at it and make it
be dead,' Drem said, and added, more for the sake of arguing
than anything else, 'Talore says that killing for the sake of
killing, in the way of the fox and the weasel, makes the Forest
Gods angry.'

'Talore! Talore!' said Luga, skimmering another flint into
the water, and trying to mimic Drem's way of speaking. 'Of
course we all know you are Talore's pet. Didn't he give you
Whitethroat just for a dead swan that you like enough found
dead of old age on the Marshes and stole from the magpies,

when *my* father would have given him a fine copper cooking pot?'

Drem rose in his place and was just about to fall on him and avenge the insult to himself and his swan alike, when White-throat sprang to his feet and stood alert, his head up to reveal the silver blaze that had given him his name, his amber eyes wary, muzzle testing the wind; and almost in the same instant, Erp, who had been lying on his stomach investigating a water rat's hole under the bank, rolled over and sat up, cocking his narrow, dark head towards the track: the ancient green track along which, as often as along the Ridgeway, the world went by; bands of skin-clad hunters from distant hunting runs; herdsmen in the droving season; warriors with stripes of woad and ochre on their foreheads, following their princes to war; traders from across the Great Water with salt and scented yellow amber and fine bronze in their ponies' bales.

Somewhere, a long way off as yet, someone or something was coming along the track between the hazels and the whitethorn trees, and instantly the quarrel was forgotten, and boys and hounds in a knot went scrambling up the bank to where they could get a view of the track through the scrub.

'Maybe it is a war-band!' said Luga, hopefully. It was exciting when a war-band came by; and there was no need to be afraid, for if their business was with the village under the Hill of Gathering, as it had been in the time when Talore lost his hand and Drem's father went beyond the sunset, then they would not be on the track at all.

'More likely it is a hunting party, now in the Fall-of-the-Leaf,' Maelgan said.

Little Erp lay with his ear pressed against the ground. 'Ponies,' he said, 'The earth speaks of ponies – I think two ponies – and one man. No more.'

'Then it must be a trader of some kind.'

They waited, peering between the hazel branches, and listening. They could all hear it now, very faintly, the light beat of hooves on the summer-hard ground, and then the pad of human feet; nearer, and nearer. There was a flicker of saffron yellow through the alder leaves; and a few moment later a man came into view: a tall, dark man in a tattered cloak whose greens and purples had dimmed with weather and mud to the colour of storm clouds, leading two dejected ponies one behind the other, the foremost bowlegged under the weight of two great bales wrapped in yellow cloth, the hind-  most loaded with the tools of a bronze-smith's trade.

A trader or travelling craftsman was always of interest, for his stories of the outside world as well as for the wonders that might be hidden in his bales. And as this one drew level, walking with the long, slow stride of a man who walks from the sky's edge to the sky's edge and knows that there is no hurry, the knot of boys swarmed from cover with the hounds at their heels, and flung themselves upon him, demanding. 'Where are you from? – Where are you away to? – Do you sleep in our village tonight? – What have you in those bales?'

The tall man looked down at them, laughing, as they padded alongside him. 'Sa hah! Here is a fine welcome, then! I am from the last village behind me, and it may be that I spend the night in your Chieftain's steading, or it may be that I shall sleep as sound under a hawthorn bush with a fire to keep the Wild away. I am for the West towards the Sunset; and as to what there is in my bales, let you see when I open them before the Chieftain's door.'

And they went on together, only Erp was not with them, for he was of the Little Dark People whose instinct was to run and hide instead of coming out to ask questions; but the others knew that he was watching them from under the whitethorn bushes.

Maelgan ran ahead to give warning of the bronze-smith's coming, and when they reached the outskirts of the village, one of the Men's side came down to meet them, with reversed spear for a sign of peace, saying, 'Greeting, stranger. We have our bronze-smith already among the huts of the Half People; but Dumnorix the Chieftain sends you greeting, and bids you come and open your bales before his threshold, according to the custom.'

'Sa, I will come as the Chieftain bids me, and open my bales before his door according to the custom,' the stranger said. 'It is in my mind that the Chieftain will not regret it. All the world knows that the finest bronze-smiths are from the Green Isle in the West; and in all the Green Island there is no smith with cunning to match mine whether in the forging of weapons for a hero, or the working of ornaments for a queen's white neck.'

When they reached the clear space before the Chieftain's house-place, the only things alive in it were an old hound sleeping outstretched on the dung heap, and Midir the Priest sitting in the last echo of the sunset, against the wind-break beside the house-place doorway, with his soft bull's-hide robe huddled about his shoulders against the chill of the autumn evening, and his chin sunk on his breast as though he also slept. But it was commonly believed that Midir never slept, only went away small inside himself and talked with the Gods in the silence he found there. He did not look up or make any sign as they drew near. But almost in the moment of checking the ponies, two older boys – next year's warriors – came across from the Boys' House to take charge of the poor tired beasts as they were unloaded; and several of the Men's side who were home early began to trickle up, gathering for a sight of the things in the yellow bales, so that the small boys who were only there on sufferance anyway, were thrust farther on to the fringe of things.

Then the dyed deer skins over the house-place doorway were flung back and Dumnorix, the lord of three hundred spears, came out; a big man with a mane of red-gold hair tumbling about his bull neck and on to his shoulder, and the bright hairs of his beard spreading over his breast almost to the bronze buckle of his belt. He was followed by his hounds and a square-built boy a few months older than Drem, with bandy legs and a pair of round, very blue eyes; his son Vortrix, who had not been one of the bathing band, because he had trodden in Midir's shadow that morning, and so had been taboo until sunset.

'Greeting and welcome to you, stranger Bronze-smith,' said Dumnorix, 'for your own sake, and for what is in your bales. It will be a while before the evening stew comes from the fire; therefore if you are not over-weary, let you open your bales now, for I am eager to see if you have fine weapons to trade.'

The stranger touched palm to forehead, then stood up straight before the Chieftain with a pride to match his own, like a prince on a journey, rather than a wandering bronze-smith in a tattered cloak. 'Greeting, Lord of three hundred spears. Did ever a bronze-smith come out of the Green Isle yet, that had not fine weapons to show? And am I not the most skilled in the craft that ever the Green Isle bred? I am on my way home towards the Sunset, and much that I had is sold, yet there are still a few treasures worth the seeing in these bales of mine.' His long, strong fingers were busy on the bale-cords even as he spoke. 'And what better way to pass the time while we wait for the food bowls to be filled?'

The Chieftain had seated himself on his stool of carved and painted wood before his door, and the others of the Men's side were squatting on to their heels, huddling their cloaks about them. Drem, squirming his way through from the outcast fringe to get a better view, came up under the arm of Talore the Hunter, and Talore made room for him, so that in the end he had as good a view as Vortrix the Chieftain's son himself.

And so, while the flame of the sunset blazed and sank behind the Hill of Gathering, as though the sacred fires burned there as they did at Beltane, and the faint smell of frost and dead leaves stole up from the forest to mingle with the sharp, blue reek of wood smoke and horse droppings, the bronze-smith brought forth his treasures, laying them first before the Chieftain, then passing them among the eager knot of tribesmen: beautifully shaped axe-heads, spear blades all of bronze, neck rings and arm rings of shining bronze and silver and copper, ornaments for a pony's harness, and a sword with studs of red coral in the unguarded hilt. There was little bargaining as yet; men looked at the things they wanted, making no comment; and in a little they would go home and think about it, and see what they had to give in exchange, and come back in the morning maybe with a length of cloth or a couple of fine beaver skins or a lathe-turned beechen bowl.

All the while Midir the Priest sat hunched in his bull's hide robe, seemingly oblivious of all that went on around him. When you saw him so, Drem thought, it was hard to believe that he was that Other One, the One red with bull's blood at the sacred slaying when the Need Fires burned on the Hill of Gathering; whose voice was like a storm wind when he spoke from the Sun Lord to the people on Midsummer mornings. He was just a tired old man making little breath-puffings in his beard, Drem thought, and then hurriedly made the sign to avert evil, because it was dangerous to think such things.

'And is this, then, the last of the things that you have to show?' Dumnorix asked at last, handing back a pony's breast ornament that had the curve of a breaking wave.

There was a little silence, and then the smith said, 'No, there is one thing more, though not of my forging – and maybe a strange thing for a bronze-smith to be carrying in his bales.'

He took up something wrapped by itself in a piece of woollen cloth, and unwrapped it and set it in the Chieftain's broad hands.

Dumnorix the Chieftain looked up swiftly. 'The light fades, and I must see this thing. Bring a torch.'

Vortrix slid from his place at his father's feet, and disappeared into the house-place, returning in a few moments with a smoking torch that he must have taken down from its sconce against the roof tree, for there was a faint sound of protest from within, as of a woman left to weave by firelight. With the coming of the torch, the misty twilight seemed to deepen behind the shoulders of the tribesmen, though it had still been almost daylight the moment before. As the whole circle gathered closer, Drem saw that there was something strange, something very strange indeed, about the dagger in the Chieftain's hands. It was the wrong colour: not the familiar sun-colour of bronze, but a kind of dim moon-colour, fish-scale colour, as the Chieftain tipped it towards the torch, and the light ran like water along the blade.

'Sa, what is this thing – this grey metal?' said Dumnorix, testing the blade gingerly with a finger.

'It is called iron,' said the stranger.

A murmur ran round the circle. They had heard of iron. It was strong magic.

'So this is iron. I have heard of it, but never held it in my hand until today,' Dumnorix said.

'Nor I, until three moons since, and I paid a heavy price for it to the yellow-haired giant out of the land of Mist-forests across the Great Water, for this one piece to carry away with me.'

'How is it greater than bronze?' someone asked, out of the torch-lit circle.

'How? It is much harder, it remains keen when bronze grows blunted, therefore it calls less often for the sharpening stone and does not dull in the midst of battle. It is to bronze what bronze is to copper, what copper is to flint. See now, and I will show you.' The stranger held out his hand. 'Let Dumnorix the Chieftain give me back my dagger, and draw his own as for battle – so.'

Dumnorix laughed, and flashed the slim bronze dagger from his belt. The stranger's blow was as swift and fierce as the strike of a viper. Bronze and iron rang together, and the smith, with a thin, triumphant smile on his dark face, and no glance at the dagger in his hand, held it out to Dumnorix again, saying, 'Take it, and look now at both blades.'

Frowningly, the Chieftain did so. Then he gave a low exclamation, half of wonder, half of disgust.

'You see?' said the smith.

'I see. Aye, I see well enough.' Dumnorix frowned at the blade a moment longer, then to his tribesmen, 'Look you, and see also.'

The two daggers were passing from hand to hand, heads bent over them, men turning to look at each other, and the murmur running from one to another, 'Ha! This is a strange thing! A strange thing indeed!'

Talore leaned forward and took first one and then the other into his hand; and Drem, peering over his arm, saw that there was a great notch in the edge of the bronze blade; but the moon-coloured blade was unmarked. Lying across Talore's thigh, it had a look of power, a lean, dark look of menace; this strange new beast that had bitten a piece out of the Chieftain's dagger. Greatly daring, he reached out and touched it; and felt that it was strong magic under his hand.

'This is a thing and a most wonderful thing, my brothers,' Talore said. 'Surely in the time to come, men armed with weapons such as this will be the masters of men whose weapons are of bronze.'

Suddenly Midir the Priest stirred in his bull's-hide robe, and leaned forward, his eyes – narrow dark eyes with a gleam of gold behind them, like dark sunlight – turned upon the strange grey dagger. Talore laid it before him with a deep courtesy; and the old man put out a thin, blue-veined hand and touched it as it lay, but did not take it up. He shook his head. 'I like not this strange new magic. The God forfend that this cold grey metal should ever master bronze. Aye, aye, I see the notch. I hear what ye all hear and see what ye all see. Yet we are the Sun People, and it is in my heart that bronze is of the Sun, and this cold iron only of the earth. As the little Dark People are the people of the blue flint, so we are the people of the shining bronze; our day is the day of bronze as theirs was the day of flint; and in a world where iron rules, we shall rule no longer. Aiee, Aiee! It will be a cold grey world, and the kings and the heroes will be dead.'

'But if we can come by such weapons as that – ' began the Chieftain, pointing.

The stranger bronze-smith shook his head, answering them both. 'The man who carries an iron dagger will be the lord of the man who carries a bronze one; but it is in my mind that there will never be many such men, nor many such weapons.'

'Why so, then?' Dumnorix demanded.

'For this reason: that it is only in the Mist-forests across the Great Water that they have the secret of the fire – ah, many times hotter than the fire we raise to work our bronze – that will melt the grey metal and make it workable. It is only the giants of the Mist-forests who have the magic of the fires and the magic of the grey metal.'

'Yet to be one of the few would be a fine thing,' Dumnorix said. 'A fine thing indeed,' and he looked up suddenly. 'I will give you the price of three bronze daggers for the grey blade.'

The smith shook his head, and took up the dagger again. 'Can strong magic be bought for the price of three bronze daggers? The thing is not for sale.'

'Yet you spoke of a heavy price that you gave for it, to the man of the Mist-forests.'

'Aye – of a sort.'

'What was it, then?'

'A woman,' said the bronze-smith. 'And I was not yet tired of her.' He saw the idea in the Chieftain's face, and laughed. 'Na, na, I want none of your little dark slave women. If the dagger was worth more to me than one woman, why should I now trade it for another?'

Midir spoke again. 'Why indeed? Let you take your dagger on towards the Sunset, friend; it is in my mind that we do better without its cold grey magic.'

The bronze-smith checked in the act of reaching for the piece of yellow cloth in which the thing had been wrapped, and cast one of his dark, mocking glances at the old Priest. 'None so cold and none so grey is the magic of this dagger of mine, Holy One. See, I will show you —' Still holding the dagger, he slipped a hand into his mantle, and brought out from somewhere about himself the flint of his strike-a-light, and struck it upon the blade. They all saw the sparks fly out, golden and fiercely bright from the moon-grey blade, and again a murmur, a marvelling ran through the circle.

'See you? It is not the warm bronze of the sun, but there is fire at the heart of it, none the less, this cold grey metal. Did I not say that it was strong magic? Who shall say what strange thing it can do?' The bronze-smith glanced about him, triumphantly, at the eager, torch-lit faces; and as he did so, it seemed that his eyes were caught and held – held so that he could not look away.

A sudden stillness took him; and his hand slackened on the dagger so that it dropped from his fingers, and stood quivering in the turf before him. 'Surely the cold iron is indeed a strong magic,' he said, as though he found it difficult to speak. 'But even I did not know that it could raise ghosts.'

Drem craned round with all the rest in the direction of the bronze-smith's startled gaze and saw that a knot of girls, returned from the bramble picking, had come to hover on the outskirts of the little crowd, eager as the others to see what treasures the stranger bronze-smith had spread before the Chieftain's door. And among them was Blai; Blai, not hanging back as she generally did when she was with the other girls, but pressing boldly to the fore, her dark gaze fixed on his face, as his was fixed on hers.

It was the time of evening, between the lights, not full dusk yet not longer daylight, when all things seem a little insubstantial; and standing there almost beyond the reach of the torchlight, Blai with her wan, narrow face and huge, dark eyes did indeed look like something not of the day-time world – as though if the wind blew she might waver in it like weed in flowing water.

But almost in the same instant before the dagger had ceased to quiver where it fell, the bronze-smith seemed to have recovered himself, and crooked a finger to her as a man might

crook a finger to a hound. 'You – if you are there in truth – come you here to me.'

And amid a sudden hush, Blai came and stood before him. She carried a rush basket half full of blackberries on her hip, and there were stains of blackberry juice about her mouth that somehow made her look more transparent than ever.

'What do they call you?' said the bronze-smith.

'I am called Blai.' The stillness that had been in him seemed to have crossed into her; only suddenly she smiled.

'From whose house-place?'

'From the house-place of Cathlan the Old, away yonder where the cattle way comes up through the Chalk from the Marshes and the Great Water.'

'So, the track inland. I remember the track,' the stranger said, half under his breath.

Midir, who, it seemed, had not gone so far away inside

himself as usual, leaned forward, his gaze narrowed on the stranger's face. 'Maybe you also remember the house-place? And the woman who died there? Were you tired of her, too?'

And suddenly Drem understood. They all understood, the big golden Chieftain and the hunters gathered in the torch-light, and the children who had crowded up to see what came out of the yellow pack bales; and Blai.

But as Drem cast a startled look at Blai, he saw that somehow she had known, even before the stranger called her out to him. This was the thing that she had clung to all her years, all those many times when she had cried out defiantly in the face of all ills. 'One day – my father will come back for me!' Now it had happened, and something about it was wrong – horribly wrong.

The bronze-smith glanced aside at the Priest, a mocking and a challenging look. 'Aye, I remember the house-place,' he said. 'But I did not know that it was so near.' He knelt upon one knee, and reaching out, set a long forefinger under Blai's chin, and tipped her face to the torchlight. But there was no gentleness in the finger, and none in his face as he stared long and hard into hers; so that slowly the smile grew uncertain, became a pathetic little grimace, and died. 'Now by the Song of the Silver Branch, here's a strange thing to come about!' he said at last. 'Aye, you're like the woman your mother; the same whey face and goggle eyes; but at least there was fire in her – like the secret fire within the heart of this grey dagger of mine; and a man might warm his hands at it – aye, and burn his fingers too! But you – faugh! You're like a damp cobweb.'

Abruptly he dropped his hand. 'So, it is enough. Away with you and carry your blackberries home.'

Blai did not move. She stood as though she had struck root, still carefully holding the basket of blackberries, staring into his face as though she were trying to understand. There was a crimson mark on her jaw bone, where his finger had been.

'Well, what do you wait for?' the stranger said; and then, as he stared, his mouth curled into a slow, cruel smile. 'Ah so, that is the way of it? You thought that I had come for you? You small fool, I had forgotten your existence until this twilight! And if I had indeed come so, what should I want with such a whey-faced thing as you are?' And he flung up his head in laughter; dark, flashing, wicked laughter.

Blai drew back very slowly, like one walking in her sleep, her eyes still fixed on his face; and there were shadows under them the colour of the blackberry stains about her mouth. As she did so, he leaned forward, laughing still, and caught up a bronze ring-brooch from the shining tumble on the yellow bale-cloth, and tossed it towards her like one tossing a bone to a dog. 'Never let it be said that I failed to furnish a dowry for my own daughter, though I'm thinking it would take a bigger dowry than that – I'm thinking it would take a whole herd of milch mares, to tempt any man to take such a grey thing to his hearth. There – take it, you poor, pale moth.'

Drem hoped that she would leave it lying there, but still with that wide, horrified sleep-walker's gaze on the bronze-smith's face, she crouched down and felt for it, and took it up, very slowly. Then she turned and ran.

Some of the other children shouted after her, hooting and

jeering: Luga called out, trying to mimic her high silvery voice: 'One day – one day my father will come! Yah! – and fetch me away on a horse with a golden bridle!'

Talore suddenly withdrew his hand from Drem's shoulder. It was a gesture like slipping a hound from leash. But Drem did not need it. He had no particular fondness for Blai; but she was of his hearth fire, and that was enough. He sprang up, Whitethroat at his heels, and began to push his way out through the circle, glaring about him at his own kind, especially at Luga, whose ankle he managed to kick in passing, and went with his freckled nose in the air after the small, desolate figure disappearing into the dusk.

She was right down by the brook before he caught up with her. Whitethroat bounding ahead to nuzzle his head against her – oddly enough she was the one person in Whitethroat's world, apart from Drem himself, to whom the great hound ever paid any attention. But Blai took no notice of Whitethroat, not this evening. She was standing on the steep bank where it almost overhung the water above the sloping cattle-place, holding the ring-brooch in her hands. And the basket lay overturned beside her, with the little, dark bramble-fruit scattered in the grass. She turned as Drem came up, and stood there like a little wild thing cornered, with the drop to the stream behind her. 'Have you come to laugh at me too? The others all laughed at me.'

'Na,' Drem said. 'I came because they laughed.'

'Did you, Drem?' Blai said, in a small aching voice. 'Did you truly?'

He scowled fiercely, swinging on his heels. 'You are of my hearth fire.' Then in a rough attempt at comfort. 'You should be glad that he will not take you away with him. We are much better to be with than he is!'

Blai looked at him in silence, her narrow white face set in the twilight; and he had a feeling that she was older than he was, much, much older, which was foolishness because he had seen eleven summers and she only nine.

'You have spilled all your blackberries,' he said, because he didn't like the silence. 'What will you do with the brooch that he threw at you?'

Something happened in Blai, like the moment when the bronze-smith had struck at the strange grey dagger blade with his flint, and fire sprang out under the blow, so that watching her with his mouth open, Drem thought that the bronze-smith had been wrong about Blai, after all. 'This!' she cried, and spat on the bronze circle in her hand, with the savagery of a cat spitting; then whirled about to the stream and flung it from her into the deep water under the bank.

It struck the surface with a plop like a trout leaping, like the stone that Luga had thrown at the kingfisher, and peering down, Drem saw the ring-ripples spreading out and out in the shadowy water, with a faint gleam of light in the curve of each ripple, as though a trout had leapt there; no more. And then the last ripple touched the bank and was gone.

Blai said, 'That was not my father. Something happened to *my* father so that he could not come back. And now he will not ever come. He will not – ever – come.'

6　The Boys' House

Next day Drem heard that the bronze-smith had moved on, taking with him the strange grey dagger with the fire at its heart, despite all the Chieftain's efforts to make him part with it; and Dumnorix the lord of three hundred spears had gone to look for a bear to kill, to ease his temper.

Blai never spoke of what had happened, and when the other children taunted her with it she cried out on them as though amazed that they could be so foolish. 'That was not my father! Something happened to *my* father so that he could not come back!' Nothing would shake her in that. It was almost as though she believed it herself. Drem's mother was gentler to her than usual in those days, but being gentle with Blai, it seemed, was no good; she merely shrank away, like a wild thing backing from a kind hand, looking sideways and showing its teeth.

So that winter came and wore away, and the year came up again out of the dark. The whitethorn of the steading hedge was curdled with blossom, and there were young calves to bring in and stall in the hurdled-off part of the house-place; that year's new warriors were made, in the night and the day before Beltane, and the Beltane fires blazed on the Hill of Gathering, before the grave mound of the forgotten champion who slept there; and it was time for Drem to go to the Boys' House.

The Boys' House stood in the garth of the Chieftain's steading, among the other turf-thatched bothies that made up the Hall of Dumnorix. From their twelfth spring until the spring that they were fifteen years old, the boys of the Clan were brought up there, as it were at the Chieftain's hearth. They learned the use of broad spear and throw-spear, sword and buckler and the long war-bow of the tribes. They learned to handle hound and pony; they hunted with the young hunters of the Clan, learning to follow a three-day-old spoor as though it were a blazed trail. They fought and wrestled together and grew strong; and together they learned to go cold and hungry, and to bear pain without flinching. And so, under the eyes of the Chieftain and of old Kylan who ruled the Boys' House with his oxhide whip, the warriors of the Clan were made.

When the morning came for Drem to be setting out, Drustic gave him much useful advice, remembered from his own years in the Boys' House, and a particularly well-balanced throw-spear of his own, which Drem thought a great deal more of than he did of the advice. And his mother gave him a cloak of thick brown wool with a stripe of kingfisher blue along the edge, a fine cloak, though it was too long for him, as yet. When he had eaten his morning barley cake and mare's milk curds – always it must be mare's milk curds flavoured with wild garlic, on the day one went to the Boys' House – he went and knelt before Cathlan the Old as he sat on his folded bearskin beside the fire, and set his hand on the old man's thigh in leave-taking.

'I go now, my Grandfather.'

'Sa, you go now, son of my youngest son, little red fighting cock,' Cathlan said, leaning forward to peer down at him with those fierce, gold-irised eyes, 'and truly I think that you will be a seasoned fighter before you come again with your Wolf Slaying behind you – if ever you do – Aiee, if ever you do. But I will tell you this: it is good, for you, that your years in the Boys' House will be the years of Vortrix the Chieftain's son, also. For ever after, the men who trained together as boys, and slew their wolves and passed into the Men's side together are a brotherhood; and the Chieftain does not forget the men who did these things with him. I know, ah, I know, I who slew my wolf in the same year with Belutugradus, the great grandsire of this one.'

Drem bent his forehead on to his hand as it rested on the old man's thigh; then rose and took leave of his mother, driving his head for a moment into the hollow between her neck and shoulder that was warm and white and soft even though her voice was often harsh with scolding. Then he caught up his new spear and flung his cloak across his shoulder, and went out into the morning, whistling Whitethroat to heel. He forgot to take his leave of Blai at all.

The parting from his family sat lightly on him, for he was used to being away from home, and had come and gone as the mood took him, since the days when he had gone up to Doli and the shepherds on the High Chalk. But at the foot of the driftway, between the waking green of the young barley, and the sleeping fallow, he halted, knowing that the time had come for a harder leave-taking. He had known that it would be no good tying Whitethroat up to keep him from following, when he went down to the Boys' House, and so for a long time past he had been training the great hound to go home alone when he bade him. And now it was the time for putting the training to the test.

Suddenly the three years that had seemed a proud thing earlier that morning, looked very long and grey; and there was an ache in his throat as he dropped his spear and called Whitethroat from snuffing among the coarse grass and the pimpernels and yellow vetch at the side of the rough chalk, and squatted down to talk to him, holding his muzzle and rubbing behind his ears in the warm hollows where he loved to be rubbed. 'I must go down to the Boys' House, brother, and I cannot take you with me. Soon I will come again, soon and often, and we will hunt together. But now you must run with Drustic's hounds, and do as Drustic bids you.'

And Whitethroat talked back in the singing growl he always made when Drem rubbed behind his ears, holding his head low and flattened, and turning it for Drem to come at yet more delicious places.

Drem stopped rubbing at last, and pressed his face down for a moment on to the top of the dog's rough head; then he sprang up. 'Go home! It is time to be going home, brother!'

Whitethroat pressed his head against Drem's knee, his tail swinging.

'Go home! Home now!' Drem ordered, pointing. And the great hound looked from his face to the pointing finger and back again, whimpering; understanding what Drem wanted of him, understanding also that this time was not like the other times that he had been ordered home.

Drem caught him by the studded collar and dragged him round to face up the driftway. 'Home! Off now! Go home, can't you!' His voice was rough and angry with the unshed tears in his throat; and he thumped Whitethroat hard on the rump with his clenched fist.

Whitethroat went then, with a piteous puppy-whimpering, his head down and his proud bushy tail that came from his wolf father tucked between his legs. And Drem caught up his throw-spear and ran, with his shoulders hunched and the ball of tears swelling in his throat.

When he reached the garth of the Chieftain's steading, he found a little knot of boys already gathered before the empty doorway of the Boys' House. Vortrix the Chieftain's son, and a boy with a round head and a mouth like a frog whose name was Gault, and Luga kicking moodily at tussocks of coarse grass that grew against the wall. Otherwise there was no sign of life in the steading, save for the old hound sleeping on the dung heap as he had been on the day last autumn when the bronze-smith came, and a half tame mallard drake with his dun wives behind him, waddling about the brushwood pile. Drem walked across to the three boys. They opened their ranks for him, and the four of them stood and looked at each other and away again, half grinning, but somehow a little uneasy. None of them spoke.

Drem leaned against the wall of the Boy's House. The flints in the wall were tawny and white and grey-blue. He had never really noticed flints before. One of them was striped grey and white and looked like a badger's mask peering out of the wall. He watched the mallard drake, seeing the glint of metallic green on his wings as he turned in a gleam of sunlight. It was a pale, dry, windy day, with a constant changing of light as cloud and clear chased across the sky; and little whirls of chalky dust hurried about the steading garth, that stung when they got in one's eyes. He wished someone would come. Old Kylan or some of the older boys – because until they did he was stuck and could not go forward into the start of the three years' training time that must be got through before he was a warrior and could be with Whitethroat again. They must all be away to the hunting or the weapon practice; and he could hear the emptiness of the Boys' House behind him.

In a while, Urian the son of Cuthlyn came stalking across the steading garth with his thumbs in his belt, and brought their numbers up to five; and then fat Maelgan appeared, with little black-eyed Tuan in his shadow; and the gathering of that year's New Spears was complete.

There before the door of the Boys' House they stood and looked at each other, still in silence. Drem saw them all with a new clearness, an awareness of them as though he had never seen them before; and it was the same with all of them. They had run and tumbled and fought together all their lives, like puppies of the same pack; but now, suddenly, they were aware of each other, and a little shy of each other, caught up in a relationship that was new to them.

A sudden spatter of rain came down the wind, freckling the ground with dark, and streaking the flints of the Boys' House wall; and a woman slave passed across the garth from the byre, carrying a high-shouldered milk pail, and turned to stare at them before she disappeared. They ignored her with an elaborate air of unconcern, trying to look as though they were not at all at a loss and were standing round the Boys' House door because they chose to.

But when she was gone, Vortrix hunched his shoulders and said, 'It grows wet, here in the garth. Let us go inside.'

'Will they not be angry?' Tuan said doubtfully. Tuan was always inclined to be cautious.

'I don't see why. No one seems to be coming to tell us what we are to do.'

Luga stopped kicking at the tussocks of grass. 'So long as you remember if Kylan comes with his whip, that it was your idea!'

It seemed a bold thing to do, to go in without leave; into the Boy's House where none of them had ever been before; and their breaths caught a little at their own hardihood, as, one after another, following Vortrix, they ducked under the door curtain and prowled in out of the wind and the bright rain, and looked about them. After the sharp spring wind and the changing light out of doors, the air in the great round hut was still and heavy, and the light was dim and brown, thickened by the inevitable bloom of wood smoke over the shadows. There were sleeping stalls round the walls, spread with sheepskin over the piled fern, but they would be for the great ones, the lordly ones who had reached their second and even their third year; the likes of Drem would sleep like hounds around the central hearth. There was a half-made hunting bow before one of the stalls, and a cloak with a green patch at the shoulder in another;

a clutter of cook pots beside the hearth and weapons stacked against the roof tree; and several pelts in various stages of curing hung from the rafters.

The twelve-year-olds felt their own boldness in their chests. Here they were, for the moment, in possession of the Boys' House, and they grinned at each other, strutting a little. The fire on the hearth had sunk low, to a red glow and a few charred logs in the midst of the white ash. 'They have let the fire sink,' Drem said. 'They should be grateful to us for coming in and mending it for them before it goes out!' And greatly daring, he kicked the logs into a blaze, and threw on a couple of birch logs with the bark still on them from the pile beside the hearth. Vortrix had led them in here, he, Drem, would be the one to wake the fire. The logs were dry and the bark like tinder; a little tongue of saffron flame licked up, and the silver bark blackened and curled back, edged with red jewels. There was a sudden flare, a flickering amber light that warmed the shadows; and they looked at each other with kindling excitement born of their own boldness and the likelihood that the older boys would make them pay for it later.

The sudden flare of the flame-light caught the bronze face of a great war shield that lay tilted against the roof tree as though some champion had just cast it down there, and woke sparks of shifting fire among the raised bosses with which it was covered. It caught at their attention, and they gathered round, looking down at it. Each of them knew a shield, maybe more than one, in their own homes; nevertheless, this one caught and held their interest. They squatted about it and heaved it up to examine it in the firelight. Truly it was a mighty shield, a hero's shield, formed of layer upon layer of bull's-hide, the whole face sheathed in shining bronze, and the bronze worked in circle within circle of raised bosses, the outermost circle lying just within the hammered strength of the shield rim, the innermost close against the thrusting swell of the central boss. And looking at it as the firelight played and ran on every curve, Drem thought it was like the spreading ripples made by a leaping fish, or when you dropped a pebble – or a brooch – into the water.

'It is a fine shield,' Maelgan said.

'Ugh! It is heavy!'

Urian thrust his arm through the straps, and staggered up-right, panting a little under the weight, his fierce brown face flushing into laughter. He pulled a spear from among those against the roof tree, and stood straddling his legs and thrusting out his chest though the weight of the great shield dragged his shoulder down. 'See! I am a man! I am a warrior already! Why should I spend three years running with little boys like you?'

They pushed him over – it was quite easy for he was off balance already with the weight of the great shield – and rubbed his nose in the fern; and Vortrix heaved the shield on to his own shoulder, and stood proud and bright-eyed in the firelight, braced under its weight. 'I am a warrior too! I am the Chieftain, the lord of all your spears!'

'Stop crowing, and let me try it,' Luga said.

One after another they all tried their strength with the great shield. Maelgan, who was the biggest of them all, with the slow strength of an ox, even managed to walk a few steps carrying it. Tuan, who was the smallest, only just managed to lift it clear of the ground. One after another, breathless and intent, until there was only Drem left to try.

'Drem! Hai! Drem, wake up!'

Drem woke up. He had hung back to the last, which was not his way: and suddenly his heart was pounding as he stepped to the great war shield. He thrust his sound arm through the straps, and setting his teeth, lurched up again. The weight bore down on his shoulder, as he stood to face the others. The war spear that each of them had taken in turn lay in the brown bracken at his foot; he felt it there. And it had already dawned on him that he could not take it up.

It dawned on the others at the same moment. They were all round him, watching him with sudden speculation. Then Luga pointed down at the spear and his face was alight with malice. 'Aren't you going to take up your spear? A warrior must needs carry a spear as well as a shield; do you forget that?'

Drem faced him, faced them all. 'Na,' he said. 'I do not forget that. But it is in my mind that a warrior might do well enough carrying only his spear and not a shield at all! I took up the shield to try its weight as you have all done. No more.'

'Ya-ee! Hark to Drem One-arm!' Luga cried. 'Drem One-arm cannot carry his spear and his shield together; he would make only half a warrior – and what use is half a warrior to the Men's side?'

Drem was sharply aware of the silence all about him, and in the silence the spattering rain on the thatch and the distant scolding of a woman. He did not move, he was too proud to move before them, even though his arm and shoulder were beginning to tremble under the weight of bronze and bull's-hide; but if he had been a hound, the hair would have risen on his neck. The others were still staring at him, not hostile as yet – though that was coming – but somehow no longer strange with each other, bonded together under Luga's leadership; and *he* was the only stranger. He understood about Luga; Luga had never forgiven him for the matter of Whitethroat and the swan; that was simple. The rest was less simple; but something far down in Drem that had nothing to do with thinking, understood that too. All their lives they had run together in one pack; a mingled pack of children and hounds from the Clan and Half People alike; but now it was different, now Erp and his dark brothers must follow their own ways, and the Clan and the

Half People were no longer one. This was the Boys' House; this was the beginning of the Men's side, the Spear Brotherhood, the beginning of the question whether Drem's place was inside with the Spear Brotherhood or outside with the Half People.

'Let you go and learn to weave with the women,' Luga said, bright-eyed and taunting, and there was a splurge of laughter.

'But you'd need two arms for that, too,' Gault squealed in sudden excitement; and – he was a great one for playing the fool – he began to jig up and down, making the gestures of a woman working at an upright loom. They were crowding in on Drem, beginning to jostle him. It was more than half in jest at first, but the jest was an ugly one, and wearing thin over what lay underneath. 'Ye-ee! Drem One-arm – Drem One-arm!'

It must be Luga or himself, Drem thought, and the only thing he could do was to fight, and if need be go down fighting. He did not stand the faintest chance, of course, but that made no difference. He let go the great shield. It fell with a ringing clash and crash against the edge of the hearth stone, momentarily scattering the little fierce knot, and in the same instant, with the life still tingling back into his arm, he hit Luga fair between the eyes, with all the strength that was in his body behind the blow. And he cried out on a shrill note of challenge, 'One arm is enough to hit with!'

Luga staggered backward, shaking his head, as though for the moment he was not at all sure what had hit him. Then he recovered himself and came in again with flailing fists.

Drem hit him again in the instant before the other boy's fist crashed into his own cheekbone, filling one eye with a red burst of stars. Having only one serviceable arm, he could do nothing to guard against the blows that came pounding in on him. He tucked his head down to save his face as much as possible, and

somehow got his back against the great roof tree. The whole lot of them were on him at once, giving tongue like hound puppies at the kill. He saw their faces pressing in on him, their open mouths and bright eyes; and their shrill clamour rose and rose in his ears. He knew that he was fighting for his place in the Clan, fighting for his whole life – all that made life worth having; and he hit out wildly, desperately, yelling his defiance. He never knew what it was he yelled, only that it was defiance. He kicked somebody's legs from under them so that they came down across the great shield with a hollow clangour; but while the thrumming of it still hung upon the air, a buffet landed on the side of his head that sent him staggering sideways, and instantly they were on him, dragging him down though he struggled and tore and bit like a cornered wild cat.

And then, when he was all but done, somebody dived low through the flailing mass of arms and legs, and whirled about at his side, flinging Maelgan off him with one shoulder, and driving his fist into Urian's howling face. And as Drem grasped the moment's respite to drag himself free and stagger upright again, shaking his head to clear it, he realized vaguely that he was no longer alone.

'Sa sa sa! Come on then! Come on all of you and see

what you'll get!' he heard his new comrade yelling. He had his back against the roof tree again now, and the other boy's shoulder was against his, guarding where he could not guard for himself, and a sudden warm sense of increase was in him. The smell of blood came into the back of his nose, far up between his eyes; the Warrior Smell. And suddenly, from feeling like a cornered animal, the joy of battle leapt in him like a flame.

He cared nothing now for the blows he got, only for the blows he gave. It was a great fight, though a short one; a stand against hopeless odds such as no warrior of the Tribe need have been ashamed of. But it was a last stand, and the odds were hopeless; five against two, and Drem had only one arm to fight with.

In their shrill and bloodthirsty absorption in the matter in hand, none of them saw the sudden dark swoop of figures into the doorway as several of the older boys came ducking in; nor the squat, hairy figure of Kylan of the Boys' House straddling there with his whip in his hand, looking on. They were not aware of anything but themselves and their own affairs; until someone behind Kylan spoke a deep-voiced word, and suddenly

Kylan was among them, wading into their midst with his lash busy in his hand, as a man wades into a fight among his own hound puppies. 'Break off! Back, I say! Back – get back!' And the long supple lash of oxhide curled and cracked again and again as he laid about him. Drem felt it sear like a hornet sting across his neck and shoulders. The shrill yammer died down, and slowly, sullenly, the fight fell apart and the fighters stood rather sheepishly looking at each other, and at Kylan and at the Chieftain himself, standing in the doorway with his great golden head bent under the lintel and the last of the shower shining behind him.

Dumnorix the Chieftain looked them over with interest, his frowning grey eyes moving from one to another in little darts and flickers that missed nothing. His gaze rested a long moment on Drem and the boy beside him; and he said to Kylan, with the merest flicker of a smile under his long moustaches, 'You spoke too soon when you swore but now that the bad days were here, and there were no more champions coming up to take their stand in the Spear Brotherhood.'

'So it seems,' Kylan said, breathing loudly through his hairy nostrils as he stood now drawing the supple lash again and again through his broad hairy hands. 'If the snapping and snarling of puppies gives any proof in the matter.'

Drem, his breast still heaving, the blood trickling from a cut under one eye, stared rather muzzily at Luga's face. Luga was working at a loose tooth, and his nose was bleeding and seemed to have spread over his face like a bannock. Yes, he'd set his mark on Luga. He'd set his mark on a good many of his own kind – he and the other at his shoulder. For the first time it occurred to him to wonder who it was; and he turned his head carefully, as though it were loose on his neck, to see.

He saw that it was Vortrix, the Chieftain's son. Vortrix turned his head at the same moment, licking a cut lip; and they looked at each other gravely, almost warily, and then, as though making up their minds, broke into slow and rather wavering grins.

The voice of Dumnorix the Chieftain called them back to the matter in hand. 'And what thing brought it about, this mighty battle?'

No one answered; they looked straight before them and scuffled among the strewed fern, while the older boys looked on as the lords of the world look on at the antics of a litter of puppies. 'Well?' said Dumnorix. 'Are you all dumb? You yelped loud enough but now!' and the frown gathered on his face like the shadow of thunder clouds gathering on the face of the High Chalk. Dumnorix the Chieftain was not a good man to defy.

For one agonized moment more, the silence held, not even Vortrix found his voice; and then Drem cocked up his head and grinned into the Chieftain's frowning face. 'We were practising to be warriors. O Dumnorix, Lord of three hundred spears, is it not for that, that we live three years as the Chieftain's hounds, at the Chieftain's hearth?'

For a moment after he had said it, he was so frightened that his mouth dried up and he could not have spoken again if he had wanted to. And then the storm broke – into a gale of laughter, as Dumnorix the Chieftain flung up his head among the rafters, and roared. His great laughter filled the Boys' House, so that a log fell on the hearth, and the sparks whirled upward, and even Kylan chuckled grumblingly in his deep chest, and the older boys nudged one another, grinning. But to the twelve-year-olds it was no laughing matter.

'Sa sa sa! We have champions indeed!' Dumnorix said, still laughing. 'The good days are not gone yet, Kylan old wolf; and we shall not be without cunning champions in the Men's side, when our time comes to sit by the fire and dream of old battles!' And then, already turning to the low doorway, he added to the knot of silent twelve-year-olds, 'It is in my mind that there has been enough *practice* for one day. Maybe now the time comes to be washing off the blood.'

When he was gone, they looked at each other uncertainly, while the older boys turned away to their own affairs as though they no longer existed. They wondered a little, now that it was over, what it had all been about. Only Luga, still working at the loose tooth, looked as though he remembered. Then Maelgan grinned suddenly, blinking pale eyelashes, and began the drift towards the doorway and the spring below the village.

Drem and Vortrix were the last to go, and as the drift became a scramble, Vortrix flung an arm of friendliness round Drem's neck. He had cut his knuckles on Urian's front teeth and a crimson trickle from the cut under Drem's eye splashed on to his hand where it was still bleeding. They both saw it, and looked at each other. Vortrix laughed, and then grew sober, for it was no laughing matter after all. 'See, we have mingled our blood. Now we are brothers, you and I.'

7 The King-Making

On an evening well into the Fall-of-the-Leaf, Drem came down the long flank of the Chalk towards the village. His hunting spear was over his shoulder, and he had just left Whitethroat at the foot of the home driftway. Two and a half years had gone by since the first time that he had left his hound there, to go down to the Boys' House – two and a half years in which Drem had become the finest spearman among his fellows and a rider who could control his little fiery mount with the grip of his knees alone when he needed a hand free for his weapons – and by now it was a thing that they were both used to. It had become a definite pattern. Always, when Drem was free to hunt with him, Whitethroat would seem to know, and would refuse to go with Drustic about the farm or on the hunting trail, though at other times he went willingly enough; and when Drem and Vortrix came up through the alder brake beside the stream, he would be waiting at the foot of the drift-way, smelling the wind for their coming, quivering with hope. Then he would leap up, baying, and come with great leaps and bounds down over the springy turf to fling himself upon his lord, and they would roll over together, laughing – the hound as well as the boy – Drem with his arm round Whitethroat's neck, and Whitethroat growling and roaring in mock ferocity while all the while his bushy tail lashed to and fro behind. And then they would go off, the boys with their spears on their shoulders, the hounds – Vortrix also had his hound – padding at their heels. And when the hunting was over, Drem would bring Whitethroat up the combe again to the foot of the drift-way, or sometimes even to the gateway of the steading where he might speak with his mother or Blai, though he might not cross the threshold while he was of the Boys' House. But if he went up to the steading, Whitethroat always came down again to the foot of the driftway with him. There, by the lowest of the little ragged corn plots, was their place for parting.

Drem and Vortrix had hunted together since that first day in the Boys' House, the day that they had become blood brothers whether they would or no; but Vortrix was never present at these partings. Drem was one to keep his loves in separate stalls; and Vortrix, though not in general over-quick to sense such things, was wise in the ways of his blood brother, and always went back to the Boys' House alone, while Drem ran his great, white-breasted hound back to the foot of the driftway.

The autumn dusk was coming up blue as wood smoke across the rolling dimness of the Wild, quenching the russet flame of the forest far below, as Drem came down through the higher field plots of the village. There was a black and white flicker of plovers' wings over the fallow, and the starlings swept home-ward overhead; and already firelight was beginning to strengthen in house-place doorways. It all looked very quiet, a faint mist stealing among the huts, made up of wood smoke and the first promise of frost and the warm breath of the cattle byres. But as he drew nearer, as he came in among the crowding bothies, Drem found that it was not so quiet as it had seemed. There was a strange activity in the village that evening; a coming and going of figures dim-seen in the dusk, a fitful mur-mur of voices, a general air of making ready for something. And in the Boys' House, too, when he reached it, was the same air of preparation. Vortrix, who had arrived some while before him, was squatting by the fire on which the evening stew bubbled in its great, slung cauldron, his light hunting bow lay beside him; and he was skinning the hare that he had shot that day, with an air of one attending to first things first. But the other boys of his year and Drem's, sprawling or standing around him, were talking eagerly as they burnished cloak pin and dagger blade, and furbished their trailing pony harness as though for battle, while Kylan sat on his skin-spread stool with his spear across his knees and watched them with a bright and vigilant eye.

'What is it, then?' Drem said. 'Is there a raid?'

Two or three voices answered him, taking up from one another. 'The King is gone beyond the Sunset!'

Drem whistled. 'How do you know?'

'The runners were here when I got back,' Vortrix said, intent on his hare.

'What killed him, then? He was not old?'

Urian tested the blade of his dagger. 'They say it was a boar. He went hunting yesterday – but it was the boar who killed, and not the King.'

Excitement shivered through the little group. There was no sorrow in them; they had never seen the King in his high Dun, they knew from their fathers that he was a hard man and a shining warrior, and that was all. And now he was dead, gone back beyond the Sunset because of a long-tusked, red-eyed boar, turning at bay.

'Now there will be a great Death Feast, and a King-Making for a new King to lead the Tribe,' said Tuan.

'A three day feast, with wrestling and foot races, and all the Men's side gathered in the Royal Dun —'

'My father says that when the last King was made,' Maelgan put in, blinking pale eyelashes in the firelight, 'there was so much cattle roasted that the smell of roasting fat reached from the Wild to the Great Water.'

There was a shout of laughter. 'That is the thing that you would care about, Fat One! ... When Maelgan was small, they drove him down with the swine in the autumn to fatten on acorns! – Let you be careful, Maelgan, that they do not mistake you for one of the fattened porkers for the cooking pits!'

Drem's eye ran over the preparations that were going on, while Maelgan, who was used to being a butt, grinned peaceably. The swift excitement that was rising in the others took hold of him. 'Is it that we also go to this feast?'

'Surely.' Old Kylan grunted, speaking for the first time. 'Are ye not of the Chieftain's household, hounds of the Chieftain's pack? Let you stop asking questions now and get to making ready for the morning. It grows late, and you are away behind the others, and I'll not have it said that any of Dumnorix's hounds looked like a mangy flint-knapper's cur when he followed his lord to the Death Feast and the King-Making!'

Luga, who was burnishing a bronze bridle bit, looked up with a sneer. 'You forget, Old Father, that Drem has always to take that most precious hound of his home, before he can come back to us in the Boys' House. Sometimes it is in my mind, Drem One-arm, that I wonder you can bear to come back at all, leaving him behind you.'

'Is it?' Drem said, stacking his spear in the rack beside the hearth. 'Maybe if you had more thought for your own hound, Luga, he would answer to you better on the hunting trail.'

It was queer how long Luga could carry a grudge and still find pleasure in it, he thought, as he clattered up the ladder to the loft in the crown of the roof, and began to delve among the gear of the rest of the Boys' House for the things that were his own. But there were other things to think about than Luga and his dark, rankling humours. He got out his brown cloak with the kingfisher stripe, which was now as much too short for him as it had been too long when his mother cut it from the loom, and his good saffron kirtle, and his belt with the bronze studs, and brought them down again. And when the evening meal was over he sat with the rest, round the fire, burnishing his dagger and the bronze belt studs, and combing and combing his hair to make it shine, as the Men's side combed their hair. For they were almost men now, he and Vortrix and the rest. The twelve-year-olds, thrust away from the fire to shiver in the door draughts, watched them enviously. *They* had no need to comb their hair, they would not be going to the Death Feast and the King-Making. That was for the third year of the Chieftain's hounds, who sat lordlywise around the fire, and talked as men, with their spears beside them.

Next morning at first light, when the village was already seething like a pan of warming yeast with last-moment preparations, the men from the outlying steadings of the Clan began to arrive, riding their small, shaggy ponies whose harness was rich with bronze and narwhal ivory, and leading others to serve as pack beasts. Cattle were being driven in from the grazing grounds, for the Royal Dun could not feed the whole Tribe, and so every Clan would drive its own meat with it, on the hoof. Supplies were being brought out and laid before the riders, or bound on to the backs of the pack animals: barley loaves and white cakes of ewes'-milk and mares'-milk curds, and meal in sewn skins. And everywhere children and dogs were under foot; children squealing, dogs barking, ponies trampling.

Drem had bitted and bridled his own mount – the Boys' House did not have ponies of their own, but rode the fiery little brutes out of the Chieftain's stable – and was standing with Vortrix near the Chieftain's door, when a cold muzzle was thrust into his hand, and he looked down to see Whitethroat beside him with waving tail. 'Greetings, brother!' he said, pulling the great hound's ears. Then to Vortrix, 'It must be that Drustic is here.' And at that moment Drustic rode into the crowded open space below the Chieftain's steading, his own hounds loping among the ponies' hooves; and a little behind him, leaving him to force their way through the throng, rode the Grandfather!

Drem had known of course that Drustic would come, but he had not thought of the Grandfather coming with him. He let out a soundless whistle. '*And* the Old One! It must be years since he had his legs astride a pony, and he's too old by far and far for such a journey!'

Vortrix laughed. 'He looks very well pleased with himself, the old Golden Eagle!'

'Always he is pleased with himself,' Drem said. 'It is the rest of the world that he is not pleased with!' and leading his own mount with him, he plunged into the throng, weaving his way through to join his kinsmen.

Drustic grinned at his young brother as he came up, but he had a somewhat harrassed look; and the Grandfather, seated on his bearskin that had been flung over the pony's back for a riding rug, splendid in his beaver-skin cloak with the scarlet lining, with his best bronze bracelets on his arms and his heron-tufted war-spear in his hand, was alight with triumph. Clearly, Drem thought, there had been a battle.

The Grandfather, it seemed, was still in something of a fighting mood, for he ignored Drem's salutation, and said in his deep crackling voice, 'So! You also think I am too old!'

'Did I say so, my Grandfather?' Drem said.

'It looks at me out of your eyes. It looks at me out of everyone's eyes. Aiee! I grow old indeed, and *because* I grow old, it is bad for me not to do as I wish! Now, I wish to see once more the full gathering of the Tribe. I wish to wear my bronze bracelets and talk with the men who stood up with me in arms when the world was young – with such as are left of them. Is it so great a thing to ask?'

'It is in my mind that you are not one for asking, my Grand-father,' Drem said, grinning, and put up his hand to caress his pony which was growing restive in the crowd. 'And surely you are wearing your bronze bracelets, and surely you are going to the gathering to talk with whoever you wish to talk with.'

'You – you were always an impudent whelp!' the Grand-father began, shooting out his lips and his ragged brows; and then unwillingly he chuckled. 'But it is true as you say. It is Sabra your mother's fault: I have argued so long with that woman that now I cannot stop. Also with so much arguing, my throat is dry. Go you and bring me some barley beer instead of standing there grinning like a frog on a hot stone!'

By the time Drem had found some barley beer and brought a cup of it to the old man, and reclaimed his own mount which he had left for the moment in charge of one of the second year boys, Dumnorix the Chieftain had come out from his house-place, burning on the grey autumn morning in his scarlet cloak and the gold-work on his arms and about his bull neck, and mounted the raven black stallion that Vortrix was holding for him before the door. The elders and the great ones of the Clan were all assembled by now; and most of them already mounted. Drem saw Talore sitting a young red mare close behind the Chieftain; Talore seeming as always very slight and dark among the tawny warriors of his kind. He saw Morvidd with a necklace of blue beads showing under his wolfskin cloak, as small and hard and bright as his hot-tempered blue eyes, and old Kylan from the Boys' House, and the rest. Now suddenly Midir was in their midst, all men urging their ponies back from him lest any should step in his shadow; Midir with the amber Sun Cross on his breast and his grey hair straggling out from under the folded eagle wings of his head-dress. The holy man settled himself on a litter of skins slung from birch poles, and was lifted on the shoulders of six runners. The great bull's horns brayed and bellowed to the mist-pearled morning sky, and the foremost riders following the Chieftain kicked their ponies from a stand into a canter. One after another they swung in a jostling stream, away between the crowding huts of the village, then up towards the Ridgeway that followed the crest of the Chalk from Sunrise to Sunset. And behind them rode Drem and the other boys, with their dogs running among them, driving the lowing, wild-eyed cattle.

All that day they followed the ancient green ridgeway along the High Chalk, with their faces towards Sunset, the Wild falling away below them on the Sword side; and on the Shield side, wherever the long upland ridges fell back, the far off shining line of the Great Water – only for Drem it was the other way round, because he used sword and spear left handed, and carried his shield, when he must carry one for appearance, on a harness over his right shoulder; and so when anyone said 'Shield side' or 'Sword side' he had to turn the things round in his mind.

Other ways branched from the way that they were following; some grassy, some white, making a spider-wed of communication along the tawny ridges of the high downs. They passed grazing sheep, who ran into startled huddles as they went by, stamping and staring at the scarlet and the bronze and the dull thunder of hooves and the streaming ponies' manes; so that the little dark shepherds sent their curses after the Golden People, who crashed by, lordlywise, startling the sheep. They passed the round grave mounds of the forgotten heroes that were strung out along the ridges, helping to mark the way. That night they camped beside one of the ancient, fortified dewponds; and about noon of the next day they came in sight of the Royal Dun, high on its vast wave-lift of the Chalk.

By that time they had become one of several such bands, following their Chiefs and great men, all drawing in by the white trails of the Chalk towards the huge fortress of turf banks that lay like a girdle, like a triple crown, like a coiled snake, about the highest crest of the downs.

The autumn day was a gleaming one, the hawthorn bushes glowing copper red with berries in the sunlight, against the staring white of the chalk-cut ramparts, and the turf below the Dun fiercely green where the autumn rain had brought it up from the tawny dryness of late summer: a day of sharp edges and colours clear and hard as the enamels on a shield boss. But away towards the Great Water, a long low bank of cloud was creeping inland, and already the distant Marshes were growing blurred as though a grey finger had been smudged across their blue and green and violet.

'Mist,' Drem said to Vortrix riding at his shoulder. 'We shall have cheerless camping tonight, up on these high downs,' and then, as the Dun drew nearer, forgot about it in the noise and excitement of their arrival.

Up the white chalk of the ancient track and over the turf on either side, the riders let their ponies out, and they leapt forward with tossing manes, shaking their heads and spilling foam on their breasts; and Midir's litter bearers, changed many times since the journey started, quickened from their long, swift lope into a run that must have all but shaken the holy man's head from his shoulders. So they swept foward towards the massive triple gateway, where the silent warriors of the Royal Clan lined the chalk-cut ramparts, their bucklers darkly glinting against the dappled autumn sky. Now they were threading the zigzag causeway that spanned the outer ditch; now the timber facings of the gateway towered on either hand; and the riders poured through. Last of all, Drem and his fellows dug their heels into their ponies' flanks and swept yelling after them, driving the wild-eyed, sickle-horned bullocks through the narrow-necked entrance.

Within the Royal Dun was an open space where the whole Tribe could gather in time of trouble, with the cattle driven into the berms between the vast concentric rings of defensive banks; and in the highest part of the stronghold the round turf roofs of the Royal Village clustered about the high hall of the King. But Drem, casting eager glances about him as he dropped from the back of his shaggy little mount, saw that from all the huddled roofs no smoke rose into the air. No hearth fires burned in the Royal Dun, nor would any, until the new King was made. And from the King's high hall he heard the keening of the women: 'Ochone! Ochone!'

When the cattle had been handed over to the men who waited to pen them, he made his way with Maelgan and the rest, down through the swarming encampment where already the horsehide tents were being set up, to picket the ponies in the inner berm. There were many ponies there already, and they were restless, stamping and fretting, made uneasy by the strangers all around them, or by the feeling that lay like a shadow, like the thick heaviness and sense of waiting before thunder, over the Royal Dun. They had almost finished picketing and feeding the ponies, when Vortrix, who had been kept back to attend on his father, came down to join them, leading the Chieftain's black stallion. They gathered round him as he set about the task that they had just finished, and looked on. But it seemed that the general uneasiness was in Vortrix's usually easy temper, for he turned on the perfectly unoffending Maelgan, saying, 'Must you stand there looking like a pig? Give me the other picket rope.'

Maelgan took up the coiled hide rope and tossed it to him. 'I do not know about a pig,' he said peaceably. 'I wish I was a pony. Nobody expects the ponies to fast until the new King is made!'

'Try pawing the ground and whinneying,' Gault said, 'and

maybe someone will give you an armful of bracken fodder.'
And he pulled his hair into a forelock between his eyes, and began to prance, playing the fool as he used to do when they were
twelve-year-olds; and the others laughed as they had done
when they were twelve-year-olds, and Urian thumped him on
the head, and suddenly they were in the midst of a rough and
tumble – anything to ease the tension, the sense of waiting that
was like something twisted too tight in their stomachs.

A young mare, pied like a wagtail, who was being led by at
that moment, chose to play startled at their laughter, and flung
up her head with a snort, dancing a little. She would have been
quiet again the next instant, but the boy in charge of her struck
at her head with the bunched reins in his hand, cursing; and
that did the mischief. Squealing between fear and temper the
mare went up in a rearing half turn, and began to swing on
her hind legs, with the boy hanging on to her headgear. She
crashed into the Chieftain's black stallion, who squealed in his
turn and flung round, dragging on the picket rope, and bit at
her crest. In an instant all was confusion.

Vortrix, struggling to quieten his father's angry pony,
shouted furiously over his shoulder. 'Oh, fool! Who let you
loose with anything on four hooves?'

There was a cry of, 'Look out, she's broken free!' and Drem
saw the mare upreared almost above him, and leaping clear of
the lashing hooves, sprang for her headgear.

'Well enough – I have her!'

A few trampling and sweating moments followed, and the
mare was down on all four legs again, trembling, but quite
docile. The two boys faced each other, both breathing quickly,
while the mare swung her head to nuzzle exploringly at
Drem's breast. 'Hasn't anyone ever told you not to jab at the
head of a frightened horse like that?' Drem said.

The other boy thrust out his jaw. 'What frightened her, then?

You all yaffling like a treeful of green woodpeckers under her nose!'

'She was well enough until you hit her with the bridle.'

The other boy flushed crimson. 'I do not need that the like of you should tell me how to handle a pony!' He caught back the bridle into his own hand, taking care, however, not to startle the mare again.

'It is in my mind that you sorely need *someone* to tell you how to handle a pony!' Drem said, laughing, and turned away to his Spear Brothers.

Behind him the laugh was caught up by the little crowd that had gathered, and another boy's voice said, 'You got the worst of that, Cuneda, *and* you deserved it! Na, na, come away. There will be trouble if you start a fight here at the King's Death Feast.'

And the thing was over; over as swiftly as it had blown up; and Drem thought no more about it as they helped Vortrix to feed and rub down the Chieftain's still angry stallion; and presently made their way back all together to the encampment below the Royal Dun.

In the crowd and the enclosed space behind the high turf banks, they had not seen how the mist – that far-off mist that had been a cloud bank along the Great Water – came creeping up across the marshes, rising higher and higher like the ghost of a long dead sea. But suddenly as they came out into the open space in the midst of the camp it was all about them, wreathing up from the trampled ground in a faint, wet smoke that seemed to gather most thickly about the King's hall in the highest part of the Dun. And with the mist, it seemed to Drem that there came upon the Royal Dun a deeper sense of waiting – waiting . . .

The waiting ended at dusk, when the household warriors, their faces and breasts daubed with the charcoal and ochre

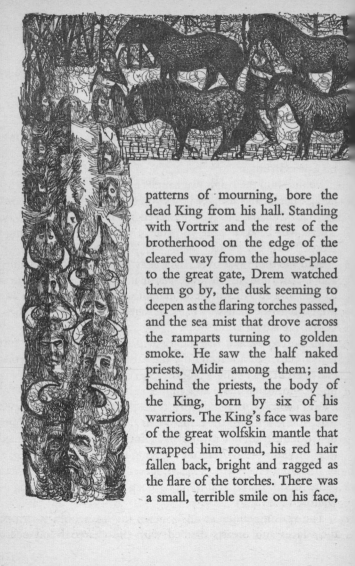

patterns of mourning, bore the dead King from his hall. Standing with Vortrix and the rest of the brotherhood on the edge of the cleared way from the house-place to the great gate, Drem watched them go by, the dusk seeming to deepen as the flaring torches passed, and the sea mist that drove across the ramparts turning to golden smoke. He saw the half naked priests, Midir among them; and behind the priests, the body of the King, born by six of his warriors. The King's face was bare of the great wolfskin mantle that wrapped him round, his red hair fallen back, bright and ragged as the flare of the torches. There was a small, terrible smile on his face,

and the same smile was stamped upon the painted face of one of the men who bore him: a very young warrior, with the same bright, ragged hair, the same great beak of a nose, so that Drem knew, though no one had told him, that he was looking at father and son, the old King and the new King, yesterday's and tomorrow's.

The crowd swayed and stirred, catching up the wailing from the women, and behind the King's body came the warriors of the Royal Clan, with his favourite ponies and hounds, who would go with him beyond the Sunset, and others driving a bull and a ram and a black, bristling boar for the sacrifice.

The Tribe turned in behind them, Men's side and New Spears alike, all with their weapons. And so, in a long comet tail of torches, they bore the dead King from his Dun and away over the downs in the mist, while the wailing of the Women's side fell away behind them.

It was quite dark when they reached the Holy Place, and the mist was thickening. Drem, far down the long tail of torches, sensed rather than saw the huge, bush-grown mass of the ancient grave-mound on their right, as they carried the dead King Sunwise about it, in a circling snake of torch light, a Sun-snake coiled about the darkness. When they had made the circle, they laid their burden on the tall pyre that had been built on the level hill-top turf. Then the bull and the ram and the boar were sacrificed by the High Priest with his black flint knife, and flayed, and the skins and fat wrapped about the King's body. Hounds and ponies were slain, though the ponies were mares and therefore almost beyond price, and their carcasses ranged upon the pyre with the flayed carcasses of the beasts of sacrifice. Great two-handled jars of honey and tallow were stacked among the logs and brushwood, and all was ready.

The High Priest with the gilded horns of the Sun upon his head, stood out with arms upraised, chanting the Invocation. 'Spear in the Noonday, Lord of Light, Lord of Life, Lord of the Cleansing Fire, take back by fire the warrior whose warring is finished, the hunter whose hunting is done . . .'

And while he yet chanted, the King's son stepped out from among his kind, and took a torch from one of the priests, and turning to the pyre, plunged it again and again into the brushwood. Then, with the flames already licking up, he flung the torch into the very heart of the great mass, and setting a foot on one of the projecting logs, mounted lightly to the muffled shape on the crest. For a long moment he crouched there, his arms across his father's body, bending his head on to the dead man's breast so that in that last moment of farewell their bright hair flowed together as one. Then he sprang down again, with the blood of the flayed skins on him, and the sparks hanging on the hem of his kirtle.

At dawn they quenched the sinking flames with barley beer, and when the dark fire scar was cool enough, they gathered the half-burned bones of the King and wrapped them in a cloth of scarlet linen, and put them in a great jar. In the growing light Drem saw that a little chamber had been cut in the flank of the grave mound, and in it the priest kind set the jar, making a singing magic as they did so. They ranged about it all that was left of the ponies and hunting dogs, the weapons and the orna- ments of a warrior, and roasted meat and jars of mead and grain for the King's journey. Then the warriors closed in, and laid back the chalk and the cut turfs over all. And only the black fire scar remained to tell that the King had gone beyond the Sunset.

And now another waiting was upon the assembled host; and all faces, eager, strained with anticipation in the thin dawn light, were turned up towards the crest of the sacred mound. The mist had thinned a little, growing ragged, and out of the trailing scarves of vapour loomed the low-growing darkness of thorn and yew and juniper that clothed the wide shoulder of the downs and the swelling green breast of the ancient grave- mound. Mist was in the hair of the warriors, a grey-silver bloom of mist clinging to the rough wool of their cloaks and the coats of the hounds who padded among them. And somewhere a bird rose crying, unseen in the drifting greyness of the morning.

Then that waiting, too, was over, with a hollow booming of bull's horns; and there on the crest of the sacred mound, where no man had seen them come, stood the High Priest, and with him the young warrior with the old King's face. A gasp, a great shout rose from the crowd. 'The King! The High Chieftain comes again!' And it seemed to Drem, staring up through the drifting mist wreathes, that the two poised high on the crest of the sacred mound were taller than any mortal man; giants and heroes, not men. The High Priest raised his arms, and his voice came down to the waiting host, thin and piercing as the bird's cry in the grey morning. 'The King is gone into the West. The King comes again. The Sun sets and the Sun rises. See and acknowledge the King, O ye warriors of the Tribe.'

And Drem saw, as he had not seen before, that between his upraised hands, between the golden sweep of the Sun horns on his head, was a twisted circle of red gold that caught a gleam of flame even in that milk-pale morning. In a silence so complete that suddenly it was as though one could hear the mist wreathes trailing through the dark juniper branches, he brought his hands down, slowly, slowly, and pressed the shining circlet low on the young King's brows.

Roar on roar of acclamation burst from the assembled warriors; a beating rush of sound, rising to the crescendo of the Royal Salute, as every man brought his spear butt crashing down across his shield. When it was stilled, the High Priest had gone, melted into the mist, no man seeing him go as none had seen him come; and the young King stood alone above them, alone with the mist and the twisted thorn trees, in the sudden isolation of his kingship. The mourning paint had been wiped from his face. He turned slowly, his hands held out, showing himself to his Tribe as the custom demanded; and when the circle was complete, cried out in a hard, clear voice, 'I am the King!'

'You are the King!' came back the shouted answer.

'I am the King! Ye who are my warriors, let you now swear faith with me!'

And the answer came back in a deep chant; in the ancient three-fold oath of the Golden People. 'You are the King. If we break faith with you, may the green earth gape and swallow us. May the grey sea burst loose and overwhelm us; may the sky of stars fall and crush us out of life for ever!'

And so the ceremony was over, and the King was made. And the new King, with his priest kind going before, led his warriors back to the Royal Dun.

8   The Hound Fight

There was a smell of roasting in the Royal Dun; the cooking smoke hung low in the mist, and there was firelight again in house-place doorways and the openings of the horse-hide tents; and in a while, when the ponies had been tended, the feasting began. It was such feasting as Drem had never dreamed of; whole baked carcasses of cattle and sheep and pig lifted smoking from the pits of hot stones, black puddings made of blood and fat roasted in the paunches of sheep, great baskets of wheaten cakes and mares'-milk curds, and jars of mead and barley beer that the slaves and the women carried round. All day it went on, while from time to time the young warriors and the champions would leave feasting around the fires, and betake themselves to wrestling and all kinds of trials of strength or skill, and then return to their feasting again. And all the while the new King sat on his stool of painted wood spread with sheepskin beside the High Fire, the Royal Fire, and with him the Clan Chieftains and the great men of the Tribe, each attended by his New Spears, who served him as cup bearers and ceremonial guard, according to the custom.

Drem, squatting with the rest of Dumnorix's New Spears, a little behind their Chieftain, and gloriously full of black pudding, could see the Grandfather and Talore the Hunter both here at the High Fire, and felt the pride rise in his chest that it should be so. He tore a last mouthful from the piece of rib he had been gnawing, and gave the bone to Whitethroat against his knee; and turned with a sigh of contentment to listen to the blind harper who sat at the King's feet, striking music like a shower of shining sparks from the slim, five-stringed harp of black bog oak in his hands. Once or twice since he could remember, such a harper had come to the home village, and played beside Dumnorix's fire, and each time he had been blind. Sometimes the power of song came to a man who was blind in the first place – as though the Sun Lord had reached out to touch him with a bright finger, that he might have another kind of seeing, another kind of light in place of the light he lacked. But if the song came to a sighted man, then as soon as it became clear that he was touched by the Sun Lord's finger, often while he was still only a child, he was blinded by the priests, that his other kind of seeing might grow the stronger. It was the custom. Drem shut his eyes, hearing the winged notes fly upwards in the darkness, above the deep surf of voices round the fire. And when he opened his eyes again, the firelight seemed brighter than it had done before, and the flower petal shape of Whitethroat's pricked ears gave him an almost painful stab of pleasure.

Vortrix, squatting at his shoulder, said, 'I suppose it is fair enough. Anyone can be a warrior and see the sky and the way the shadows run, but only one in a host can make the Harp Magic.' It sometimes happened like that between him and Vortrix; they did not talk to each other much, but often they knew what the other one was thinking.

Dusk was again creeping over the crowded Dun by now, and much mead and barley beer had been drunk since the feasting started; eyes were growing brighter and tongues looser, and there were wild bursts of laughter and swift flaring quarrels as men grew fierce and merry in their cups. The main business of eating was over, and there was a breaking up and shifting all round the great fires; but the drinking would go on for a long while yet. The young King, lounging sideways on his painted stool with the head of a favourite wolfhound on his knee, held up his great cup of wrought red gold, and looked about him at his Chieftains and warriors in the firelight. 'My Chieftains, my

brothers, I drink to you. The Sun and the Moon on your path.'
And flinging back his head he drained off the thick yellow
mead.

And from all round the fire the answer came back as the
Chiefs and Warriors raised their cups and horns in reply. 'The
Sun and the Moon be on the King's path also.'

Dumnorix drank with the rest, and turned, laughing his
deep, slow laughter, to drink again with the man whom the
general shifting had brought to sit beside him; a fat man whose
paunch bulged over his gold studded belt, and whose eyes
bulged also, on either side of a mottled nose. Drem rose swiftly,
taking up one of the tall mead jars that stood ready, and stepped
forward to pour again for his Chieftain; and it was so that he
saw the thing . . . As the fat man flung up his arm and leaned
back to drain the horn he held, his fine plaid cloak fell back, and
Drem and his Chieftain saw, both in the same instant, the dagger
that he wore thrust into his belt; a little grey dagger that caught
the firelight fish-scale colour instead of golden.

Dumnorix stopped laughing and set down his mead cup, and
leaned forward. 'Brother Bragon, show me the dagger that you
wear in your belt.'

Bragon hiccupped, clearly gratified, pulled the dagger from
his belt and held it out. 'Sa. I show it to you. It is in my mind
that you will not have seen a dagger the like of that before?
There are few such daggers, and they are strong magic. Have a
care, therefore, how you handle it.'

Dumnorix's hand tightened on the haft. 'I have seen the like
of this dagger before; aye, more than that, for I have seen and
handled this very dagger before. But the bronze-smith in whose
pack it was would not sell it, not for the price of three bronze
daggers nor yet for a fair woman slave. How then comes it
about that you wear the thing in your belt, brother Bragon?'

'Did you think, then, that yours was the only fire at which a bronze-smith might open his bales?' said Bragon, with blurred triumph, holding up his mead horn to be filled by one of his New Spears.

'Said I not that he would not sell the thing?' Dumnorix leaned closer still, his frowning gaze fixed on the mottled face of the other Chieftain. 'I asked you how it came to be in your belt; now let you answer me my question!'

'Sa. I will answer you your question. It comes to be in my belt because maybe I have sharper wits than you, my brother Dumnorix!' Bragon laughed jibingly, showing wolf-yellow teeth. 'What a man will not sell, he may be got to throw the knuckle bones for, if he be first made drunk enough. They are great gamblers, the men of the Green Isle; and I – I have a way with the knuckle bones. If my brother Dumnorix also wished for the little grey dagger, my brother Dumnorix should have shown more wit in the matter!'

So the bronze-smith had lost his grey dagger with the fire at its heart, Drem thought. He would tell Blai that, when he got home. He would say, 'That bronze-smith who came once – *you* know – has been cheated of his grey dagger with the fire at its heart.' And Blai would be glad; it was pleasant to make Blai glad, now and then when it wasn't any trouble.

The frown had deepened between Dumnorix's eyes until the thick golden brows met in a single bar, and he drew his legs under him and rose as though to find another place to sit, where the air was fresher. 'It may be that I lack the wit of my brother Bragon – Bragon the Fox! But I do not make drunk the stranger at my hearth, to cheat him of what he will not sell!'

Bragon leapt up after him, with unlikely swiftness in so fat a man, thrusting his face into that of his fellow Chieftain. 'When any man crows to me in righteousness of what he does or does not do, that is the time that I look to my goods and gear!' he shouted, his voice thick with passion and much mead. 'Give me back now my grey dagger, lest maybe you confuse it with your own!'

There was a moment's deadly silence. Then Dumnorix, whitening to the lips, cast the dagger down at the other's feet. 'Take it, then. Mine is no more than bronze, but it will serve its purpose well enough!' And as he spoke, deliberately, he drew his own dagger from his belt.

It had all flared up as swiftly as the sudden spurt of flame when a log falls on the hearth. A few moments ago they had been laughing together, and now . . .

One of Bragon's New Spears slipped in low, and caught up the grey dagger and gave it to his lord almost before it had ceased to quiver. A kind of rustling and murmuring hush had fallen on the circle of watchers, and in the silence, there was an ominous forward thrust of men out of the farther dusk, as Clansmen from the lower fires, drawn by the raised voices of their Chieftains, came up to their support. Daggers were out in a score of places, and any moment now there was going to be trouble; bad and tragic trouble.

Then the young King flung aside his half empty drinking cup, spattering those nearest to him with the sticky golden mead, and crashed up from his painted stool. 'Na na, my brothers!' He stood over the scene, dominating it, young as he was. 'Will you fight like dogs at my father's Death Feast and my own King-Making? Here is no time nor place for such brawling; put up your daggers – put them up, I say!'

The two chieftains never turned their gaze from each other's faces. 'He has put an insult on me,' Dumnorix said, 'and I demand fighting to wipe it out.'

'If ye must have fighting, then let it be the fighting of dogs indeed,' the King said, and glanced about him, laughing, at the many hounds among their masters' legs. 'Surely there are dogs enough about my Dun tonight. Let you take each a dog – nay, three dogs will make a better showing. Bragon, let you take three hounds from among your own pack, and Dumnorix, let you take three hounds also, and let them fight to the death, here in the circle beside the fire. So, we may have good sport with our mead, and the insult will be wiped clean.'

There was a little silence after he had spoken. Then Bragon slid the grey dagger back into his belt. 'It is as the King says.'

'It is as the King says,' Dumnorix growled, echoing the action.

All around them there was a sheathing of daggers, a sudden slackening of the tension that had sprung up so swiftly; and the danger was past. A splurge of voices rose, eager, fiercely laughing. 'So, it is good – a dog fight. Come, Cerdic, there is going to be a dog fight.'

Bragon called to one of his warriors. 'Ho, Llew! That dog of yours is a fighter; bring him here.' And a man came shouldering through the throng, holding by the collar a big, heavily built dog whose ragged ears and scarred muzzle told their own tale.

For answer, Dumnorix whistled. 'Whee-ee!' and a young prancing hound of his own sprang up at his side. Again Bragon called out a hound; and Dumnorix glanced over his shoulder. 'Fynn, have you the red devil with you?'

'He is here,' said an old warrior, and thrust forward into the open space a reddish hound whose ears and muzzle were scarred like those of the first.

The King looked them over. 'Sa, two pairs we have, and I the King, will make choice for the third.' Under the twisted golden circlet, his gaze went carelessly to and fro among the nearest of the hounds, and singled out from among those of Bragon's Clan a huge brindled brute with a mane on him like a full bred wolf. 'That one I choose. And for the other –'

At that unlucky moment, Whitethroat, standing beside Drem, flung up his head to nuzzle the boy's arm, in one of the sudden little bursts of affection that he was given to; and the firelight caught the silver blaze that had given him his name. 'Sa! That one!' the King said, pointing. 'That one with the white throat.'

For one shocked instant of time, Drem did not believe it. It couldn't be Whitethroat he meant – not Whitethroat. But there was no mistaking the direction of the King's gaze and his pointing finger. Drem looked down at the great hound standing against his knee. Whitethroat's tail was swinging, and he gazed up at Drem trustingly, with amber eyes a little puzzled as though he caught the smell of something around him that he did not understand.

Drem looked at the other dog, the cunning, scarred veteran of many fights, his head lowered, the hackles already rising on his neck as though he understood perfectly what was expected of him; and in his eyes the red glint, the unmistakable red glint of the killer. Whitethroat could fight when need arose, though he was no fighter by nature, but Drem knew with a sickening certainty that if they were matched together, Whitethroat would be killed because he himself was not a killer.

They were looking to him to thrust the dog forward. The pause could only have lasted a couple of heart beats, but it seemed to Drem to have dragged on for a hundred. And then, setting down the mead jar that he still carried, he walked forward, with Whitethroat as usual pacing beside him, and turned, head thrown up, to face the King, to face Dumnorix his Chieftain and the big-bellied Bragon. He heard his own voice, level and challenging, though his heart had lurched into the base of his throat. 'We also, the New Spears, are called the Hounds of Dumnorix, and should we then have no part in this setting-on of hounds? Let one come out to me from among the New Spears who are the Hounds of Bragon, that we may fight it out here, beside the fire, for the third pair!'

There was a startled grunting, a startled rustle of voices round the fire. It was an unheard of thing that a boy who had not yet come to his Wolf Slaying should raise his voice in challenge before the Great Ones of the Tribe, before the King himself. But his challenge suited the wild humour of the assembled Tribesmen none the less; and the King smote his knees with an open hand, laughing. 'Well spoken, Hound of Dumnorix! And what say the Hounds of Bragon to that?'

Bragon stuck his thumbs in his belt under his broad paunch, and whistled. And one by one his New Spears slipped through the throng of Chieftains, and came to him. Eight of them, Drem saw: and one was the boy Cuneda, of yesterday's scene in the pony lines.

'Well,' said Bragon. 'Which of you takes up the challenge?'

There was a long pause, a harsh, dragging pause. And Drem, looking bright-eyed and defiant from one to another of the eight faces that looked back at him without any sign, understood it all too well. Understood that none of Bragon's Hounds was eager to face the possible shame of being defeated by a one-armed champion, nor yet of defeating him, for that, in its way, could carry almost as little honour. His mouth was dry, and he ran the tip of his tongue over his lips, smiling at them, a smile that was as much an insult as he could make it. If they refused him fight . . .

He was aware of the Grandfather, of Talore, of Drustic who had come thrusting up with the Clansmen from the lower fires; the whole Tribe, it seemed, looking on. Dumnorix had not whistled up his Hounds; but suddenly they were there, all the same, slipping through the crowds as Bragon's had done; and Drem felt their coming as they gathered in a knot behind him, Vortrix's shoulder against his; the bond of the Boys' House, the Brotherhood, close drawn between them. Save perhaps for Luga, he thought, they would stand by him whatever happened. If Bragon's Hounds refused him fight, they would stand by him still, in the face of the world, and make a mock of Bragon's Hounds who feared to fight a one-armed champion; but when they were by themselves they would look at his right arm again, as they had looked at it on their first day in the Boys' House, and he would have lost the strong place that he had won for himself among them. Drem knew his world; and it was a harsh one in which the pack turned on the weakest hound, in which little mercy was asked or given.

Bragon straddled his legs and wagged his thumbs under his belt, grinning. 'A pity it is that none of my young Hounds runs on three paws. It is in my mind that after all –'

The sickness rose in the pit of Drem's stomach. And then close beside him, Luga turned his head a little, and looked the boy Cuneda up and down with a faint sneer. 'And yet even a hound on three paws has his uses,' he said, and then, as though on quite a different subject, 'Is it that you need anybody to help you hold a pony?'

Drem flashed a startled look at him. He had thought – if he had given a thought to the thing at all – that Luga might be glad to see him humiliated before the Tribe; glad even, to see Whitethroat killed. Was it that he would be even more glad to see Drem killed? Even as the thought came to him, he knew that it was not that; but there was no time to seek the answer now.

To the Chieftains and elders about the fire, the taunt had no meaning, but Bragon's Hounds knew what it meant, and so did the Hounds of Dumnorix, and each knew that the other knew. There could be no escaping it. The boy Cuneda shrugged with an attempt at carelessness, though the angry colour flushed up to his forehead as it had done yesterday; and caught the dagger from his belt. 'I'll take you, then, with an arm bound behind my back if need be.'

'Na,' Drem said, smiling, though he felt the sweat prickle on his upper lip. 'That would be to tip the chances all one way. I have learned to fight one-handed.'

Men were crowding in on them more and more thickly from the other fires; the hounds, scenting what was in the wind, were straining at their broad studded collars, snarling and with raised hair. The King stood looking down his great beak of a nose, fondling the pricked ears of his wolfhound. 'So, it will be a dog-fight indeed . . . Wait though, should the third of our pairs go up against each other as it were naked, while the rest have their wolf collars to their throats? No shields, I think, in this dog fight – no, no shields. Irdun, bring out the hunting straps.'

And so the strips of thick yet supple pony-hide that men wore on the wolf or boar trail were brought out from the King's Hall; and Drem pulled off his saffron kirtle, and stood as though in a dream while Vortrix, thrusting the others aside, bound the straps about his belly and loins and left forearm; Vortrix, very bright and truculent of eye, and with an odd grimness about his mouth. And all the while, Whitethroat thrust and fawned against him, whining.

'Here, let you give me your dagger, and take mine,' Vortrix said when he had finished. 'It is better than yours.'

It was not, it was almost identical; but Drem knew that if this had been Vortrix's fight, he would have done the same thing because to lend Vortrix his own dagger would have been the only thing he could do for him in help and friendship. 'So, I take your dagger,' he said. 'Hold Whitethroat for me.'

The crowd was falling back, clearing a space beside the fire. The King had seated himself again on his painted and skin-spread stool with his blind harper at his feet. The four hounds dragged against their collars with renewed urgency, their snarling rising to a sing-song note of hate and menace; most of the others had been thrust out of the circle, lest they seek to join in. 'Good hunting, my brother in blood,' Vortrix said, and Drem heard him through the advice that the rest of his kind were showering upon him and which he did not hear at all. Then he stepped out into the clear space.

Across the crowding circle he saw the Grandfather sitting with his beaver-skin cloak huddled to his ears, gazing into the middle distance, for it was not the custom for any of the Men's side to show a public interest in a young kinsman who had not yet slain his wolf. Drustic, close beside him, was clearly deep in trouble; poor Drustic, who took life heavily and was always troubled about something, and was now in all likelihood wondering what he was going to tell their mother afterwards. Talore was looking straight at him despite the custom; Talore, slight and darkly fierce in the firelight that glowed in the brilliant folds of his scarlet cloak and struck shifting sparks of light from the coils of the great copper snake about his maimed forearm; and between the man and the boy, across the cleared space, unseen by the rest of the Tribe, there passed the old salute.

Then he was walking forward with stiff legs, houndwise, to meet his enemy.

They came together in the midst of the circle, and checked. The mist seemed to have thickened again, a golden smoke in the firelight, dimming a little the farther shapes of the crowd. He was aware of the moment's hush, everything save for the sing-song snarling of the hounds caught into stillness; of the eyes of the Men's side upon him. He was not aware, for his pride did not run on that particular trail, that standing there poised in the firelight and the golden mist, on the edge of intense and deadly action, he was beautiful to see. A tall, red-haired boy, with the lean, strong grace of the King's wolf-hound; all the more beautiful, in a queer, crooked way, because he carried his right arm trailing, like a bird with a broken wing.

Then the hounds, slipped from leash, sprang snarling past him, for each other's throats, and the frozen instant was over.

Drem and his enemy did not spring as the hounds had done; they were circling warily, crouching a little. Drem was watching the other boy's eyes. 'Watch his eyes.' How often old Kylan of the Boys' House had said that: 'Watch his eyes, and let his dagger hand look after itself.' Cuneda was the first to spring, but Drem had seen the flicker in his eyes in the instant before, and slipped sideways, feeling the wind of the dagger past his shoulder. Then he sprang in himself, to be met by a lightning guard-stroke. Dagger and dagger rang together, and he felt the jar of the impact all up his arm. On either side, all around him, the snarling tumult of the dog fight rose, and the voice of the crowd surged to and fro; but Drem heeded neither the one nor the other. His world had narrowed to a circle of sea-smelling, fire-gilded mist, and he was alone in it with his enemy. Once before, he had fought in deadly earnest – on that first day in the Boys' House; but this was a very different thing, no wild, squealing hurly-burly of random blows, no warrior's smell of blood at the back of his nose. This was something almost of ritual, a duel rather than a battle, and the more deadly for that. Yet it was linked, as the other had been, with his Warrior Scarlet.

Cuneda sprang in again, and again there was that ring of bronze on bronze; and Drem, breaking free his dagger, leapt in under the other boy's guard and drew blood from his upper arm before he could spring back out of range. One of the dogs had begun to howl, and there was a hideous worrying noise. For a few moments the boys circled at a distance, then sprang in again in a swift, fierce flurry of thrust and counter-thrust.

Drem felt a hot flick of pain in his side, as though old Kylan's bull's-hide whip had flicked him there. He laughed, and drove

in for closer fighting, momentarily pressing the other back. He saw Cuneda's face, the lips drawn back and nostrils flaring. Cuneda was losing his temper, as yesterday he had lost it with the pony mare; all the better, for with temper gone, judgement went too.

For a few moments the thing had the swiftness of a battle between wild cats rather than a dog fight, before both sprang back out of touch, and the wary circling began once more.

The end came suddenly; and by chance rather than his enemy's skill, very nearly in disaster for Drem. He saw again the warning flicker, just in time, and again side-sprang clear of

the other boy's stroke, but even as he did so, he heard a shout behind him, and something crashed snarling into the back of his legs, and he went down sprawling over two hounds locked together, the one with jaws fast in the other's throat.

Cuneda was on him in the same instant. He saw the flash of the descending blade, and twisted wildly, flinging up his arm. There could be no parrying the blow. He took it on his dagger arm instead of in the breast, and the keen blade, landing square, sheared through the pony-hide straps and laid his dagger arm open from wrist to elbow, and in the same instant he stabbed upward and felt the blow go home in the other boy's shoulder.

The King, on his painted stool, bent his head to listen to something that it seemed his blind harper had to say; then nodding briefly, rose to his feet, and stood hands on hips, surveying the scene.

Drem knew nothing of that. But as Cuneda grunted and lurched sideways, and he got to his feet panting, he heard the King's voice raised above the splurge of other voices. 'Finish! It is enough! The fight was good and it is over!' And just at first he did not understand. But he saw a flicker of a new kind in Cuneda's eyes, as the other boy scrambled up, clutching his shoulder; a flicker of relief.

For a moment Drem and his enemy, no more his enemy now, stood and looked at each other, while the uproar of the Men's side rose about them. Of the two victorious hounds, one was being dragged off by his master, and the other, bleeding from a score of wounds, stood licking his muzzle over the body of his foe. The fourth dog writhed horribly on the stained ground with his throat torn open. One of the warriors bent and put the poor brute out of its agony with a thrust of his dagger.

Drem turned and walked back to meet his own kind, stiff-legged still, swaggering his shoulders as he went. But the blood from his gashed forearm was trickling over his hand, and it was hard to hold the dagger. Whitethroat, tearing free of the hands on his collar, had come leaping to meet him, with bushy tail flying. They were all about him now; Vortrix had an arm across his shoulders. 'My heart is glad!' Vortrix said. 'It was a good hunting.' And then old hairy Kylan of the Boys' House was there, and one of the priest kind with linen strips and evil-smelling, black salve.

Meanwhile the King stood with his Chiefs about him, swinging a little on his wide-planted heels, the golden mead cup again in his hand. 'Nay,' he said, in answer to the grumbling protest of an old Chieftain, that the fight should have been allowed to find its own end. 'We have had our sport: why should the Tribe lose a warrior, maybe two?'

'Aye, but see,' said another Chieftain. 'The matter of the dagger is not yet wiped clean, for look you, a dog of Bragon's clan and a dog of Dumnorix's have won their fight, and you called off the boys with their fighting not yet finished. Therefore the thing stands equal and unfinished still.'

'You speak truth, Findabair,' said the King, and there was a small and rather grim smile in the shadow of his young golden beard. 'The matter of the dagger is not yet finished. Therefore we will make an end of it now . . . It is in my mind that surely it is not fitting that a strong magic such as this grey dagger seems to be, should lie in the hands of a Clan Chieftain – even so great a Clan Chieftain as you, Bragon my brother – while the King carries only a bronze dagger such as all men have in their belts. Therefore doubtless it has been in the mind of Bragon the Chieftain to give the grey dagger into the hands of the King.'

Bragon swallowed thickly, and turned as red as a withy when the sap rises. 'The King – surely the King jests.'

'Na, the King left jesting behind him on his father's death-pyre,' said the big golden man, smiling still, and he held out his hand.

Bragon, now almost purple, took the little grey dagger from his belt, and pressed it to his forehead, then gave it into the out-stretched hand.

The King took his own dagger rich with inlaid silver and red amber from his belt, saying. 'So. Now let you take this in exchange, that the gift of a knife may not break the friendship between the King and his Chieftain.' And so the thing was robbed of its sting.

Dumnorix flung up his big russet head and laughed, and the laughter was caught up by the Chieftains and the warriors around him, until even the red face of Bragon cracked into an unwilling grin. The King's dagger was a fine one, after all. And on the outskirts of the throng, Cathlan the Old gave a deep appreciative chuckle, and said to Talore who stood beside him: 'Sa, sa, the young bull has an old head on his shoulders. Behold, he has turned aside the trouble that there might have been between the Clans; and he has the grey dagger for himself.'

Talore showed the dog teeth at the corners of his mouth, in that swift, dark smile of his. 'Surely the young bull is a wise one – or has a wise counsellor in that blind harper of his. It is in my mind that it was wisdom to call off the fight when he did, that Bragon's boy should not be put to shame by a one-armed fighter – a thing which also might have bred trouble between the Clans at a later time.'

The Grandfather peered up at him under his thick, grey-gold brows. 'You think it would have ended so?'

'After that shoulder blow, I – think that it would have ended so,' said Talore the Hunter. 'He is a born fighter, that hound cub of yours.'

Drem heard the laughter of the Men's side, though he did not know what it was about. The small gash in his side had been salved, and his forearm tightly bound with linen strips to stop the bleeding and bring the edges of the wound together;

and his own kind were thronging about him; and he was very thirsty. 'I am thirsty,' he said. And it was Luga who brought him a pot of barley beer, and held it for him to drink, because his arm was so stiff in the tight binding that he could scarcely bend it. And looking at Luga's dark face over the tilting rim of the pot, he thought suddenly: 'I know you; you're a trouble-maker, always one to pick a quarrel and bear a grudge; but you're one of the Brotherhood still, and let any threat come against the Brotherhood from the outside, and you'll stand with the rest of us until the threat is beaten back.' Nothing was changed between himself and Luga, they would be hackles-up with each other tomorrow as they had been yesterday. But today they grinned at each other across the beer pot as Luga set it down empty.

The firelight was in Drem's eyes, and the taste of triumph in his mouth was hot and sweet as wild honey. He had made a good fight with his enemy, Whitethroat was safe, and he had held and strengthened his place among his spear brothers; now, surely, nothing but his Wolf Slaying was between him and his Warrior Scarlet.

And his Wolf Slaying would be before the spring came again.

9   The Black Pebble

Drem walked proudly among his fellows of the Boys' House in the moons that followed, while the long gash on his forearm healed and faded to a pinkish line that would be silvery by and by, and autumn gave place to winter, and the mid-winter fires blazed on the crest of the Hill of Gathering. And when the year turned towards spring and the wolves left the winter pack to mate, it was time for the Wolf Slaying to begin.

For two winters, Drem had watched the boys in their third year go out to the Wolf Slaying; and now the time had come for him and Vortrix and the rest of them. The time that, he realized now, had lain like a kind of darkening gulf across his path ever since he entered the Boys' House, making everything on the far side of it seem fiercely bright and at the same time remote. That was the same for all of them, he knew; they did not speak of it, but it was in their eyes as gaze caught gaze, every time they drew the sacred lots.

Since the choice of the Tribe's warriors must lie with the Sun Lord, the boys drew pebbles out of a narrow-mouthed jar – one black pebble and the rest white – to determine each time who should have the next hunting. And after each Wolf Slaying, one pebble was cast away, so that there were always so many pebbles in the pot as there were boys with their Wolf Slaying yet before them; one black pebble, and the rest white.

And in the dawn after each lot drawing, the hunting would begin. There were no hounds with the Wolf Slayers, but the whole of the little brotherhood would set out together as a hunting band; and together they would track down the beast and bring it to bay. Only the actual kill must be left to the one of them who had drawn the black pebble. For at the last, the thing must be fought out in single combat between the hunter and his wolf, matched together by the Sun Lord, so that from that time forward there was room for only one of them in the world of the living.

The time of Wolf Slaying went by slowly, and the white pebbles dwindled in the narrow-mouthed jar; and one white pebble was smeared with red ochre before it was cast away. That was for Gault who had missed his spear thrust and would never play the fool again. They made his death fire as it had been made for the old King; but this was a small fire, for a boy who had never come to the Warrior Scarlet.

Vortrix drew the black pebble and killed his wolf; Luga also, and Tuan and fat Maelgan, while still Drem drew only white pebbles, and waited for his turn to come. Spring came early that year, and the curlews were calling over the upland country and the first blackthorn foaming on the forest fringe, when Urian and he drew the last two pebbles from the jar. Once again, Drem drew the white pebble. And after Urian had slain his wolf, the weather turned wild and wet, so that for many days on end the white rain drove lashing before the spring gales across the roof of the Boys' House, and there was little to do but crouch over the smoking fire and go out to try one's weapons and come in half drowned and deaf with the wind, to crouch over the fire again; waiting, waiting, no hope of a wolf in this weather, while the days went by. Drem scarcely ate in those days of waiting; he grew gaunt as a famine wolf himself, and tense as an over-strung bow, so that even Vortrix scarcely dared to speak to him.

Then one evening the wind died, and the sun set wetly yellow over behind the Hill of Gathering, and the rain drifted away, leaving the world sodden and gale-weary. 'Give it two days,' old Kylan said. 'Two days, and the game trails will be alive and fit for following again.'

Drem looked up from beside the fire, where he sat burnishing his wolf spear. 'Give it two days, and the storms may return on their track. Already there are too few days left of Wolf Slaying. Give the word, old Lord of the Boys' House, and I go tomorrow.'

Kylan considered, his eyes that were yellow like a wolf's frowning into the eyes of the boy before him; and at last nodded his ragged head. 'So be it then; it is your trail, your wolf trail. Let you follow it.' And he gave the black pebble into Drem's hand.

And so in the dark before the next day's dawn, the hunting band rose and began to make ready. Standing naked by the fire, with the others about him, and the whole of the Boys' House awake and eager in the shadows as always when there was a Wolf Slaying in the wind, Drem tied back his hair with a thong, that it might not get in his way; and stood for Vortrix to bind the supple, sweat-darkened straps of pony hide about his belly and between his legs and round his left forearm, just as he had done beside the Royal Fire when the King called for a hound fight.

'Too tight?' Vortrix asked.

Drem twisted and crouched. 'Na, not too tight – tight enough, though.' And their eyes met in the light of the roof-tree torch, one pair very blue, the other suddenly golden, remembering that other time. The others stood looking on; one less of them than there should have been, and Drem, glancing round at them, saw in his own mind the missing one among them; a smallish ghost in the firelight with a mouth like a frog, and felt the skin prickle a little at the back of his neck. Beside Gault's death fire he had felt that quiver for the first time. Each of the New Spears were well aware, when they went out to the Wolf Slaying, that they might not come back, but he had realized then, as he had not quite realized before, that for him, because of his arm, the chances of not coming back were greater than for the others. Maybe tomorrow they would build the death-fire for him . . . But he would not think of that. He would think of coming back to the village at Sunset with the blood of his wolf on his breast and forehead, and the newly flayed skin on his shoulder.

He reached out and took his broad wolf spear from the rack beside the roof tree, and turned to the door, while behind him the others caught up the spears and the light wicker hunting shields that they carried for self-defence, and Vortrix took down the flaring torch from its sconce. Kylan was waiting for him in the doorway, old fierce Kylan with his bull's-hide whip laid aside, oddly gentle as he always was at this moment, and set his hand on Drem's shoulder, saying, 'Show the wolf kind that I have taught you well. Good hunting, my son.'

The sky had begun to lighten, a luminous water-green above the dark peaks of the turf roofs, as Drem with his hunting band behind him crossed the steading garth towards the doorway of the Chieftain's house-place; and his own shadow ran dark and spider-tall before him, in the light of the torch that Vortrix carried. Midir came to meet them on the threshold, with the golden eagle cap upon his head, and the amber Sun Cross on his breast catching the warmth of the torchlight.

'Who do you bring here to the sacred threshold of the Chieftain's house?' said Midir as they halted before him; and to the ritual question, Vortrix, the torch bearer, gave the ritual answer. 'A New Spear to be marked for his Wolf Slaying, Holy One.'

'Let him kneel down,' said Midir.

And while Drem knelt before him on sacred ground – every threshold was sacred, the Chieftain's above all others – the old priest made the three slim lines of the Wolf Pattern with charcoal and red ochre on his forehead. Lastly, with a hand so thin, despite its strength, that the torchlight seemed to shine through it, he took the amber Sun Cross on its thong, and touched Drem with it on the forehead above the Wolf marks, and again on the breast.

'Go forth and slay the wolf that waits your coming, my son. The Light of the Sun be with you through this day.'

And Drem rose, marked for his Wolf Slaying, set apart from the world of other men, and turned away to his hunting.

'What is the plan?' Vortrix asked softly, when they had left the still sleeping village behind.

'It is in my mind that the Under-Hill track is a good place to pick up a trail,' Drem said, moving a little ahead of the rest; and as they went down through the village barley plots he lifted his head and sniffed the morning, his nose almost as sensitive as a hound's, so that for him, running water and bare chalk and the north side of trees all had their clear, distinctive smells. The morning smelled chill and fresh, the wind still blowing in long, soft gusts that died away into stillness between; but his questing nose could discover no scent of wolf in it as yet. He felt the Wolf mark on his forehead as though the charcoal and red clay pressed against his skin. The light was broadening in the sky when they came down to the track under the steep northern scarp of the Chalk. The ancient trackway was sticky and slippery after so much rain, set with great pools that reflected back the pale shining colours of the sunrise beyond the interlacing hazel and sallow twigs. And for the trained eyes of the boys who came down to it spear in hand through the scrub, it bore a complete record of all the coming and going that there had been on it since the rain stopped yesterday evening.

Drem, his eyes moving unhurriedly here and there, as he checked beside the way and then began to follow it, was reading the signs with the ease of long use. Here a hedgehog had crossed the track from left to right, there a herd of deer had followed it for a little way, then turned off into the scrub towards the river: four head of deer, with three yearling fawns among them. A little farther on, a fox had crossed the track, going down to drink at sunset, and his spoor was crossed by that of a hunter coming that way a little after, carrying his kill on his left shoulder. Drem saw where he had halted to change it to the other shoulder, and left the tale in a single blood spot on the sodden ground, and in the changed balance of his footprints when he went on again. And then, just beyond that place, clear in a patch of fine gravel, were three padmarks that might have been the prints of a huge dog.

Vortrix saw them in the same instant as Drem, and said softly, 'Here's your wolf, brother.'

Drem nodded, slipping to one knee and bending low over the prints for a closer view, for the light was still poor, though growing stronger every moment. The tracks were new; the wolf could not have passed much before first light, and the depth and spacing of the pad marks showed that he was travelling easily, almost lazily. Probably he had killed somewhere up on the hill, and was now on his way back to his lair.

The others were standing round him, careful of their feet and where their shadows fell, in the way of the trained hunter. 'Well, do you take it?' Luga asked impatiently. 'Or is it that you need that dog of yours to tell you what to do?'

'I take it,' Drem said quietly, 'when I am ready.' And he went on studying the tracks, learning all that he could about his wolf. It was a big dog wolf, and from the angle at which the prints crossed the open ground, he judged that it was heading for the shallows of the stream below, as though to cross over into the dense forest that choked up the valleys on the farther side. He rose from his knee at last, his hand tightening on the white ash shaft of his spear, his heart giving the little lurch of excitement with which he always began a hunting; and with his hunting band at his back, melted into the budding hazel scrub beside the way, leaving the wet track empty in the day-spring until a magpie flew down on to it to drink at one of the puddles.

They forded the stream, picking up the pad marks again in the soft earth on the far side, and pressed on. All that morning while the sun rose high into a sky of drifting cloud and storm-washed blue, and the broken tumble of light and shadow sailed lazily across the High Chalk, Drem and his companions followed the trail of the big dog wolf through the deep mazes of the forest; very occasionally by a pad mark, more often by a single brindled hair on a low-hanging thorn branch, by a few side-brushed blades of grass, by the distant alarm call of a jay; by all the thousand and one signs, not there for any save the trained hunter, that told of a wolf passing that way. The hazel scrub and wild fruit trees and the red, sap-bloomed alders of the forest fringe had given way by little and little to the small, dense damp-oaks of the Wild, and as they pushed farther and farther into the dark heart of the forest, dense tangles of yew and holly crowded ever more thickly about them. It was not a tall forest, but a dark one; grey-misted, brown-shadowed, green-gloomed, and the hunting band, moving with the light swiftness of questing hounds, moved in a twilit world, where the sunlight splashing in through the tangle of bursting oak twigs overhead or between the black rook-wing branches where a yew had fallen, seemed to burn with a brilliance that was sharp-edged as a sword cut and gave off none of its light into the misty glooms of the surrounding forest. When summer came and the trees were in full leaf there would be no sunlight at all, even to stripe and dapple the darkness. A cold and heavy smell hung between the trees, and there were few birds here. Only suddenly, not far off, a jay screamed its warning.

Drem checked an instant, the little cold thrill closing round his heart; then he began to run, circling wide so as to come up-wind on the place where the jay had sounded its alarm call. And the rest of the band were hard behind him; a swift and silent running of shadows among the trees.

Stronger light glimmered through the twisted and crowding trunks ahead, and somewhere to the right the jay called again; and slipping low under the drooping branches of a great forest yew, he found himself crouching on the edge of a clearing. In the midst of the open space, a dense mass of thorn and elder and wayfaring trees thrusting up into the light and air, almost hid from sight a kind of low, overhanging cliff of earth and rock, caused maybe by some landslide in the rains of a long past winter, that closed the far side of the clearing. But Drem knew as surely as though he could see the cave mouth with his own eyes, that somewhere in there, under the dark overhang and the crowding bushes, was the lair of the wolf that they had trailed so far.

He made a small, swift sign to the others behind him; and knew, though no breath of movement told him so, that they had slipped away, right and left, to draw their ring about the place. Drem crouched motionless in the brown gloom under the yew branches, his hand clenched on the spear shaft until the knuckles shone white. His nostrils widened, and little tremors ran through his body, houndwise, as the smell of wolf came to him down the wind.

The faintest movement, the swaying of a branch in one place, the stirring of a tall bramble spray in another, signalled to him that the others were in place all round the clearing. This was the moment, then! He stood up. The others were up almost in the same movement; he could see them all round the circle, closing in towards where, somewhere in the dense scrub before them, the wolf must be aware of their coming and watching them come. The time for silence was past now, and they began to shout, their voices chiming together and rising into the tree tops. 'Ty-yi-*yah*-eee!' And with the rising voices, Drem's heart seemed to rise too, beating upwards with a wild exultancy: 'Ty-yi-ee! Yah-ee-ty-yi-yi!' as they came closing in through the long grass and the brambles.

And then suddenly the wolf was there. With a crashing of twigs and small branches it sprang into the open, then, seeing the hunters all about it, checked almost in mid spring, swinging its head from side to side, with laid-back ears and wrinkled muzzle: a great, brindled dog wolf, menace in every raised hackle. Then, as though it knew with which of the hunters it had to deal, as though it expected him, it looked full at Drem. For a long moment it stood there, tensed to spring, savage amber eyes on his as though it knew and greeted him. The rest of the band had checked at a small distance, spears ready; but Drem was no longer aware of them; only of the wolf, his wolf. The thing was between him and his wolf, life for life, and the Warrior Scarlet.

It seemed to him that the open jaws with their lolling tongue were grinning at him as he leapt forward and ran in low, his spear drawn back to strike. And at the same instant the wolf sprang.

Quite what happened he never knew; it was all so quick, so hideously quick. His foot came down on something agonizingly sharp that stabbed through the soft raw-hide of his shoe and deep into his flesh – a torn furze root perhaps – throwing him for one instant off his balance. It was only for the merest splinter of time, but twisting to regain his balance, somehow he missed his thrust; and the wolf was on him. He had one piercing flash of realization; a vision of a snarling head that seemed to fill his world – yellow fangs and a wet black throat; and then sky and bushes spun over each other. He was half under the brute, he felt a searing, tearing pain in his right shoulder, he smelled death. The wolf's hot breath was on his face as he struggled

wildly to shorten his spear for a dagger-stab, his chin jammed down in a despairing attempt to guard his throat; while at the same moment something in him – another Drem who was standing apart from all this – was knowing with a quiet and perfect clearness like a sky at summer evening: 'This is the end, then. It is Gault's fire for me . . .'

He heard shouting, and at the edge of his awareness caught the downward strike of another spear blade. There seemed to be another struggle rolling over him, and confusedly he knew that the wolf had turned from his throat. He heard its snarl rise to a sudden yelping howl; he was aware of a great weight gone from him, a crashing away through the bushes, a burst of more distant shouting; a moment of oddly terrible quiet. And in the quiet, scarcely knowing what he did, he dragged himself to his knees, shuddering and gasping for breath, his spear still in his hand. And Vortrix's arm came down to him, helping him to his feet.

Blood from the long fang-slash in his shoulder spattered down, bright on to Vortrix's hand, just as it had done on the day so long, long ago, when they had become blood brothers. They looked at each other across the silence, and then, ashamed to look at each other because of what had come between them, looked away. The other boys were gathering about them, breathing fast. Someone said, 'The brute is clear away – na, the lair is empty. We shall not see that one again.' And someone said: 'It was no ordinary wolf. Surely it was a ghost wolf, or it could never have escaped after that thrust of yours, Vortrix.'

Drem leaned weakly on his spear and looked at Vortrix again. 'You should have left the thing between my wolf and me,' he said, but his mouth was so dry that the words came out only as a choking whisper.

Vortrix was deadly white, grey-white to the very lips, and his eyes looked blind. He shook his head, but said no word. There was nothing to be said, Drem knew, nothing to be done. Even if he could stop the bleeding in his shoulder and track down the wounded wolf again and slay it – before sunset, it must be before sunset – it would do no good, for Vortrix would have had a hand in the killing; and the killing must be between wolf and New Spear alone. That was the custom.

Everything seemed unreal and far off. Somebody brought him a handful of moss to press against his shoulder, and he took it, slipping his arm through the thong of his spear, and gathered himself slowly upright. He looked about him at his fellows; and the familiar faces looked back, silently, not quite meeting his eyes. He saw that as though by common consent, they had parted their circle about him, and understood that the gap was for him to walk out through; out and away. His brothers of the Boys' House were offering him the only mercy that they had it in their power to give; that he might go now, to live, or more likely die, as the forest chose, instead of coming back to face the shame. He was free to turn to the forest as he had turned to it that night six summers ago, when it had all begun. It would be the easiest way. But that night six summers ago had been the last time that Drem had turned tail. He had fought so long and so hard that now he couldn't stop fighting; he couldn't take the easy way, though he longed for it.

'The forest is all around you,' Luga said.

Drem shook his head. 'Na,' he said. 'Na.' And could say no more because of the dryness in his mouth. He gathered himself together, and slipped the spear thong up to his shoulder; then, still pressing the reddened moss against his hurt, turned back in the direction that they had come. The others fell a little behind, but Vortrix walked with him.

10 'Brother, My Brother!'

At dusk that evening, having faced Kylan, having faced the Boys' House, Drem went home.

They were all at the evening stew, round the hearth in the familiar house-place; and they looked up and saw him leaning in the doorway, on the dim edge of the firelight, with the remains of the Wolf Pattern still on his forehead, and the dried and clotted wound in his shoulder. And for one moment it was in the hearts of all of them that he was a ghost. He saw it there; he saw the fear in his mother's eyes. Well, in a way he was a ghost – dead to the Tribe. A boy who failed in his Wolf Slaying and did not die was dead to the Tribe. It was the custom.

Then Whitethroat, who had sprung up with the other hounds at his coming, gave a piercing whine and came running to him, crouching low, in very different manner from his usual joyous greeting, and the still moment, the icy moment, was past. His mother had risen swiftly to her feet. 'What is it? Ah, you are hurt – your shoulder –'

Drem looked about him. He saw that the loom by the door was empty, and a piece of cloth lay folded at its foot as though it had been newly cut from it; fine chequered cloth of Warrior Scarlet woven with the dark green of juniper leaves. And his heart twisted with a physical pain under his ribs. He said hoarsely, 'If that was meant for me, my mother, let you take it for a new cloak for Drustic. I have failed in my Wolf Slaying.'

He thought that he should never forget his mother's cry. It was not loud; quite a little cry, but it seemed to be torn from her raw and bleeding, and it hurt him as he had not known that it was possible to be hurt.

Cathlan, the Grandfather, on his folded bearskin beside the

fire, leaned forward to peer at him through the wreathing smoke fronds, his golden eyes almost hidden under the down-twitched grey-gold brows. Then he tossed the bone he had been gnawing over his shoulder to a waiting hound, and spat harshly and disgustedly into the flames. 'What did I say, son's wife? What did I say, six summers ago?'

Drustic was staring at him, too, his pleasant square face bogged deep in trouble. He opened his mouth and then shut it again, as though he wanted to say something but couldn't think what.

Drem came in to the fireside – the first time in three years that he had crossed the threshold of his home; the last time, maybe, in all his life – and squatted down, with Whitethroat crouched against his knee. 'Is there no food for me?' he demanded, harshly defiant. 'I have not eaten for a night and a day.'

His mother was pressing her hands across her forehead. 'Food? Yes – yes, there is food. But first – at least let me bind your wound.'

'It will do well enough as it is,' Drem said. 'I want food before I must be away, no more.'

Blai, unnoticed in the shadows until that moment, had risen to her feet. 'I will see to it,' she said; and brought him a bowl of stew and a barley cake, and gave them to him without another word.

He took them from her and ate furiously. He had not eaten for a day and a night, as he said; one did not eat before hunting, and besides, he had been too afraid. But there was nothing to be afraid of any more, because the worst thing that could possibly happen to him had happened. So he ate fiercely and swiftly, tearing the meat from the bones with his teeth, and tossing the bones to Whitethroat against his knees. It was his mother and brother and the silent Blai, watching him, who did not eat. The Grandfather ate, but then nothing in the world would come between him and his food.

When at last Drem could eat no more, he rubbed his hand in the brown, piled fern to cleanse it, and looked round him; a long, long look; at the faces of his kin, at the familiar, firelit, shadowy house-place. He saw the firelight falling saffron coloured across the hearth stone, the long, jagged knot high up on the roof tree where a branch had been when it was a growing oak tree in the forest, the dappled cream and tawny deerskin hanging before his mother's sleeping stall, and the bronze and bull's-hide shield hanging from the edge of the loft, that would never now be his to carry. All the long-familiar things that he had not seen for three years, and after tonight, would never see again.

Then he got to his feet, saying to Whitethroat, 'Come, brother, it is time that we were away.'

His mother, who had remained standing all the while, braced against the roof tree, as though she were bound there, came and set her hands almost timidly on his shoulders. 'Where are you away to? Cubbling, what will you do?'

'I will go to the Half People, as you said six summers ago – you and the Grandfather both – that I must go if I failed,' Drem said. 'I will go to Doli and the sheep.'

'So you heard,' his mother said; and he saw her eyes straining in her beautiful, dagger-thin face, and the desire to hurt as he had been hurt rose within him. He had not forgiven her for that small, agonized cry.

'You always wondered, didn't you? Aye, I heard, every word. I was in the loft; I had come in by the roof strip meaning to drop on you like an earwig out of the thatch – a child I was; but I was never so much a child again, after that day . . . That was why I ran to the forest; only Talore One-hand found me and bade me come back and fight for the thing if I would have it. And I have fought, the Sun Lord knows that I have fought, these six years gone by. But the Grandfather was right after all.' His voice, which had become a man's voice in the past year, cracked, and steadied again. 'Let you be glad of Drustic, as you bade the Grandfather to be glad of Drustic. You'll not be without a son to stand with the Men's side, when I am herding sheep.'

She cried out again at that, and her second cry seemed to undo what the first had done. He wanted to put his arm round her and drive his head into the warm, soft hollow of her neck as he had used to do when he was small, but he did not dare, lest he should weep like a woman. It was better to go on being angry. Anger was a kind of shield. His mother had dropped her hands from his shoulders. 'Drustic is a good son, but it is better to have two sons – better two sons than one . . . And this time there will be no coming back.'

'Na, this time there will be no coming back.'

He turned, with Whitethroat at his heel, blundering past Blai, whose pinched, white face swam for an instant into his sight as though it floated in dark water, and went out into the spring dusk. The ponies in the fore porch advanced soft muzzles to him, but he blundered past them also. Behind him he heard a movement as though his mother made to rush after him; and Drustic's voice saying urgently 'Na na, my mother, there is no good that you can do !'

And he plunged on into the dusk with the sound of sudden wild weeping in his ears.

He was going out, stripped and alone, from his whole world, leaving behind him his people, the comradeship of his own kind, even his own gods. Many of the Half People bowed themselves to the Sun Lord, but he was going not only to the Half People but to Doli; to the little Dark People, the children of Tah-Nu; and he knew that little by little he would lose his own faith that was sharp and fierce and bright as a spear blade; turn from the Sun Father and the open sky, to the older faith of Doli and his kind, to the warm suffocating darkness and the Earth Mother who gave all things birth.

He turned his steps towards the sheltered fold of the downs high above the village, where the turf-walled lambing pens stood for use each winter. In a little now, after the Beltane fires were burned out, the shepherd kind would take the ewes and their lambs up to the High Chalk again, to the summer sheep runs, but now sheep and shepherds would still be there, and Doli with them.

It was long after dark when he came up the combe and saw the gleam of firelight from the doorhole of the low turf bothie beside the pens, and heard the faint rustle of the penned flock and the bleating of a lamb that had woken to find itself apart from its mother; and a great baying of herd dogs broke out, making him stoop quickly and catch Whitethroat by his bronze-bossed collar. Then a voice sounded, silencing the dogs, and a little bent figure came ducking out through the firelit doorway, and turned to peer down the combe.

'Who comes?'

'It is I, Drem,' Drem called back.

Doli, for it was Doli, spoke to the dogs again, and they lay down on either side of him. He stood without any movement, leaning on his broad-bladed spear, and waited for Drem to come up to him.

'It is past barley harvest,' he said, when the boy stood before him; and that was all.

'It is past six barley harvests,' Drem said, 'but I am come at last. You said once that I should make none so ill a shepherd. Do you think so still?'

'How shall I say, I who have not spoken with you these six barley harvests past?' And then as a silver wing of moonlight slipped over the shoulder of the combe and spread towards them, the old man looked up at him, slantwise under the grey tangle of his brows. A long considered look. Then he shook his head. 'I am none so sure. I think that you are more ungentle than you were, six barley harvests ago. Yet it may be that you are gentler with the four-footed kind than with men and women. Why do you ask?'

There was a little silence, filled by the delicate riffling of the wind through the short grass, and the stirring of the sheep in the fold behind them. A curlew cried from the head of the combe, and one of the herd dogs, still lying obediently at Doli's side, gave a warning growl as Whitethroat's exploring muzzle came too near. Then Drem said, 'I have had too much fighting of late, to care much for the gentle things. But I have lost my fight. I have failed in my Wolf Slaying.'

Doli showed neither surprise nor sorrow – but then Doli very seldom showed anything. 'Sa, that is a bad thing,' he said. 'And so now you come to me and the sheep.'

'So now I come to you and the sheep,' Drem said dully.

'Then let you come in to the fire, and I will salve that shoulder,' Doli said. No surprise, no questions asked. And deep in his raw and angry heart, so deep that he did not realize it, Drem was grateful, as he ducked under the low lintel and followed Doli into the shepherd's bothie. Someone sat beside the fire, a dark boy of his own age, and he saw that it was Erp who had run with the rest of them in the days before the Boys' House. Their eyes met, black eyes and golden, and then both looked away again.

Doli brought rank-smelling yellow ointment in a pot, and smeared Drem's shoulder as though he had been a wolf-bitten ewe, saying, 'This is good against a wolf gash, whether in man or sheep.'

Drem bore with the salving, then sat down with Whitethroat against his knee, beside the fire, not avoiding Erp's dark, curious gaze any more, not seeking it out, too tired to care either way. He felt oddly adrift, like something with its roots hacked from under it, spent and empty. Even his rage had gone from him, and there seemed nothing to take its place, nothing; just emptiness where yesterday his life had been: and he was so tired.

By and by he lay down beside the fire, with his head on Whitethroat's flank, and fell asleep like a tired child, the traces of the Wolf Pattern still on his forehead. So deeply asleep that he did not wake even when Flann and his brother came back from the village.

It was the eleventh morning after that, and his shoulder, thanks to Doli's salve, was three parts healed, when he looked up from helping the old shepherd to spread the same stinking yellow stuff on a ewe's back where she had been pecked by ravens – and saw Vortrix standing by the opening of the fold.

He was not surprised, he had known that Vortrix would come, before his initiation cut them off from each other for all time. And this was the last day of all.

No word passed between them, only one long look, and when the ewe had been released, bleating after her lamb, he said to old Doli, 'I will come back in a while,' and whistling Whitethroat to heel, walked out of the fold to where Vortrix waited for him.

Still without a word, they turned together, and walked up the combe, with their hounds loping behind them.

'Why did you not come before?' Drem asked at last, staring straight before him as they walked. He had not meant to ask it; but he asked, none the less.

'I have been nine days and nine nights enclosed. Taboo in my father's house,' Vortrix said. 'Midir sealed the door with clay, and sealed it again every time he came – he and the warriors with him – and I might not break the seal.'

Drem had not thought of that; that Vortrix had broken custom by coming between him and his wolf, and would have to pay for it in ritual purification. 'Was it bad?' he said.

'It was – not good,' Vortrix said, quite quietly, but it sounded as though he had spoken through shut teeth. Drem looked at him sideways. Vortrix's square, cleft jaw was set, and there were great stains like bruises under his eyes. What had they done to him, those nine days and nights, in the hut with the clay seal on the door? Drem realized that he would never know; that he must not even ask.

All that day they hunted together as of old. They killed at last among the wooded combes of the High Chalk, and evening found them making their way home with the carcass of a young roe hind slung from Vortrix's spear between them. The hounds padded at their heels; the shadows of boys and hounds and kill long-drawn on the downland turf. All as usual, everything as usual, save that it was for the last time.

They came over a last lift of the Chalk, and on the edge of a little solitary wood of wind-stunted oak and thorn trees that crested the ridge, halted to rest. But they had carried home heavier kills before now, and never thought of resting. And there among the budding oak trees, with the body of the hind at their feet, they turned to look at each other. All day they had contrived somehow to hide from themselves the fact that this was their last hunting together, but now they could not hide it any longer. It was in the sea-song of the wind in the budding oak branches, and the distant crying of the gulls, in the cool scent of the moss that grew thick under the trees, and in the bleak and hopeless desolation of their own hearts.

'We have had good hunting,' Vortrix said.

Drem nodded. They had had good hunting; not only today,

but all the days of their hunting together. He would hunt again, and so would Vortrix, but never again together. That was over. The fore-shadow of tomorrow's parting hung over them; a parting as sure and more final than it would have been if one of them was to die in the morning, and one to go on living. It was not that they would not see each other again, but that they would see each other only across the gulf that divided the Men's side, the free Tribesmen of the warrior cast, from the Half People without the Tribe. There was nothing they could do. They were in the grip of the custom of the Tribe; and the custom was stronger than they were, stronger than all the men of the Tribe together.

Drem stared down at the roe hind at his feet. There was a scarlet stain on the white of her belly, like the scarlet stain on the white breast feathers of the swan. Warrior Scarlet . . .

He cried out hoarsely, as though under sudden sharp pain. 'Why did you come between my wolf and me?'

'I had no time to think – even now I cannot think. I – it is none so easy a thing to stand leaning on one's spear to see a brother die.'

'And so tomorrow I must stand to see you and all our company go away from me – and turn back alone, after you are gone.'

'My brother – oh, my brother – we have hunted the same trails and eaten from the same bowl and slept in the same bed when the hunting was over. How shall I go on or you turn back alone?'

'I do not know,' Drem said. 'It must be – it must be; but how, I do not know.'

They reached out their hands to each other, Vortrix's two hands, Drem's one, gropingly as though both of them were blind. Their arms were round each other in a close, hard embrace. They had always been equally matched, a team that had

neither leader nor follower; but now in their parting it was Drem who was the stronger of the two, and Vortrix who cried like a woman, with his head bent into the hollow of Drem's shoulder, while beyond the wind-stirred branches of oak and thorn the low sun set fire to the clouds, and the west was suddenly kindled to furnace gold.

Higher and higher burned the fires of the sunset, deepening from gold to copper, to fierce and glowing red. The branches of the oak trees were black against it, and the wings of the gulls were black as they swept by; and the crimson light splashing far in through the little wood flushed the vivid moss under the trees, and stained the breast of the roe hind so that it was as though the blood spread until the whole of the white fur was stained pink.

When the fires began to fade, dying out into pale rose-flecks overhead, so that all the sky was freckled like the skin of a trout, and the shadows thickened among trees, they stooped again to their kill. The village, though out of sight below them, was not far off, and, 'I will come no farther with you,' Drem said. 'It is in my mind that you can carry her alone from here.'

'Aye, I can carry her. I will take your half of the kill to your mother.'

He helped Vortrix to get the carcass of the deer across his shoulders, fore feet in one hand and hind feet in the other, and to settle his spear. Then without another word between them, he turned and went blundering down through the little wood. He could not bear any more. He did not even remember to whistle Whitethroat after him, did not remember the great hound at all, until a brindled black and amber shadow brushed past his knee and circled before him with bushy tail flying. He had forgotten Whitethroat; he would not be quite alone.

It was dusk when he got back to Doli and the shepherd kind; and he settled down to his evening stew keeping well away from the fire, that the light of the flames might not show them his face.

Drem tried to keep away from the village the next day, but nevertheless, when sunset drew near and it was time for the start of the ceremonies, he came up the stream, through the alder brake, and stood among the alder trees in their haze of young leaf, looking across the irregular barley plots to the familiar huddle of turf roofs. He heard the soft, formless murmuration of the gathering crowd that rose to a long-drawn cry as the boys appeared from the Boys' House doorway; and he bent his head on to his fist on the spear shaft, seeing against the darkness of his closed eyes the scene that he had watched so often before. He saw them coming down through the now silent crowd, walking one behind another, very proud and erect, and looking straight before them. Another cry – almost a wail – told him that the first boy had stepped out into the open space about the Council Fire where Dumnorix stood with the greatest of his warriors about him. That would be Tuan, the youngest of them; always it was the youngest first, the eldest last – the eldest who this year would be Vortrix. Against the darkness he saw two warriors step out from the

Men's side, to either side of him. But it was no longer Tuan between them, and the warriors that he saw in his mind were not Tuan's father and his friend but a huge and stooping old grey-gold man with a beak like an eagle's, and a slight, dark one with a great copper snake twisted about a left forearm that lacked a hand. They were bringing him to Midir beside the Council Fire; Midir bending a little to receive them, his thin hair straggling from beneath the golden eagle cap of the priest kind. He seemed to hear the ritual questions and answers. 'Who is this that you bring before me?'

'It is a boy, that he may die in his boyhood and return a warrior to his Tribe.'

'And who speaks for the boy?'

'I, Cathlan the Old, Cathlan the Mighty, I his Grandfather, speak for the boy –'

Drem, leaning on his spear among the alder bushes, drew a hoarse breath that was like a sob. Why had he come? But he knew that his coming had made no difference; if he had stayed with Doli and the sheep as he had tried to do, the thing that was happening beside the Council Fire would have reached him just as surely.

Across the little barley plots and the young flax, he heard the women taking up one from another the death chant for the sons who were going out to their ritual dying, and knew that it was over; it never took long, that first ceremony. Now they would be coming down after Midir, through the crowd that swayed back to let them through, the boys who had been his companions of the Boys' House, who would have been his fellows of the Spear-ring – Vortrix . . . He raised his head, and saw them, no longer against the darkness of his inner eyes, a slim line of young proud figures, with the winged figure of Midir at their head, and the first of a stormy sunset that he had not seen come, blazing behind them; and as they walked, their

159

shadows reached out towards him across the springing barley as though in farewell. Now, for a night and a day, until the fires of tomorrow's sunset flared beyond the Hill of Gathering, they would be as dead to the Tribe; and then they would come back, as warriors from victory, with the tattooed patterns of their new manhood raw on their breasts, and there would be a great rejoicing, a triumphal blowing of war horns before presently the Beltane fires were lit.

But Drem knew that he would not see that triumphal home-coming. He had come because he must, to see his brothers of the Boys' House away; the return of the young warriors was no more to do with him.

They had turned right hand, now, and were walking straight up the slopes of the Hill of Gathering, while behind them the women lamented still. 'Ochone! Ochone!' And the death chant fell heavy on Drem's ears and on his heart. The boys dwindled smaller and smaller on his straining sight, winding up the long slope towards the sleeping-place of the unknown champion on the crest, and as they dipped over the skyline towards the Place of New Spears beyond, it seemed as though they walked straight into the blazing brightness of the sunset. And the brightness opened for them, and they were gone.

Drem turned away alone, blind with more than the sun in his eyes, and plunged back through the alder scrub. And still behind him rose the wailing of the Women's side. 'Ochone! Ochone!'

11   The News-Bringers

The next night Drem stood alone by the empty lambing pens, when the flocks and herds had all been driven down to the village, and watched the Beltane fires blazing red on the crest of the Hill of Gathering; and knew that the young warriors had returned out of the sunset. Behind him in the shepherd's bothie the hearth was black and cold, just as his own heart felt black and cold within him, and with the same empty desolation. But the hearth only waited, like every hearth throughout the Clan and the Half People, to spring to life again at the touch of the sacred fire . . .

Then far down the combe a red bud of flame pricked out in the darkness and Erp came running with a torch, as all up and down the Clan territory the youngest man of every household would be running. And the black hearth in the shepherd's bothie woke and kindled and uncurled petals of living flame. But the coldness and darkness within Drem was as cold and as dark as ever.

Next day, when the Beltane fires were burned out, the sheep were taken up to the high summer pastures, and Drem, whose life was now the life of the shepherd kind, went with them. And little by little, as the days went by, the slow, solitary rhythm of the new life closed round him. Every night at twilight they folded the sheep in the great, turf-banked enclosures. (Even in summer the sheep only had to be left unfolded for a few nights for the wolves to come up from the forest and hunt the grazing lands. They were no fools, the wolf kind.) Every morning, when the light returned to the world, they were let loose again. And morning and evening they must be taken to the dew-pond a bow shot from the enclosures, to drink. All day long as they

grazed, they must be watched and guarded, moved from place
to place so that there was always fresh grass, kept from the parts
of the Chalk where harmful herbs grew, and from danger
spots such as the old flint quarries; rounded up when they
became too scattered; tended when they were sick or hurt. At
night when the sheep were safely folded, there was the low turf
bothie by the dew-pond, and stew – mutton stew for the most
part, from the carcass that hung in the hearth smoke out of
reach of the dogs – cooked by one of the Little Dark Women
who came and went and seldom seemed to belong to any of the
shepherds in particular. There were sheep salves to be mixed
and shepherd's gear to be mended; while sometimes old Doli
would blossom into a story, and sometimes young Erp would
play a little wandering, tuneless air on the elder pipe that by
day he played to his sheep. But for the most part they sat in
silence. They were a silent people, the shepherd kind.

When Drem had been more than a moon with Doli and his
people, it was time for sheep shearing.

Three times a year the Tribe and the Half People without
the Tribe came together at a common need. One was at the
great cattle round-up at the Fall-of-the-Leaf, one was at lambing time, when every able-bodied man, Dark or Golden, must
take his turn in the Wolf Guard; and one was at sheep shearing.
But it was chiefly the women of the Tribe who came to mingle
with the Half People at the sheep shearing.

It was early summer as yet, but already the rolling chalk hills
quivered in the heat. Swifts darted high in the blue air, or
skimmed low above their own shadows along the flanks of the
turf, and the whole wide sky shimmered with lark song. Drem,
bringing down a small flock from the high Chalk to the shearing
pens above the village, heard the larks and smelled the dry
thyme bruised under his feet and the little sharp hooves of the
sheep, and felt the sun hot between his shoulders. But the old

fierce joy that he had once taken in such things was lost to him. He kept his ears on the bleating of the ewes and their half grown lambs, his eyes on their bobbing rumps, and on the grey herd dog circling on the flanks of the flock. Cu, the older of Doli's two dogs, who had been the young one, six summers ago, would not work with anyone but his master, but Asal, the young one now, would work with Drem well enough, and there was no trouble between him and Whitethroat so long as Drem remembered never to fondle Asal when the great hound was by. Whitethroat padded at his lord's heels now, with a long fluted strap of pink tongue dripping from his mouth. He would never make a herd dog, he had been a hunting dog too long, but he understood that the sheep were not for hunting but for protecting, and already he had proved that he could earn his keep as a guardian of the flock.

It was the first time that Drem had been within sight of the village since the day when he had watched the opening cere-monies of the New Spears from afar; and as he dropped lower, and the distant blueness of the Wild was lost to sight behind the rolling bluffs of the Chalk, he looked for the familiar roof-huddle under the Hill of Gathering, and the full and noisy scene on the level turf above the corn plots, where the shearing pens had been set up and the shearers were already at work; half longing for the sight of familiar things, familiar faces, half flinching from it.

Drem could not work among the shearers. There were few things that he could not do one-handed, but to deal with a struggling and indignant sheep and work the heavy bronze shears, one must have two hands. So through the rest of that crowded and sweating day, when the droving was over, he worked at the pens, and ran the sheep down, bleating and pro-testing, to the shearers, from whose hands they were turned loose at last, pale and shorn, to trot quietly off in search of their bleating lambs. It was hot work. His hair stuck to his forehead and his kilt to his thighs, and his hand was greasy with the yolk of the fleeces that seemed to have got inside his nostrils so that he could not smell anything else.

When a girl, passing with a tall jar full of buttermilk for the shearers on her hip, paused beside him, he turned to her eagerly – and it was Blai.

For almost the first time in his life he was glad to see her. She would be able to tell him of his house, of the old life that he had left behind him. For the moment, in his swift surge of longing, he forgot even his thirst and the buttermilk, and letting go the sheep he had just taken from the pen, stretched out his yolky hand and caught her wrist as though he was afraid she might be away before he could get out the things he wanted to say, the questions he wanted to ask. 'Blai! Blai!' He was almost stammering. 'It is good to see you!'

She looked up quickly, and for a brief moment it was as though a light sprang up in her face. 'Is it, Drem?'

'Of course.' He was impatient at her stupidity. 'You can tell me how it is with my kin at home! How is it with my mother, Blai?'

The light died again, and Blai said after a moment, 'Yes – I can tell you of your home. It is well with your mother, Drem.'

'She is – not here?'

'Na. She is not here.'

They looked at each other a moment, then Blai raised the wide-necked jar, holding it for him because he had not the two hands to take it. 'Now drink. You must be thirsty.'

Drem drank. The buttermilk was cool and thin and smooth, and he drank his fill. When he had done so, he stood back, wiping his hand across his mouth; and then wished that he had not because of the yolk on it.

In swift little scattered sentences, Blai was telling him the news of his home; of the Grandfather's cough and Drustic's hunting, of the birth of hound puppies, of how the half wild fruit trees did, of his mother, and the red mare who was ready for breaking.

When it was all told, she was silent a short while, staring down into the jar. Then she said a little breathlessly, 'I could come and bring you news of your home again – sometimes – if you would like.'

'I shall be up on the High Chalk again tomorrow. That's a long way,' Drem said quickly; and then, without meaning to say it, heard his own voice adding, 'It is lonely, up on the High Chalk, Blai.'

Blai was still staring into the jar. 'I could come – sometimes,' she said. 'I would not mind the long way, and – then maybe it would be – less lonely.'

Drem looked at her with a little frown between his eyes. He was puzzled. 'Why would you do that – come all that way, for me, Blai?'

Blai raised her head, and a slow painful wave of colour flowed up over her narrow face. 'You came after me once – years ago – when *that man* came, and all the other children laughed. You came after me because I was of your hearth, you said; and so now – surely if I am of your hearth, then you must be of mine.'

There was a little silence – silence to Drem and Blai, though filled with all the crowding sounds of sheep shearing going on around them. Drem was still puzzled, not so much by Blai now, as by something in himself that was strange to him. Just for a moment he seemed to be looking at Blai for the first time, and for the first time really seeing that she was there. He saw that there was a knot of white elder flowers caught into the dark coils of her hair. The other girls often wore a flower caught in the neck pin of a kirtle or braided into their hair, but he had never seen Blai, who was not like the other girls, with a flower about her, before. Or maybe it was that he had never noticed before. Somewhere deep inside him, a small faint fellowship curled open, delicately like a bud curling back its petals. And yet with the fellowship, with his sudden awareness of her, he was shy of her for the first time in his life.

'Blai – ' he began uncertainly. 'Blai – '

A triumphant bleat awoke him to the fact that the ewe he had been taking down to the shearers had of course wandered off. Fool that he had been to forget about the ewe! It was at a little distance by now, already mingling with the shorn sheep that had been turned loose. One of the Half People shouted to him, pointing. As though he could not see! He began to run, and the ewe, seeing him coming, broke away and began to run too, bleating as though he were the butcher, her matted fleece flouncing up and down above her thin legs. He caught her in a few moments, but before he could get a firm grip on her fleece she whirled about, bawling, and dived between his legs, tripping him up. Somebody at the pens laughed, and as he picked himself up and went after her again, he felt that he was a fool – one armed, humiliated. He shut his teeth, and getting her again, twisted his hand in the fleece at her neck, and swung her round with a savage thrust of his knee in her flank, all but bringing her down. She cried out in earnest that time, in pain and terror; and in the same moment Erp passed him, carrying the pot of wood ash that was for dabbing on any cut made by the shearers. 'It is a poor shepherd that loses his temper with the sheep,' Erp said, not quite looking at him, as usual. 'Also it is foolishness, for she will remember and be the more trouble another time.'

From one of the older men, Drem might have taken it, but from Erp, who was no older than himself, who was not even shearing, but only ash-boy to the shearers . . . 'Maybe I should find it easier if I were like you, you little black bush-creeper, born for nothing better than to tend the sheep!' he began furiously; and then he caught sight of old Doli, standing leaning on his spear beside the opening of the lower pen; and what he saw in the old man's weather-wrinkled face made him swallow the rest. With shut teeth, and the blood burning up to his forehead, he ran the ewe down to the shearers, and then returned for the next. Doli was still leaning on his spear beside the lower pen. 'You should not lose your temper with Erp, either, as though he were another sheep that would not go your way,' Doli said. 'That also is foolishness.'

Drem stood before him, his breast heaving a little. 'I forgot that the Little Dark People are my equals now. It is a thing still strange to me. Maybe I shall learn in time!' he said. It was the most insulting thing that he could think of to say.

But Doli, it seemed, was not insulted. That was one of the

maddening things about the Dark People; they were often in some way beyond the reach of an insult. 'Nay, there is no question of equals,' Doli said. 'Since you have come to us, by our standard you must be judged. Hunno and Flann and I are older than you, and wiser; and even Erp knows more about the sheep. Therefore you are the least among us . . . Go now, and bring down another sheep lest there be a shearer waiting.'

Drem brought down the sheep, and another, and another. He worked on, furious and heart sick; and when, a little later, he straightened to wipe the sweat out of his eyes and thrust back the heavy red hair that was stuck to his forehead, and found Blai with her jar beside him again, he turned on her so roughly that she shrank back as though he had struck her. 'No need that you follow me about with the buttermilk, for I am not thirsty. No need that you follow me up to the summer pasture. I shall do well enough – better maybe – without news of my home, for I have no home now. I am no more of your hearth!'

Blai was white enough now, a grey, thin white like the buttermilk in her jar; she stood looking at him for a moment, in the way that he had seen her stand looking at someone once before, but he didn't remember who it had been, or when, and he didn't care. He noticed with a kind of savage satisfaction that the elder flowers in her hair were limp and tarnished already.

He turned away with hunched shoulders, and went after another sheep, leaving her standing there.

Summer wore on. Below, along the skirts of the downs, the wild garlic flowers were gathered and spread to dry on the roofs of the village, and the flax harvest was got in, and the barley stood tall and golden, rustling when the wind blew over, in the village corn lands and the little lost plots among the downland folds that belonged to Tah-nu's children who had known the secret of the barley before ever the Golden

People came. But up on the High Chalk there was little sign of how the seasons passed. The turf grew dry and tawny, and the noon-tide shadows of shepherd and flock grew shorter, and then began to lengthen again, and that was all, save that the elder trees that grew in the corners of the sheep enclosures for a medicine, shed their creamy blossom and began to darken with blue-black berries that the birds loved.

Drem was no happier than he had been, but he began to grow used to what had happened, as one may grow used to the ache of an old wound until it is possible almost to forget about it and to think of other things, though the ache is still there, just the same, and the weariness of the ache.

Harvest came, and among the clustered turf hummocks in the high combe that was the nearest thing Tah-Nu's children had to a village, the Little Dark People made strong magic of their own that had nothing to do with the harvest of the Golden People on the lower slopes. Magic that was made with the open palm on stretched sheepskin drums, while one of the young men danced the dance of the Corn King until he fell twitching to the ground. 'Once we killed the Corn King every year, that the next year's harvest might be good, but now there are not enough young men among the Dark People, and we kill him only once in every seven harvests,' old Doli said to Drem, when the ceremony was over. 'And the harvests are not what they used to be. Na na.'

On an evening a little after harvest, Drem took part of the flock to the dew-pond, to drink before they were folded; a task that sometimes fell to him and the young dog Asal, now that they had begun to learn the ways of the sheep and how to handle them. He had half the flock with him; if you took the whole flock together half of them would never get near the water. Whitethroat was loping at his heels as usual, Asal circling on the flanks of the sheep. As they came over the last rise, and saw the water before them, they surged forward in a bobbing flood, suddenly purposeful. He heard the quick putter of their little sharp hooves on the turf. The pond had sunk very low in the long, hot summer, a shining round boss of water in a great shallow buckler of puddled clay that was almost white at its upper edge, deepening to the pinkish brown under a mushroom as it neared the water. Sometimes it was blue and staring, that water, sometimes changeable with cloud shadows, or sullen grey when the mist came up. Now it lay pearl and palely golden, quiet in the sunset, and a magpie rose from the water's edge, chattering, as the flock swept down towards it. There were always birds at the dew-pond; they dropped feathers round the margin of the water, wagtail and hawk and magpie; warm, russet curlew feather curved like a flower petal, speckled starling feather; once, far out on the water, the white pinion feather of a swan.

The sheep were spreading out all round the margin of the pool, working down over the hard clay to the water. Drem stood leaning on his spear and watching them, the two dogs at his side. The dogs were thirsty, panting and with dripping tongues, but they knew – even Whitethroat knew by now – that they must wait their turn until the sheep had drunk. The sheep drank thirstily, the water riffling round their muzzles, every ripple with a flake of the sunset caught in its spreading curve. It was a very peaceful thing to watch.

In a while the sheep had drunk their fill, and began to lose interest in the water and turn away. Asal and Whitethroat were looking up into Drem's face, their tongues hanging from their jaws, their tails giving little beseeching flicks and flutters. 'Go then,' he said, and they bounded away into the longed-for water, crouching belly deep in the coolness as they lapped.

He had just whistled the dogs out, shaking the shining drops from their rough coats in showers, and set Asal to rounding up the flock – not that much rounding up was needful now, for the sheep, their thirst gone, were beginning to drift of their own accord in the direction of the night enclosures – when little dark Erp came over the brow of the Chalk carrying a meal-skin on his shoulder, and headed down for the bothie beside the pond.

Drem lingered a little behind his sheep, half waiting for the other boy to draw near. Erp had been down to the village that day, for fresh barley meal; and it was seldom that he came up from the abodes of men without news of some kind; he was all eyes and ears, was little dark Erp. And so now Drem, sick for the news of his own kind that he was too proud to ask for, lingered behind his flock, making belief to do something to the belt that held his sheepskin close about his narrow waist, while the other boy flung down the meal sack before the bothie door.

'Surely you have been a long time down in the village,' he said, his eye half on the flock, as Erp came up to him a little sideways as a dog comes.

'The meal sack was heavy,' Erp said, and wriggled his shoulder. 'And it is a long way from the village, and the meal sack grew heavier all the way.'

There was a little silence. Drem longed to say, 'Well, then, and how was it with the village? How is it with my house? What word runs through the Clan?' but pride stuck in his throat; and Erp glanced sideways into his face, torn as he always was between his wish to please the boy who seemed to him so tall and golden and splendidly heedless of where his feet fell, and his wish to be revenged on him for being what he was. At last he said, 'There is a new man-child in the house of Talore.'

'So?' Drem said.

'And a new red bull calf in the Chieftain's byres, and Urian has slain a bear, but they do say that it was little more than a cub. And Caradig and Morvidd have returned to their quarrel – the old quarrel about the line where their corn plots come together.' He looked at Drem again, sideways under his brows, bright-eyed and curious. 'And Drustic the brother of Drem has asked Belu from above the ford for the third daughter at his hearth.'

Drem looked round quickly. He remembered that third daughter: Cordaella he thought her name was. A plump, pink girl who smelt like new bread. So she would be coming to spin beside the fire in his old home. Suddenly, and rather oddly, since he had never troubled about it himself, he hoped that she would be kind to Blai.

'And Drustic is not the only one,' Erp said. 'They do say that Vortrix also has a girl under his cloak.'

Drem did not answer for a short space. Then he said: 'What girl is that?'

'Rhun, the daughter of Gwythno of the Singing Spear. I have seen her myself, grinding corn before her father's door, and she grows very fair.' Erp grinned. 'See now, do I not bring you back news – much news, from the Golden People?'

'Much news,' Drem said. 'Much news, little Eyes-and-Ears. But now it is time that I go after my sheep, lest they begin to scatter.'

It seemed to him that the sunset was fading very quickly tonight. The gold of it was quite gone, as he turned from the dew-pond; and there was a new and sharper ache in the old wound. He had a harsh desire to make the sheep suffer for it, to set Asal snapping at their heels, and hustle them along, and see their silly fleeces flouncing above their thin legs as they ran; but he had learned that lesson – among other lessons that summer on the High Chalk. He walked slowly, using his spear as a staff, the dogs on either side of him, the flock drifting ahead, a grey cloud of sheep along the tawny downland turf. One of the ewes swung out sideways from the rest, and he whistled to Asal, pointing with his spear, and the dog streaked off to gather her in. 'Easy!' Drem called after him; Asal, being young and over-eager, was sometimes inclined to chevy his charges exactly as he, Drem, was longing to see them chevied. Despite the warning, he was doing that now, snapping over close at the heels of the straying ewe. Drem whistled again, shrill and compelling, and the dog checked and looked back. 'Softly,' Drem called. 'Softly, brother.' And the dog returned to his task more gently, heading the ewe in again to the main flock.

'Sa, that was well done,' said Doli's voice, and he found the old man beside him, leaning on his spear, and looking, as always, as much part of the downs as did the elder trees in the corner of the sheepfold; as though he had not moved in a hundred years.

'I begin to learn,' Drem said. 'It is well that I begin to learn.' There was a hard and heavy note in his voice, and the old shepherd gave him a swift, searching look under his grey brows.

'Erp is a great one for hearing news.'

They were walking together now, behind the flock; and Drem looked quickly at the old man, realizing that he must have met with Erp as the dark boy came up with the meal sack, and also heard the news of the Golden People. 'Little Eyes-and-Ears could always hear the thoughts of a man's heart a day's trail away, by putting his ear to the ground.'

They were drawing near to the entrance of the great turf-walled fold, where Flann and his brother waited with their notched tally sticks to count in the sheep as they did every night; and Drem fell back a little, for Doli to take over the task of getting the flock through the narrow opening; but Doli shook his head. 'Na na, if the old dog does all the work, how shall the puppy ever learn? Let you take them through.'

So Drem went on; he and Whitethroat and the young dog Asal, while old shepherd and old dog watched behind them. He was lost in a great loneliness; he thought he had not really known what loneliness was, until now. He tried to be glad about Vortrix – glad that now Vortrix would be comforted and would forget his blood brother. But it was lonely – so lonely, for the one forgotten; and the downs looked very wide and dark and desolate in the fading light. And surely the wind had grown cold.

But he got the sheep safely through the gap between Flann and his brother with their tally sticks; and later that evening, when they were safely folded, and Drem and the old man were alone for a moment in the bothie, Doli said, seemingly to the red heart of the fire: 'It is a good shepherd that can think of his sheep when his heart is full of other things. It is in my mind that maybe Drem will make none so ill a shepherd, after all.'

12 The Wolf Guard

Autumn came, and the rams were turned loose to run with the ewes, while far below in the rolling distance of the Wild, the weary green of late summer caught fire and flamed tawny and amber, bronze and gold, the wild apple trees of the woodshore were bowed with little russet crabs, and the brambles dark with fruit among their gold and crimson leaves, and the village swine were driven down into the valleys to fatten on acorns. And then it was Samhain, and with the last leaves falling in the forest, they brought the sheep down to the winter pastures, where there would be more hope for them in snow or hard frost. There was all the tumult of the great cattle round-up and the winter slaughtering. And when the slaughtering was over, only the best and strongest of the rams and the ewes were left, for there would not be enough food for the hoggets or the weaker ones through the winter.

So winter came, and in the long dark nights the shepherds huddled close about the fire in the turf bothie, with their sheepskin or wolfskin cloaks drawn close about them, listening, as somehow one never seemed to listen in the summer, to the great loneliness of the Chalk beyond the firelight. It was an open winter at first, a winter of gales and rain, but not cold, and there was little danger to the folded sheep from their ancient enemy; and the midwinter fires of the Golden People had burned out, and it was within a moon of the start of lambing time when the first hard frosts came.

A few nights later, they were huddled round the fire in the smoke-filled bothie, over the evening meal of barley stirabout and broiled deer meat – Drem and Whitethroat had been hunting. They were all there save Flann, who had a woman among the little green hovels of the Half People, and so was often missing when winter brought flocks and shepherds alike down to the lower pastures. Drem, who had finished eating, was polishing a new spear shaft with a piece of sandstone. The white ashen shaft came up silvery pale and smooth in the firelight; the rubbing stone, crumbling a little under his fingers, shed an occasional trickle of yellow sand, like pollen, like dust of gold, into the lap of his sheepskin mantle. From time to time he glanced across through the smoke at Erp and the girl who had cooked the evening meal. More than once, that particular girl had come up, in the past moon, and Erp had bought her a necklace of jet and blue glass beads, paying an otter skin for it to the trader. She showed her teeth like a young vixen when he sat too near her; but she was wearing the necklace. Drem could see it in the opening of her sheepskin. Pretty it was, with little blue sparks where the firelight caught the glass beads.

Drem shifted his hold on the spear shaft under his arm to come at another length of it; and drew closer to the fire, though his shins were scorching under the cross-bound deerskin leggings. That was always the way in frost or wind, one's front scorched and one's shoulders froze. He hunched deeper into his cloak, and said, because he was tired of the silence: 'See, the fire burns red all through. There is a frost tonight.'

Hunno looked up from the piece of rib that he was chewing. 'I should know that without a fire to tell me,' he growled, 'by the gash that I carry here in my shin where the she-wolf caught me seven winters ago. Always it aches in a frost.'

And in that moment, as though the mention of wolf had been a spell, first one and then another of the dogs pricked its ears and growled softly. Old Doli raised his head to listen. 'So. It comes,' he said. 'Always it comes; later in some winters than others, but always it comes.'

Drem listened, aware of Whitethroat suddenly tense and

quivering beside him. They all listened, dogs and men alike, hearing afar off in the starry darkness the long-drawn, desolate, cry of the wolves on the hunting trail.

'So, the time comes to be keeping the Wolf Guard,' Hunno said.

It was the thing that Drem had been dreading; knowing that it must come, yet unable to bring himself to face it. The Wolf Guard would bring his brother Drustic, and the young warriors who had been boys with him in the Boys' House – and Vortrix. At shearing time he had not had to face that fear, for the Men's side did not concern themselves greatly with the sheep shearing, considering it work only for the women and the Half People; but the Wolf Guard was another matter, that was man's work, and all must take their turn when the wolves hunted among the sheep runs and the lambing time drew near.

The rubbing stone slipped in Drem's fingers, a jagged angle of it making a long score in the silvery smoothness of his new spear shaft, and he cursed with the small, bitter, adder's-tongue curses of the Dark People.

So the men of the Tribe stood the Wolf Guard with the men of the Half People, through the long bitter nights that followed. Men who had been great warriors and hunters before Drem was born, men who had been boys with him only a year ago.

He did not mind the older men so bitterly – even Talore, who never tried to speak with him, but set a hand on his shoulder once in passing, as he bent over a sick ewe. But his own fellows he minded with a minding that cringed in his belly. They talked easily enough with Doli and the Half People, squatting round the fire that had been built at the mouth of each fold, easily and with no sense of barriers between; there had been no barrier between Drem and the Half People before the Grandfather raised it, six summers ago. But they did not know how to speak to Drem, nor he to them; their eyes slid away from meeting; and in the end they pretended, both he and they, not to see each other. Even when Drustic came, they pretended not to see each other. It was better that way.

As yet, Vortrix had not come at all.

At least, when lambing began, Drem had plenty of work to fill in days and nights, and that helped. Never a night went by for the next two moons or more, that several lambs were not born in it; and all the while the ewes must be watched and tended, the lambing pens constantly crossed and re-crossed to keep a look-out for trouble. When there was a moon it was easier, with the silver light to see by; in the darkness there was only the ewe's bleating, and your own hands – hand – to tell you when she was in trouble; and then she must be got down to the fire, where there was light to work by, for you could not carry a torch among them without frightening the whole flock. And trouble came more and more often as the time went by, and the winter shortage began to tell on the ewes. There were foolish ones too, who would drop their lambs in the trampled fern and wander away; that also was a thing that must be watched for, for a lamb left long to lie on the frozen ground was a lamb dead. Then there were lambs who lived though the ewe died, and must be reared beside the bothie fire, cared for as a woman cares for a babe, until maybe they could be given to a ewe who had lost her lamb. Yes, there was work enough for Drem as for all the shepherd kind, now that the lambing time was here.

On a night midway through the lambing season, Drem squatted with Hunno beside the fold fire, working over a straining ewe, while the men of the Wolf Guard leaned on their spears and looked on. It was a bitter night, with a shrill north-east wind blowing, and snow whirling down the gusts; snow that became visible like a cloud of eddying and swirling feathers as it entered the firelight. They had got the ewe close in against the turf wall for whatever shelter there was, but even there the snow reached her, pale-freckling her fleece that the wind parted in zigzag lines. But Drem doubted whether she felt it. He doubted whether she felt anything clearly, any more. She was beautiful, too. Sheep had ceased to be just sheep to Drem by that time, and he had begun to see them as the shepherd kind saw them, as he saw men and women; this one beautiful and that one sour-faced, this one cross grained and that one placid. Beautiful and proud she was, but old Doli had said for some time that it would go hard with her when the lamb came.

And now the lamb was here; a fine little black-faced ram lamb limp and sprawling on the handful of brown bracken fronds that they had hastily spread to keep it from lying on the snow; and they left it to itself for the moment while they turned themselves to do what they could for the ewe. Small, surly Hunno rose and turned to the fire for the barley gruel that was warming beside it. But the ewe was already stretching herself out.

Drem leaned over her. 'Quickly, Hunno!'

And then Hunno was kneeling beside him again, with the bowl in his hands, and the growling gentleness in his voice that was only there when he spoke to a sick sheep, and never for his own kind. 'So now, the work is over. Now gruel, my girl.'

The ewe seemed to know that they were trying to help her, and raised her head a little. But a shudder ran through her under Drem's hand, and her head fell back on to the snow. And they were left, Drem and Hunno, as they had been left before, with a lamb flickering into life, and a dead ewe between them.

It had happened before, and each time Drem had hated it, but tonight, perhaps because he had actually felt the shudder that was the life going out of her under his hand, perhaps because she had been proud and beautiful like the great swan

that had been his first kill, he hated it more than ever; and the old wailing bewilderment rose in him, crying out to know where the life had gone to . . . but it was no time to be asking such questions, with the movements of the lamb already growing fainter.

'Sa, the thing is over,' Hunno said, setting down the gruel with a slow, expressive shrug. 'Let you take the lamb down to the bothie before it goes the same way. I must see how it is with the speckled one with the torn ear.'

So, carrying the lamb like a mere rag of wet wool trailing from his hand, Drem made his way across to the bothie that looked more than ever like a little knoll of the hillside, with the snow to muffle its outlines. The bothie was empty but the fire burned low and red, and a crock of ewe milk stood ready as always in the lambing season. Drem set the lamb down on the spread fern beside the hearth, and left it to be licked and nuzzled by Whitethroat, who, though no sheep dog, seemed to have the love of all small and young things that some very big dogs possess, and an instinctive feeling for what to do with a new-born lamb, while he set some of the milk to warm in a bronze pipkin, and with fingers numb with cold brought out from the dark recesses of the bothie the feeding bottle of stitched sheepskin, and a short length of elder twig with the pith scraped out. When the milk was warm, he poured it into the bottle, wrapped the elder twig in a scrap of rag so that it would be soft and the lamb might be persuaded to suck on it, and pushed it into the neck of the bottle; then, taking the lamb from Whitethroat, he settled down beside the fire, with the little creature against his knee, to the business of getting it to suck.

Patience never came easily to Drem, but he had more patience with animals than he had with people; and besides, he was learning. He was learning many things, those days and nights. Again and again he dipped his fingers into the drops of warm milk left at the bottom of the pipkin, and painted the lamb's mouth with them; again and again the little thing wavered its head away, or merely lay there making no response whatever. But it was stronger; he was sure that it was stronger. That was Whitethroat's licking and the warmth of the fire. Little sprawling tremors began to run through it; and then quite suddenly the battle was won, and it began to suck. 'Sa, that is the way of it, small one,' Drem said, and dipped his fingers again in the warm drops and gave them once more to the little sucking mouth, and then hastily took up the feeding bottle; and the lamb butted at it as though it was its mother's flank.

It was half standing against Drem's knee, its tail awag behind it as it sucked, while Whitethroat looked on with prick-eared interest, when old Doli came ducking down the entrance step, with the snow thick in his sheepskin mantle. Drem looked up with a kind of wry triumph. 'If we are no good for anything else, Whitethroat and I, at the least we do well enough in the place of a dead ewe.'

The old man crouched down beside the fire, taking in the little scene with those shrewd, weatherwise eyes of his. 'There are worse things for a man or a hound to do well at,' he said.

The next night it happened the other way round; a lamb dropped in the snow that no skill even of old Doli could stir to life, and a ewe was left bleating pitifully without understanding. Drem went across to the shepherd's bothie with the dead lamb hanging from his hand as yesterday the living one had done. And there, leaning against the squat roof tree, with a barley bannock in one hand, the firelight flickering upwards warmly saffron over his square, bandy-legged figure and steady face, was Vortrix.

Drem checked an instant, crouching in the low doorway, and as he did so, Vortrix's head went up; and for a long moment their eyes met through the drifting, firelit smoke, while Erp and Hunno looked on.

It seemed to Drem that there was a pain, a physical, dragging pain, under his breast bone. Then, deliberately, as Vortrix made the beginning of a movement towards him, he turned away, as he had done from the others of his kind. Only this was not just another of his kind, this was Vortrix, with warrior patterns blue upon his breast; and the sudden wild weeping rose against the base of his throat as he bent to the next thing he had to do.

Laying the dead lamb down beside the fire, and thrusting away Whitethroat's exploring nose with a, 'Na na, brother, not this time,' he drew the knife from his belt.

'The ewe?' Hunno grunted.

'It is well enough with the ewe,' Drem said, and his voice sounded hoarse and heavy in his own ears, as he set about the task of skinning the dead lamb.

'You will give her the other one in its place, then?' Hunno jerked his head towards where last night's motherless lamb slept curled into a little grey hummock against the wall.

Drem nodded and went on with his task. Hunter though he was, he had never found an easy way to skin an animal one handed. It would have been much simpler to pass the task over, lordlywise, to Erp. The other boy would have done it for him, he knew, though he was in the middle of his evening bannock. But if he did that, he would have no excuse to keep his head bent over his hand; he would have to look up. He did look up once, and saw Vortrix watching him, the bannock still untouched in his hand. Then he bent his head again over his flaying-knife.

When the skin was off he did turn to Erp. 'Bring the small one and help me get him into it.'

So Erp brought the live lamb, bleating in scared protest, and between them they worked his back legs into the pelt of the dead one; then his forelegs, finally drawing up the head over his own like a little hood. Hunno laughed, and little dark Erp laughed; there was always something funny in the sight of a lamb wearing another lamb's skin over its own; and the little creature's shrill, indignant clamour made them laugh the more. Only Drem, tying the skin lightly at neck and belly to keep it in place, did not laugh; nor did Vortrix, looking down on them from his stance against the roof tree.

When the thing was done, Hunno tossed a bannock towards him, saying, 'Best eat before you take it out.'

Drem shook his head, and left the bannock. 'Later, maybe.' He got up without looking again at Vortrix, and carrying the living lamb in the pelt of the dead one, shouldered out blindly into the grey, snow-lit darkness.

He went down, Whitethroat as always at his heels, through the big lambing enclosures, parting the ewes and turning them aside with his knee where they were most densely packed, until he found the ewe he sought. The ewe was restless, calling for her lamb. He set his small burden down beside her, and stood to see that all was well. The little creature staggered to its feet, bleating, and made instinctively for the warm woolly flank that meant milk. The ewe swung her head and sniffed at it, suspiciously; but the smell was the smell of her own lamb; all was well. Seemingly quite satisfied, she stood, passive and peaceful, while the fosterling, accepted as her own, butted at her flank to make the warm milk flow faster. Both of them were perfectly content.

If only there was as simple a cure for all ills, Drem thought dully, and turned away, holding himself bent a little as though to ease the ache of a physical wound.

Another figure, short and bandy-legged and dearly familiar even in the darkness, had come down towards him through the sheep, and Vortrix's voice said, 'They are happy now.'

'They are happy now,' Drem echoed. He drew a quick breath. 'Why have you come down after me?'

'You left your bannock lying,' Vortrix said. 'Therefore I have brought it down to you. Why did you turn from me as from a stranger, up yonder in the bothie?'

'Maybe because I was a fool,' said Drem wearily. 'I am tired of things that hurt in my belly.' And he took the bannock that the other held out to him in the darkness, and began to eat; but the bannock seemed to be made of dust instead of barley meal, and his stomach revolted at it though he was wolf hungry.

'I also. I am tired of things that hurt in my belly,' Vortrix said.

Wading through the grey, huddled shapes of the flock, they had come out to the opening of the great fold, and stood together, looking away down the curve of the snowbound valley. It was a very still night, still with the brittle, waiting stillness of hard frost. The seven stars of the Great Hunter seemed to hang out of the sky, pulsing with cold fires; the Great Hunter, swaggering as he always swaggered, above the pale shoulder of the snow-covered downs. Far off in the distance a wolf howled, and the sheep stirred uneasily, and were quiet again, their breath and the warmth of their bodies making a faint smoke in the starlight. With their backs to the fire beside the fold open-ing, Drem and Vortrix

might have been the only living men in a frozen and forgotten world.

They were standing very close, and Vortrix brought up his arm and laid it across his blood brother's shoulders. Drem felt the warm weight of it through the thick rough sheepskin of his mantle, and let it lie there. But the gulf was between them, nevertheless, and neither of them could cross it to the other's side.

'How is it with you, my brother?' Vortrix asked, very quietly, in a while.

'It is well enough with me,' Drem said. 'I have let go my

own kind, and I hunt with the Dark People in all things now.'

'Is it truly so? – in all things?'

There was a long silence, and again, far off among the woods that lay dark and soft like furs flung across the whitened hills, the wolf cried, and again the sheep stirred in the fold, snorting and stamping. Then Drem said, 'Na, we cannot think with one mind, the Dark People and I. We speak the same words but they do not mean the same things. We laugh together, but I do not know the things that stir behind their eyes. Maybe one day I shall learn . . .' He turned to Vortrix. 'And with you? How is it with you?'

'I am – lonely without my brother.'

'One was telling me that there is a girl – the daughter of Gwythno of the Singing Spear. One was telling me that she grows very fair.'

The silence fell between them again. Only a short silence this time, and then Vortrix said, 'If there was a girl under your cloak, though her hair were as bright as the sun and her arms as white as mare's milk, would she fill my place?'

There was no more to be said; and in a little they went out from the lambing pen, drawing the gate hurdle to again behind them, and turned towards the watch fire, round which several of the Tribesmen stood or squatted, leaning on their spears. Vortrix's spear picked up the firelight in a slim leaf of flame against the bluish darkness of the snow and the stars; but Drem saw only the dark side of the blade, a leaf of darkness against the firelight, for he had dropped behind a little, walking not as brother with brother, but as one of the Half People behind one of the lordly Golden Ones.

13   The Grey Leader

The winter had been late in starting, but before it ended, it was one of those winters which men speak of years afterwards, round the fire when the earth is frost-bound and snow comes drifting down the wind. And when the first signs of spring should have been waking in the forest and the curlews coming up from the seaward marshes, the earth was still deep in snow and held by frost as keen and deadly as the blade of the strange grey dagger that the King wore now in his girdle. On fine days the snow melted a very little in the sunshine; in the shade where it was blue as the hyacinths in the woods at Beltane (but surely that was in another world) it froze without ceasing, day after day; and it seemed that as the days grew longer the cold increased. The sheep had to be kept folded all day as well as at night, and with no grazing the fodder ran short. Drem and his fellows cut branches all along the woodshore and stripped the lower-slope birch trees of their bark, pressing farther and farther afield as time went by. But there was little good in such fodder, and the sheep grew thinner and thinner, the weaker of them scarcely able to stand on their legs, and many of the late lambs were born dead. They killed the more weakly sheep and lambs, so that the strong ones might have their share of the poor fodder; and there was so little flesh on the poor, starved carcasses that even when they could get them down to the village they added nothing to the meat supply for Clan or Half People.

The wolves, driven by famine beyond their normal fear of the guard fires, were growing ever more bold, howling closer and closer in the darkness about the folds. Farther along the run of the Chalk, the sheep folds themselves were attacked; and everywhere a sheep that strayed was a sheep lost, and no man cared to step beyond the firelight and the sound of his brother's voice after dark.

On a day about the end of the lambing, Drem came up from the woods, carrying on his shoulder a bundle of hardly-gathered fodder branches; and flinging it down beside the gate-gap of the fold, looked about him hastily as he always did, for Doli. The old man, spent with over-much labour and hardship that was sharper even than the shepherd kind were used to, had been ill on his feet for days, after becoming chilled to the bone over a lambing ewe, and Drem had been constantly anxious about him; but to all suggestions that he should go down to the village, or even remain beside the fire in the shepherds' bothie, he had only replied impatiently, 'Na na, there is too much that I have to do.' And now, not seeing him, Drem's anxiety flared up. 'Where is Doli?' he demanded of Hunno, who was spreading fodder.

'One of the ewes has broken out.' Hunno jerked his head towards the High Chalk that closed the head of the valley. 'A strong one such as we can ill afford to lose, and she near her time with the lamb. Doli is gone after her up towards the summer folds. He said it was in his mind that she was gone that way.'

Drem hitched his sheepskin higher on his shoulder, frowning. 'Is Flann with him, or Erp?'

Hunno shook his ragged head. 'Na. As for Flann, his woman has come to her time also, and all men know the fool that he is about her. One brought him word to come, and he went. Therefore, with Drem away down the woods, and the Golden Folk not yet come up for tonight's Wolf Guard, there were but the three of us here when we found the ewe gone.'

'And of the three of you, it must be Doli that went after her? Why not you or Erp? You are younger than he is, also he is sick.' He swung round on Erp who had come ducking out from the bothie. 'Why did you let him go alone?'

Behind him Hunno growled something only half spoken about an old man being of less worth to the village than a young one, and Erp gave him a swift upward look under his dark brows. 'Not to us the blame. Doli said to us that being old and wise he knew more of the ways of the sheep kind than we could do. Therefore he bade us to stay and guard the fold, and left us Asal and took Çu with him and went. There will be no harm come to him; not to Doli in his own sheep runs . . . There is lamb stew in the hut if you are hungry.'

If he was hungry. As if any of them were ever not hungry these days. Drem hesitated, looking about him. It was drawing towards dusk already; low sky and snow-covered hills alike yellowish grey in the fading light. In the fold, the ewes and lambs – such as were left of them – huddled close, standing or lying in the puddled snow and the litter that was frozen hard where they had wetted it. Icicles hung from the long wool under their bellies, that rang together when they moved so that the fold was full of a faint chiming as well as the pitiful bleating of the ewes as the weight of ice tore at their skins. A bitter wind was gusting over the shoulder of the downs from the north-east, making jagged, bluish partings in the wool of the sheep and the rough hair of the herd dogs; and Drem, sniffing at it, could catch the faint but unmistakable smell of more snow on the way. He shrugged, and turned into the shepherds' bothie, where the dung smoke stung his eyes, and the warmth of the fire seemed to mix with the icy eddies of wind as oil and water mix together but without ever mingling. One of the Little Dark Women was within, huddling over the rough hearth. She looked up as he ducked through the door hole with Hunno behind him, and pointed to the pot that she had just taken off the fire. And Drem took himself a bannock from the basket in the corner, and settled down to stay his chilled and empty belly with the lamb stew.

He began hungrily enough; one mouthful, two mouthfuls, scooping up the lumps of meat with bits broken from his bannock. He ate the third mouthful, more slowly; the fourth he swallowed at a gulp, and drawing his legs under him as he did so, got up, pushing the remains of his bannock into the breast of his rough woollen kirtle, and reached for one of the spears that lay against the turf wall.

Hunno looked up, his mouth full of lamb stew. 'Where away?'

'Up towards the summer folds.'

'There is more snow coming.'

Drem was already half turned to the door. He checked, looking down at the little surly man beside the fire. 'I too can smell other things than garlic with my nose. There is more snow coming, and that is the more reason why I should go after Doli.'

'It is in my mind that you are a fool if you do,' Hunno said simply. And as though to give point to the words, at that moment there came to the ears of both of them, far off and faintly down the wind, the long-drawn and infinitely mournful cry of a wolf. They were silent, looking at each other, while the cry was taken up by another wolf, and then, still farther off, by a third. '*They* are early on the trail tonight,' Hunno said.

Drem's grip tightened on his spear shaft. 'The men from the village will be here soon. Meanwhile keep a good fire up by the fold,' and heedless of Hunno's growling retort that he had been keeping the Wolf Guard when he, Drem, was not yet thought of, he turned again to the door hole, whistling Whitethroat to heel with lips so chapped by the cold that he could scarcely form the sound, and plunged out into the bitter dusk, past the guard fire where the boy Erp stood leaning on his spear, with the herd dogs beside him, and away into the great, white loneliness.

All around the fold the snow was cut up, trampled to a frozen brown mud by the feet of men and dogs and sheep, but within a spear throw the tracks thinned out, and in a little there was only Doli's track and the strayed ewe's, and that of the dog Cu, faintly visible in the whiteness, reeling out before him into the gathering of the winter dusk.

Drem huddled his sheepskin mantle more closely about him, and trudged on, head into the wind that came swooping down the combe. Something like a tiny frozen feather eddied past his face to alight on the thick fold of sheepskin in which his chin was sunk, and clung there. Another settled with an icy touch on his right eyebrow; another on his lip, and suddenly there was snow flurrying all about him.

It was snowing hard when he came up out of the combe-head on to the open Chalk, and already Doli's track was becoming blurred by the fresh fall. There was still some light left to see by, for there was a moon behind the cloud roof, and the snow threw a faint upward light of its own. But the wind was rising steadily, blowing up from the dark immensity of the Wild far below, with the sea-surge roaring of wind through bare branches and the desolate, long-drawn hushing of wind across open snow. And the snow was worsening with every bow-shot that he pressed on. It was whirling down the gusts now in a fine, choking powder to mingle with the dry snow already fallen that the wind drove sideways across the ridges in a mealy spray. It was growing hard to find the trail, harder all the while. Growing harder, too, to know exactly where he was, in the whirling icy cloud that blotted out the familiar shapes and smells and underfoot feel of the downs.

Drem, already weary from a hard day's work, pressed on in a desperate attempt at speed, stumbling in the deep snow, crouching double at times to search out the faint hollows in the smooth whiteness that were all that was left now of old

Doli's track, then struggling on again. Whitethroat, long since trained not to spoil a trail by running on it, floundered at his heel, belly deep in the snow. On the north side of the slope, Drem lost the track in the drifting of the new fall. He struggled down to the bottom of the little dip, casting desperately to and fro, houndwise, and on the farther side, where the snow lay thinner, picked up the faint trace again, and with a gasp of relief, pressed forward once more. But on the farther crest, where the whole flank of the hill turned over into a long, level slope towards the north, the tracks faded out into the drifts, and for all his searching, and the great hound's sniffing to and fro, he could not find any trace of it again.

As he stood at fault, rather desperately, it seemed to him that the snow was passing. A faint cobwebby gleam of moonlight slid through the clouds; but only to show him the whiteness ahead as pure and unmarked as though no living thing had passed that way since the first man was a thought in the darkness of the Earth Mother. Then the gleam was gone again, as swiftly as it had come, and the snow came whirling back as though in triumph. With very little hope of any answer, Drem propped his spear in the crook of his arm, and cupping his frozen hand about his mouth, shouted at full pitch of his lungs. 'Coo-oo! Coo-aoh-ee-*yah*!' The seeking cry of the hunters and herdsmen of the High Chalk wailed out into the storm. Boy and dog listened, head up into the wind, but there was nothing to hear save the desolate hushing of the wind and the whisper of the snow. They pushed on a short way farther, as nearly as Drem could judge it in the direction of the summer folds, but his sense of direction was confused by the whirling whiteness, and he had no clear idea of his own whereabouts, let alone that of the folds.

In a while he halted, and called again, 'Coo-oo! Coo-aoh-ee-yah!' and this time, to their straining ears, there came a reply – a long-drawn howl from far ahead of them, at sound of which Drem's mouth dried and his hand tightened on the ashen shaft of his spear. But the howl ended in a burst of barking. 'That's Cu!' Drem said aloud, his numbed lips scarcely moving; and his heart leapt between relief and an added fear. He called again, and tried to run, stumbling, floundering in the deep snow. Ahead of him he heard the dog howling, and he called again, gasping, 'I come! Doli, I come!' and plunged on.

A few moments later a wolf-like shadow seemed to scramble from the whirling paleness almost at his feet, and old Cu was weaving round his legs, panting and whining. And Drem realized that he had all but gone straight over the edge of the old open flint quarry in the steep hillside. A torn-away place at the edge told its own story, and below him as he peered down, the chalk dropped away so sharply as to be clear of snow save where the whiteness clung about the roots of the bushes that grew here and there on the sheer surface of the drop. The darkness of more bushes gathered thick at the foot; and among them, something moved and bleated; and he thought that there was something else down there, darker than the bushes, that lay unmoving.

The old dog had launched himself from the crest again, and gone slithering and scrambling down at a rush, to the dark thing that did not move. Drem never paused to remember that there was a perfectly easy way down the hillside and into the old working at its lower end. He took the steep chalk slope much as Cu had done, in a landslide of snow and falling chalk and grass tufts. Whitethroat went past him as a rushing shadow, and somehow, with most of the breath driven from his body, he was at the bottom. The sheep was on her legs, so she was not likely to have come to much harm, although she bleated distressfully at his coming, and made no attempt to move. Drem was kneeling over the still figure of old Doli, lying face

downwards with the snow already building up against his
weather side. In frantic haste he turned the little shepherd over
with hand and knee, and felt for his heart. His own was
drubbing so that for a moment he could not be sure; then he
felt the faint beat of life under his fingers, and a sob of relief
burst from him. 'Doli! Doli!' But Doli never moved. His
exploring fingers found a hard lump on the old man's temple
and the stickiness of blood among his hair. The ewe must have
scrambled and slithered down much as he and the dogs had
done, but Doli, following on her track before it was swallowed
up, ill and blind weary, and away north of where he thought he
was, even as Drem had been, and maybe giddy with the whirling snow, must have pitched clean over as from a cliff, striking
his head somewhere on the way down.

Drem thought desperately, crouching over the old shepherd.
What was the thing to do now? At fifteen he had not yet come
near to his full strength, and he knew that, one-armed as he was,
he could not get Doli across his shoulders and carry him back
unaided. Even if he had had the strength of an ox, to carry
Doli he would have had to leave his spear behind, and that
would most likely mean death for both of them, with the wolf-
kind abroad and the smell of Doli's blood to draw them. Here
at the foot of the old flint quarry the bushes gave some shelter
from the wind and snow, and in case the wolf kind came he
would at least have his spear-arm free and the solid chalk behind
him. He was fumbling with the bronze pin of his sheepskin
cloak even as he thought. He tore it off and spread it over Doli,
feeling the wind strike like a knife through his own body without it. Then he turned to Whitethroat and pointed. 'Back – go
back, brother. Fetch the others.'

Whitethroat looked along the line of his pointing finger and
then up into his face, whimpering. Drem got up and caught
his collar, and urged him out to the open mouth of the quarry,

where the chalk cliff sank into the hillside; then pointed again.
'Back! Go back to the fold! Fetch Hunno!' He had no means
of sending any message, but there was no need: anyone seeing
Whitethroat apart from his master would know that it meant
trouble – bad trouble, and there would be plenty of men at the
fold, for the men of the village would have come up long since
to keep the Wolf Guard. Maybe even Vortrix; Vortrix had
come up more than once in the past moon. He held the hound's
big rough head for a moment with his hand under the raised
muzzle. 'Go back, brother *Bring Hunno!*' Then he pointed
again, and gave the hound a light, open-palmed blow on the
rump.

Whitethroat looked up into his face again, whimpered, and,
turning, ploughed away into the darkness and the flurrying
snow.

Drem waited until he was lost to sight, then turned and went
back to Doli. Cu, crouching over his master, greeted him with
an agonized whine, and he spoke gently to the old hound, and
began to drag the shepherd farther back against the chalk cliff,
where there was more shelter. It was not easy, with only one
hand for the task, but he managed it little by little. When he
got Doli where he wanted him, in a little bay of the chalk
where a dense clump of spindle bushes broke the wind, he
spread his cloak again over the old man, and saw with relief
how Cu crawled close and lay down almost on top of his
master. That should give him a little warmth.

He turned to the ewe, running his hand over her as best he
could in the dark. Her lamb was on the way, but it would not
come just yet. Like enough the wolves would be here first, he
thought grimly. Her also he urged in close against the foot of
the chalk, into the same sheltered spot where he had dragged
Doli. Then he found Doli's spear and laid it beside his own,
where it was easily come by; and fell to collecting loose turfs

and lumps of chalk and frozen snow – anything to throw when the time came. And when that was done, there was nothing more that he could do. If only he could have made a fire! That would have helped to keep away the wolf kind, at any rate for a while. He had his fire stones, but there was nothing in the frozen bushes that would make a blaze, nothing at all. All that he could do now was to wait.

How far would Whitethroat have got on his way back to the fold by now? He had no idea, no means of knowing how time was going by, as he crouched, spear ready to hand, over the old shepherd, trying to add the shelter of his own body to that of the spindle bushes. Maybe Whitethroat would never get back to the fold at all; maybe he would meet the wolves, his father's kind, instead. Peering out through the bushes, with every strained sense on the alert for danger, it seemed to him once again that the snow was slackening. A little later he was sure of it. That was one thing to the good. It was scarcely snowing at all now; there might be something left of their track for the others to follow – if Whitethroat ever got through. It was growing lighter, too, the low sky breaking up into hurrying masses through which every now and then a greasy blur of tarnished silver showed where the moon rode high. Behind him the ewe was becoming restless. The lamb would be here soon.

Ah, but it seemed that he had been right in his thinking. The wolf kind would be here first!

From somewhere ahead of him in the grey murk, it rose; long-drawn, savage, and unutterably sad, the cry of a wolf on the hunting trail. Another cry echoed it, nearer than the first – and then there was only the wind in the silence. Drem felt as though all the blood in his body had jumped back to his heart, and an icy stillness took him. The ewe stirred behind him, snorting and stamping her foot; he prayed that she might not bleat in terror – not that it would make much difference if she did, for the wolves were down wind of them, and the gusts would carry their scent, if indeed the brutes were not running on it already. Something brushed against his knee, and Cu was crouching beside him; he could feel the tremors running through the old dog's body: tremors of fear and fury and hate. He laid his hand for an instant on the dog's neck, and felt the harsh hairs rising against his palm.

Nothing more happened for so long that he felt he could not bear the waiting for a heart-beat longer; he must yell, beat his spear against the chalk, anything to break the thin-drawn agony of waiting. But still he crouched silent, his heart beating with a slow, heavy drub that seemed to wait to listen between each beat, and the old hound crouching against his knee. The ewe was snorting again, in pain and terror. She had gone off her feet, and Drem thought she needed help, but he could not help her; not now. The moon swam out suddenly, free of the scudding, curdled cloud into a lake of clear sky – and in the sliding silver light, something moved on the smooth whiteness of the snow before the quarry mouth. Something dark, and running low, like a great hound. But it was no hound; and behind it came two more.

Now that the moment had come it was almost a relief; and as the wolves swerved in their tracks and headed in towards him, Drem began to yell; yell and throw the lumps of chalk that he had gathered. That might frighten them back for a while, but not for long. If only he had some means of making a fire – fire to singe their hides! The great grey leader flinched from the lump of chalk that caught him on the shoulder, and gave back a little. But they were famine-driven; even in that fitful light Drem could see how their bones stared through their hides; and seeing that there was none against them but one lone shepherd and a dog, they would not be long held from their attack by yelling and lumps of chalk.

They slunk to and fro, dodging the clods he flung at them, and he saw their shining eyes in the moonlight, their lolling tongues and the thick, raised hair of their manes. There was a kind of hideous mirth about them, as though they knew that there could be but one end to the thing, and could afford to laugh.

Already the great grey leader was slinking forward again, his belly almost on the snowy ground, his jaws widening in that obscene grin . . . Drem had no idea how long he had held them off with his lumps of chalk. He had nothing to throw now, except Doli's spear. He caught that up and flung it; but the broad fighting spear was not meant for throwing, and in the uncertain light it did not more than graze the leader's shoulder as it flew. He had nothing left to throw at all now; and the wolves knew it. This was the kill. Drem had caught up his own spear and half risen to his feet, crouching there, his eyes wide and fixed on the oncoming grey leader. His mouth was very dry. The old hound crouched snarling at his side, and behind him he was aware, though he did not know how, that the ewe had struggled to her feet again, bleating in wild pain and terror.

Nearer and nearer, circling warily, came the grey leader,

squirming and slinking low-bellied over
the snow. In the last moment it seemed to
Drem that he had known this wolf before;
and the wolf had known him. The wicked
grin, the welcome in the savage yellow
eyes belonged to a before-time as well as to
now. But then it had been the wolf who
waited for the meeting. Now it was Drem.

Then the great beast gathered himself on
his haunches, and sprang. Drem leapt to
meet him, while Cu flung himself with a
snarl at the throat of the second wolf, the
she-wolf. Even as they came together, there
was a distant shout – a burst of shouting –
but Drem did not hear it. In all his world
there was only himself and his wolf, and old
Doli; and the ewe struggling to bring her
lamb to birth behind him.

And then not even Doli and the ewe,
only himself and his wolf. He had side-
slipped as the wolf sprang forward, and his

spear took the great brute behind the shoulder and was all but wrenched from his grasp as it turned, yowling, almost in mid leap. Fiery pain slashed at his right shoulder just as it had done before; but he scarcely felt it as he drove his shortened spear home again. He was dragged to his knees, the wolf almost on top of him, tearing at his shoulder, striving to come at his throat. He drove his chin down on to his breast, and stabbed his spear dagger-wise again and again into its body as they rolled together in the snow. The third wolf was on him now; there was a terrible stricken howling – he did not know whether it was himself or his wolf that howled – a worrying and a snarling and a yelling. There was the taste of blood in his mouth, and a darkness flaring into ragged lights before his eyes . . .

And then the yelling was a different yelling, neither his own nor his wolf's; and the lights were the saffron mares'-tails of torches carried by running men – and it was all over. In some unbelievable way it was all over. He was crouching with hanging head in the churned and trampled snow, staring down at the red that blotched and spattered the whiteness. Scarlet on white; Warrior Scarlet; and for a moment he thought hazily that it was the scarlet on the white breast of the swan that had been his first kill. Then his brain cleared somewhat, and he saw that it was blood on snow – hot blood on cold snow, steaming a little in the flaring light of the torches. Old Cu and the she-wolf lay sprawled together, both with their last fight fought, and at a little distance; the third, a young one, snapped and snarled in its death agony, with somebody else's spear through it. But the torch light fell fullest and fiercest on the body of the great grey leader lying outstretched almost against Drem's knee.

There were men all around him; Whitethroat nuzzling into his face, trying to lick all at the same time the torn and streaming wounds in his right arm and breast and shoulder. Someone was supporting him, and he knew that it was Vortrix; and

Vortrix's voice was in his ears, lit with a ringing triumph. 'He has killed his wolf! See, Luga, Urian, a fine Wolf Slaying there has been here! He has killed his wolf!'

'And I think that his wolf has killed him,' Urian said.

But Drem only heard them vaguely and a long way off. 'Look to Doli,' he mumbled. 'The ewe too – she –'

'It is well with the ewe.' That time it was Hunno's voice. 'She needs no looking to.' And suddenly he was aware of the thin crying of a new born lamb; and a moment of swift exultancy leapt in him, not because he had slain the great grey leader, but of all unlikely reasons, because a lamb had come unscathed into the world.

It was the last thing he knew with any clearness for a long time.

14 The Warrior Scarlet

After that there was a time that Drem remembered only as a darkness and confusion, with two fires burning in it, one in his head and one in his shoulder. Sometimes the confusion thinned a little, and there were faces in it; his mother's face, and Blai's, and Midir the Priest's with its eyes like dark sunlight; and sometimes the face of Vortrix. But he knew that it could not really be so, because all those faces were of the Tribe, and something had come between him and the Tribe, between him and Vortrix – a kind of black gulf. He couldn't remember what it was, and always when he tried to, the confusion came back and all the faces were lost to him again.

And then, like someone waking from a sleep that has been uneasy and full of crowding dreams, he opened his eyes and knew by the angle of the sword of sunlight striking through the smoke hole in the crown of the roof, that it was evening; knew also that he was lying on piled fern, under deerskin rugs in his own sleeping stall, where he had lain before he went down to the Boys' House a whole lifetime ago – or maybe only yesterday. He felt quiet and clean, and he was sharply and shiningly aware of the delicate, fork-tongued flicker of the fire on the hearth, and the golden dust dancing in the beam of sunlight, and the little rhythmic sounds that meant somebody weaving – his mother, or Blai. The hairs of the dappled deer-skin were tickling his neck, and he made to thrust it down, finding to his surprise that he had barely the strength to fumble his hand clear of the folds. There was a swift movement beside him, and Blai leaned forward and did the thing for him. She bent closer a moment to look into his face, and then cried out something – he did not know what, but the sound of it was glad; and the sounds

of weaving stopped and next instant his mother was kneeling at his side, feeling his forehead, looking into his face with eyes that looked as though they were aching in her head, her bright, heavy hair bursting as always out of its net. 'Small cub! Heart-of-my-heart – ' She gave a little laugh that broke in the middle, and put down her cheek against his. 'You have me back. Soon, quite soon you will be well again.'

He tried to come up towards her, and press his face in the soft hollow of her neck as he had used to do when he was small. But at the first movement, pain tore at his shoulder, where the fire had been, and he realized that shoulder and breast were tightly bound. That must be where the wolf had mauled him. There had been a wolf – or was that only another dream?

Blai had risen, and brought a bowl from the fire, with warm,

strong broth in it, and his mother fed him, calling him all the while by the small soft names that the Women's side kept for the smallest of their children. And by and by, when he was already beginning to grow sleepy, she rose and went back to her weaving.

Drem lay still blinking at the disc of singing gold that was the sunset beyond the smoke hole. Then Whitethroat crawled up from where he had been lying at his feet, to thrust his muzzle under the palm of his lord's hand. Drem fondled the great rough head, drawing the twitching ears through his fingers with a small, sharp-edged pleasure in their warm, silken texture. Odd how soft the ears of even the harshest coated dogs were. 'Greetings, brother,' he said. He could hear the sounds of his mother weaving, and somebody scouring the cook-pots – that must be Blai – and the buzzing, sing-song snore of the Grandfather who must have fallen asleep over the fire after his supper, as he so often used to do. There were other sounds behind these, too, little formless, green, trickling sounds; a dripping under the eaves. An indefinable sense of relief and quickening reached him even under his piled deerskins and told him that at last the thaw had come.

The faint, familiar rattle of the loom weights teased at his ears. He wondered what his mother was weaving, and managed to turn his head to see. The big standing loom by the door had been set up afresh quite lately; there was a new piece of cloth just begun on it – scarlet cloth.

Was it for the Grandfather? Or for Drustic? he wondered. Drustic must have had the piece that she had woven for him, Drem, a year ago. Vaguely he seemed to remember something heard in one of his dreams: the Grandfather saying with the familiar, wide-nostrilled snort, 'Let you wait to see that the boy will live, before you set the loom up and maybe have your trouble for nothing!' But that did not seem to fit in anywhere;

and he was too tired to think it out, too tired and spent even to care that the scarlet could never be for him. He had spent so much caring over that, that his caring seemed to have grown numb.

All that he cared for now, was to sleep.

He slept that night, a long, dark sleep without dreams, and woke at dawn to hear the thaw still dripping under the eaves, and feel the life running back into his own torn and battered body, and with the life, old unhappiness, old complications that he did not want to look at as yet; the beginning of a half formed idea that there was something odd about his being in the home house-place at all.

But in a little, he slept again, while the rest of the household woke around him; and when he roused the second time, they had already scattered to the work of the day, Drustic to see to the beasts, his mother to the store shed, even the Grandfather gathering his huge frame together and hobbling out to see how much snow had gone from the world since yesterday. He was alone save for Whitethroat, and for Blai grinding the day's corn beside the doorway, until suddenly a pony whinnied in the entrance porch and somebody came ducking in over the threshold.

Drem turned his head towards the doorway, thinking to see his mother or Drustic; and saw instead Vortrix with something that looked like a brindled wolfskin under his arm.

He gave a little croaking cry, and fumbled his hand clear of the coverings, and next instant Vortrix had come striding across the house-place and flung down the bundle and was squatting beside him with Drem's hand in both of his. 'My brother – oh my brother, they told me that you were come back into your body.'

Drem looked at him, frowning a little. 'I thought – I dreamed – that you were here before.'

'One may dream many things, with a wolf-mauled shoulder such as that,' was all Vortrix said; but looking into his square steady face with the very blue eyes, Drem knew that it had not been a dream.

'That was a great fight – a great Wolf Slaying!' Vortrix said; and his eyes were shining. 'I shall not forget how we came down the slope at Whitethroat's tail – running we were, running until our hearts were like to burst – and saw you down there, with a whole pack it seemed upon you, and the snow trampled and scarlet as though two wolf-packs had fought there. Aiee! They speak your name round the fires in the village, these nights!'

Things came rushing back to Drem as he listened; things that had been hovering on the fringe of his memory since last evening, but they brought with them no triumph in his Wolf Slaying. He was too weak for triumph. 'Doli!' he said. 'What of Doli?'

'Doli went to his own place, back to the Earth Mother, five days since,' Vortrix said. 'The little man was worn through, and there was the breathing-fever on him.'

There was a small harsh pause; and then Vortrix laid Drem's gaunt hand back on his breast with a kind of clumsy gentleness, and took up the brindled wolfskin. 'See, I have brought you your wolfskin. I have scraped it and begun the curing, lest it should be beyond curing before you could come to it. But now it can wait until you are strong again to finish the task.'

Drem looked from him to the wolfskin and back again; and his heart began to beat heavily, unevenly, though he did not as yet understand – did not dare to understand. Vortrix was brushing aside the harsh, brindled hair at the shoulder of the pelt, high up near the base of the neck, showing him a scar that there was on it, a place where the hair had not grown again over an old wound, saying something about his own wolf. 'It is your own wolf!' Vortrix was saying. 'Your own wolf! Here is the mark from the first time!'

Drem stared at the puckered, hairless line on the pelt, and his hand on the soft deerskin coverings clenched into a fist. 'I did not so much as scratch the hide of my wolf.'

'Na,' Vortrix said, 'but I did. A brindled dog wolf, and I wounded it here, high on the shoulder; here where I found the scar when I came to flay this one, nine days since!'

They looked at each other with the great wolfskin lying half across Drem's body between them. And Drem's hand crept down to rest on the harsh hairiness of it. 'It was between him and me in the first place. My heart is glad that I have slain my wolf, even though – it is too late.'

Vortrix said, 'It is not too late. Do you not see that there is scarlet on the loom for you already?'

Drem stared at him, his breath caught in his throat. Vortrix could not really have said that; it must be that he was still dreaming ... But Vortrix was saying it again, bending close over him, suddenly ablaze with his own eagerness. 'I thought they would have told you! Wake up, Drem, you have slain your wolf, and your place waits for you among the New Spears!'

Drem shook his head, denying it because he did not dare to believe it. 'Many times the Half People kill their wolves as I killed that one. There can be but one Wolf Slaying, and – I failed in mine.' His voice dried up into a cracked whisper. 'It is not true; it could not be true.'

Neither of them was aware that Blai had left her grinding and stolen out like a grey shadow, leaving them alone. They had not noticed that she was there. And the only sound in the world was the drip of the thaw under the eaves.

'I am your blood brother, not your sorest enemy,' Vortrix said at last. 'Why should I tell you this thing if it were not true?

Listen, Drem. Three days since, it was spoken of round the
Council Fire. It is true, I swear to you by – my own spear hand
that it is true.'

And Drem knew that it was so. He reached out and caught
the other's wrist, straining up from the piled fern, heedless of
the pain that clawed at his breast and shoulder. 'How then – ?
I – I do not understand. Tell me what passed at the Council
Fire – all that passed – '

Vortrix pressed him back again. 'Let you lie still; if you
burst the wounds, I shall be blamed . . . See then; when I had
flayed the wolf and found the scar on it, then I went to Dumnorix my father, and showed him the scar as I have showed it
to you.' Vortrix grinned. 'It is useful, now and then, to be the
Chieftain's son. And my father laughed that great laugh in his
chest, and said, "Sa. The cub was always a fighter, from his
first day in the Boys' House, as I remember; and the Men's side
may have need of its fighting men one day." And so when the
Spring Council gathered three nights since, he took and showed
the pelt to the Men's side of the Clan, beside the Council Fire,
and said, "See, the Shining One has sent to Drem One-arm his
Wolf-Slaying again, and this time he has not failed!" Then there
was much talk, and some among the elders said – even as you –
that there can be but one Wolf Slaying. And at last the thing
went to Midir where he sat gone-away-inside-himself beside
the fire. So Midir came back and looked out of his eyes again,
and said, "I have seen the wounds in the boy's shoulder; they
cover the scar of that first Wolf Slaying, so that the scar of that
first Wolf Slaying is no more. The thing was not finished, and
now it is finished; therefore let one among you be found to
stand for the boy, beside Cathlan his Grandfather, on the Day
of the New Spears, for the Sun Lord and the Lords of the
Tribe and the Hunting Trail have shown that they would have
it so." And truly I think that there would have been more than

one come forward to stand with Cathlan; but before any other man could move, Talore sprang up – you know how swift he is, like a wild cat when it springs – and stood there before the Clan, smiling so that his lip curled up over those great strong dog-teeth; and he cried out: "Seven summers ago, I found the boy curled under the roots of an oak tree, like a wolf cub himself, far into the Wild, where he had run from his own kind, fearing to fail in this very thing; a small, hairless cub and very much afraid, but fierce even then, and bit my finger to the bone before I had him out of his lair. Because he was small and valiant, and one-handed even as I am myself, my heart turned to him; and I promised him that night that when he had slain his wolf and the time came for him to stand before the Clan on the day of New Spears, I would stand for him beside Cathlan his Grandfather. Therefore the thing was settled seven summers ago." (You never told me that, Drem.) And then all the elders – all the Men's side looked at each other and nodded their heads, and said, "Aiee! It is well!" And Maelgan and I and the rest of us drummed our spears on our shields and made a great noise – and so the thing was done.'

Drem lay with his eyes fixed on the other's face, trying to lay hold of what had happened and draw it in and make it part of himself. He began to laugh at Vortrix's attempt to mimic Talore's swift dark vehemence; and then, because he was to be let in to his own world after all, returned to the company of his own kind after all, and because he was very weak, found the laughter breaking in his throat, and hid his face in his sound arm and cried.

The days went by, and Drem grew steadily stronger. Every third day Midir came and pointed the Fingers of Power at the wounds in his breast and arm and shoulder, driving new life into them; and his mother and Blai dressed them with salves made of yarrow and comfrey and the little pink centaury that grew on the High Chalk, reciting the proper charms over them as they did so, so that they healed cleanly, leaving only the puckered, thunder-purple scars behind. There was a third woman in the house-place, these days, for Drustic had brought home the plump, pink Cordaella to be his wife; but she took no part in tending Drem. It was not that she was unwilling, but the only time she tried to bring him his food bowl, Blai took it from her, showing her teeth like a young vixen; so that Drem, watching in bewilderment, thought that he had been wrong in hoping that Cordaella would be kind to Blai, he should rather have hoped that Blai would be kind to Cordaella.

As soon as he was strong enough, he crawled out to sit in the sunshine before the house-place doorway, and work at his wolf-skin pegged out on the ground there, curing it with herbs crushed in salt, and working in grey-goose grease until it was as supple as the finest deerskin. He wanted to be quiet, in those spring days, while suddenly there were washed-faced primroses in the hollow banks of the driftway, and the alders by the brook were dropping their little dark catkins into the water; he wanted a kind of threshold time between one thing and the next.

There was something else, besides his wolfskin, that he must have ready before the time came for him to stand with the New Spears before the Clan. And one evening when the supper stew was finished, he took down from its place among the smoky rafters, the heavy bronze and bull's-hide shield that had been the Grandfather's and would be his after all when the Feast of Beltane was over; and squatting beside the low fire with the rest, fell to fixing the shoulder harness of pony-hide straps, such as he had carried his buckler on in the Boys' House.

The Grandfather, looking up for a while from his bygone battles in the fire, eyed him as he worked, with a grudging interest that increased until he was leaning far forward to see more clearly how the straps went. 'Sa, this is a cunning thing,' he said at last. 'I see – ah, I see. Not even Talore carries his shield that way.'

'No need,' Drem said round the strap he held in his teeth. 'Talore has his shield arm almost to the wrist.'

The old man glanced up at him under the shaggy, grey-gold jut of brow. 'Why did you never tell me of that promise between Talore and you, seven summers ago?'

Drem did not answer at once. There were hard and hurting things that he could have said to the Grandfather about that. Once he would have said them, but not now. He spat out the strap and turned the buckler round to come at it from the other side. 'It is good to have a secret, when one is small. With a secret in one's chest, one feels larger.'

Drustic, mending a piece of plough harness, looked up with his slow grin. 'There was never anything needed to make you feel large, little brother.'

'Surely the cub who comes behind so fine a brother as mine – with so long a whip – has need of *anything* that makes him feel larger,' Drem said with an answering grin. 'Let you throw me over that piece of thong.'

And then it was the day before Beltane. Time for Drem to go down to the Boys' House. He did not eat when the rest of the household ate that morning; for a New Spear must go fasting to his initiation. He washed all over in the brook, a ritual washing, and came up naked and shining and scarred, to stand beside the hearth stone, while his mother and Blai belted on his new kilt of scarlet cloth – Warrior Scarlet; he felt it lapping about him like a flame – and settled the finely dressed wolfskin over his shoulder, belting that also about his narrow waist with a strap of leather dyed violet blue and bright with studs of bronze, and combed his hair and bound it back with thongs; so that when all was done he stood up like a warrior for battle, but with no war paint on his face, and no weapon in his hand. He looked up and saw the Grandfather's shield hanging in its usual place. Tonight they would take it down and lay it beside the hearth with his new war spear that he had not yet seen; tonight when he was – where? No one who had been that way before him, not Drustic, not even Vortrix, could tell him. They were bound by the oath of silence, as tomorrow, he also would be bound.

Blai was doing something to the fold of his wolfskin; he looked down at her, but saw only the top of her bent head, before she turned away without looking up. She never looked at him now. She had stopped looking at him when he began to get better. She did anything he wanted, willingly, but she didn't look at him any more, and he felt vaguely hurt.

But now it was time for him to go. He knelt and set his hand on the Grandfather's thigh as custom demanded; and as custom demanded, the old man put his huge, blue-veined one over it and said: 'Go forth a boy and come home a warrior.' Then his mother kissed him on the forehead with the same words, and took him to the threshold and sent him out with a light blow between the shoulders. Whitethroat followed him as usual; and at the foot of the driftway he parted from the great hound as he had done so many times before, and went on to the Boys' House alone.

There was a little wind running through the grass, and the hawthorn bushes of the lower slopes were in flower, the scent of them coming and going like breath, and a small brown bird flashed through the alder brake ahead of him. It seemed to Drem suddenly that the world was very kind. He had known its beauty often; a fierce and shining beauty like that of his great white swan, but he had not had time for the kindness. After this, maybe he would not have time for it again, but he thought that he would not quite forget . . .

He had been wondering what it would be like in the Boys' House, with the New Spears who were not of his year at all, but the year behind him. But he found that his name had become great in the Boys' House, greater even than after he fought Bragon's Hound at the King-making; and his companions were more interested in the purple scars on his shoulder than in the fact that he belonged to last year. But they had none of them much time or thought to spend on anything save what lay before them.

There were long rituals of strengthening and purification to be gone through under the eye of old Kylan; and Kylan himself painted the white clay patterns of initiation on their foreheads. And when all was done and made ready, they sat in silence about the low fire in the Boys' House, from which the younger boys had been sent away, listening to the sounds of life going on in the village around them; and even Vran, the stupidest of them, was afraid.

At last the sounds of life began to fall away, and in the quiet a distant voice or the barking of a dog sounded unnaturally loud. They heard feet and then more feet going down towards the centre of the village. And then Kylan rose and ranged them before him and looked them over with those wolf-yellow eyes of his, and said: 'So, it is time. Remember the things that I have taught you, children.' And to Drem he said: 'You also, who have already had a year to forget them.'

And they ducked out through the low doorway, and stood blinking in the sudden blast of sunlight after the gloom of the Boys' House.

The familiar ritual that came then seemed not quite real to Drem, like an echo of something real that had come before. He saw the faces of the Clan as the line of New Spears went winding down towards the space beside the Council Fire. He saw the Chieftain's face and the Priest's face with the sun behind its eyes; he heard the ritual questions and the ritual answers.

'Who is this that ye bring before me?'

'It is a boy that he may die in his boyhood and return a Warrior to his Tribe . . .'

But he had lived through it all so vividly, a year ago, that now it seemed to have little meaning, less reality than the pressure of his own spear shaft against his forehead as he crouched in the alder brake . . .

And now, one behind another, looking neither to right nor left, they were following Midir out from the village and away up the long slope into the eye of the setting sun, while behind them the women raised the death chant, 'Ochone! Ochone!'

The fires of the sunset still flamed behind the Chalk as they came up over the broad shoulder of the Hill of Gathering, passing close by the grave mound of the champion who slept on its crest, and dipped down again on the far side towards the hollow place among the hills where the warriors of the Tribe were made. And the hollow was brimming with shadows, so that as they looked down the ancient turf circle with its nine thorn trees seemed drowned in them as though it lay under water. They dropped down out of the sunset into the shadows that rose about them and closed over their heads.

The place seemed empty of all life; lost in its own solitude. But as they drew near a horn brayed somewhere ahead of them from within the thorn trees, and out of the shadows there sprang up smoky golden light; and out of the brightness figures came filing to meet them. Naked and golden in the light of the torches, hooded with the heads of animals; the animals that the Tribesmen hunted – the wolf, the wild, black boar, the red fox and the brindled badger. They closed round the boys in

silence, and turned back with them towards the half moon of
piled brushwood that had been set up screening the entrance
to the sacred circle.

Here there was a kind of low bier of turfs spread with a huge
red oxhide, and still without a word, they took the youngest of
the New Spears and laid him upon it as for sacrifice. One with
the head of a badger took up something that lay beside the bier,
and for an instant Drem's breath caught in his throat. Then he
saw that it was only a wooden haft set with slim bright pins of
bronze, and realized that this must be the time and place to
receive the warrior tattooing of the Men's side.

It was a long time before it came, last of all, to Drem's turn;
and when he flung back the wolfskin from his shoulder and
gave himself proudly into the hands of the tattooers, it had
grown quite dark, and looking up past the tawny flare of the
torches and the snarling masks of those who bent over him, he
saw the stars very far off and uncaring, and already, behind the
Hill of Gathering, the silvery snail-shine spreading before the
rising moon. The man with the badger's mask took up his tools
for the seventh time, and began to paint the zigzag and flowing
lines on the skin of his breast and shoulders with a wisp of
sheep's wool dipped in his woad pot, and then to prick along
them with the sharp bronze pins, grinding in more woad as he
went. It felt like being stung by a crawling trail of insects, and
where the lines crossed the newly healed scars the insects
became hornets, and it was all he could do, lying there with

shut teeth, not to flinch under the small, merciless, stinging points. And all the while he was knowing that this was the easy part; that the real thing, the dark and terrible and shining thing was yet to come.

Save for that first blaring of a war horn as they drew near the Holy Place, complete silence had held the scene; not even a night bird's call or the whisper of a little wind over the turf to break the stillness; but now Drem became aware of a sound – no, a sensation rather than a sound, a rhythmic pulsing that might almost have been his own heart. But even as he listened, it grew and strengthened, changing – changing – from a pulse beat to a fierce, confusing rhythm that made Drem think of that harvest magic of the Dark People, beaten out with an open hand on the sheepskin drums. It never grew loud, that drumming, but moment by moment it became more intense, more potent, until it seemed to Drem to be inside himself, in his head, in his heart, so that he could no longer think clearly, like a man who was drunk with much mead.

He was vaguely aware of getting up from the bier and standing with the other New Spears, the proud new patterns smarting like fire on his breast – on all their breasts, for while the drumming lasted they all seemed to be part of each other, so that each felt the sting of the others' wounds and the sharp, confused fear in the others' hearts – and then, suddenly, as though it had been cut by the swift downward flash of a sword-blade, the drumming stopped, and there was silence again; silence that was more potent, more clearly and irresistibly a call than any blare of war horns could have been.

The New Spears looked at each other, their blood jumping oddly within them. And while the silence yet seemed to tingle, two of the beast-headed figures took the youngest of the New Spears and led him to the shielded entrance of the sacred circle, and in a while came back alone.

Then the drumming started again.

Again and again came the tingling silence, and each time another of the New Spears went away into the sacred circle, and none of them ever came back.

And then the drumming ceased for the last time of all, and the call was for Drem. He stepped forward, with a sense of moving in a dream, the two beast-headed figures on either side of him, out from the shelter of the brushwood curve, and turned to the entrance of the sacred circle. There was light, a smoky dazzle of torchlight among the thorn trees; he glimpsed figures like the figures of a dream – beast-headed as the others had been, striped badger mask and upreared antlers and snarling grey wolf muzzle – and the torchlight under the thorn trees making the white blossom shine against the moony darkness, and the sparks flying upwards. But his whole awareness was caught and held by the tall figure of Midir the Priest, naked as the rest, and crested with the folded wings of the golden eagle, standing in the midst of the circle, in the very heart of the brightness. He was no longer aware of the men on either side of him, not aware of walking forward, until suddenly he was close before Midir; not aware of anything but Midir's eyes.

But Midir's eyes, that were like dark sunlight, were no longer eyes at all. They had contracted to two pin points of intense yellowish light, and the light ate into his very soul . . . Yet even as he gazed and gazed, his whole spirit caught up and held powerless, they were eyes again; yet such eyes as he had never seen before. Eyes that burned with a fire beyond fire, a blasting and shrivelling glory; and he was aware of a face growing up around them, and a figure, but not Midir's. He had forgotten Midir. This was One who leaned on a spear as vast as the shaft of light when the sun strikes through storm clouds. And the face –? Afterwards Drem only remembered that looking into it was like trying to look into the sun at noonday. He was aware of a shining and unbearable glory, a power that seemed to beat about him in fiery waves; and he knew in a moment of terror and ecstasy that he was looking into the face of the Sun Lord himself, which no man might see and live. The voice of a thousand war horns rang in his ears, and he was flying forward, plunging, swooping like a hawk, like a shooting star, into the heart of the singing brightness, the heart of all things.

15 The Flower of the Sun

The warmth of the sun was on his body, and above him great grey and white clouds were drifting across a sky that had in it already a hint of evening. There was a lazy, blustering wind blowing – a south wind, it must be, for there was the salt of the sea in it: the honey of hawthorn flowers in it too, and garlic, which was odd and did not seem to fit with the rest. He felt as though he had been on a very long journey; so weary that he wanted to do nothing ever again but go on lying on his back and staring up past the lazy clouds into the blue heights of heaven. But he had a feeling that somebody had called him by name, and he stirred himself to look about him.

He was lying at the heart of the ancient circle, and the other New Spears with him; lying with their feet to the centre and their heads towards the ring of thorn trees, like the rays of a seven pointed star. And instantly he remembered the splendour and the terror that had been. The warrior patterns on his breast and shoulders were sore and stiff, and as he moved, a knot of dried garlic flowers fell from his breast, where they must have been set to keep his body safe while he was away from it.

The others were stirring now, sitting up one by one and looking about them. Nothing remained of last night's mystery; no beast- and bird-headed figures among the thorn trees; no smoky blaze of torches; nothing left of the supremely beautiful and terrible moment when each had looked into the face of the Shining One – only Midir the Priest, sitting peacefully under one of the thorn trees and gone away small inside himself, with his bull's-hide robe about him and his thin, grey hair wisping out in the wind from under the eagle head-dress, and the amber sun cross on his breast catching and losing the light with his old, quiet breathing, and a few fallen hawthorn petals lying in his lap, as though he had sat there unmoving all night.

Then as they stirred and rubbed their eyes and looked about them with an air of having lost something, the old Priest stirred also, looking out of his eyes again, and brought out from under his cloak a bowl of black lathe-turned shale. 'Sa, it is over,' he said, and smiled a little, the bowl between his hands. 'Come now to me, ye who return again out of the West, new and weak as thy mothers brought thee into the world aforetime. Come now and drink, and grow strong again.'

One after another, still a little dazed, they got themselves to their feet and went to him, and took the bowl he held up, passing it among themselves from one to another. There was milk in the bowl, and other things in the milk. What they were Drem never knew, things that tasted bitter, with an under-taste that clung evilly to the back of one's throat after the milk was swallowed – but new strength ran through him as he drank, and some of the weariness fell away.

'Now ye are warriors and men of the Clan, and of the Tribe,' Midir said when they had all drunk. 'Now ye have seen those things which are forbidden to all save the Priest kind and the warrior at his initiation, and which none may speak of afterwards. Therefore now ye shall swear the silence, by the ancient threefold oath of the Golden People, that no boy not yet come to his manhood shall ever learn from you the things that lie before him.'

And so, each in turn, kneeling before the old priest, they swore, just as the warriors had sworn fealty to the new King. 'If I break faith, may the green earth gape and swallow me, may the grey seas burst out and overwhelm me, may the sky of stars fall and crush me out of life for ever.'

It was near to sunset again when they came down the last sloping shoulder of the Chalk towards the village, following

Midir, one behind another; and their long shadows ran away before them, pointing the way home.

The village was swarming with life, the poor thin sheep and cattle left from the famine winter all driven in close to wait for the Beltane fires. As the New Spears drew nearer, suddenly the voice of a war horn rang to and fro between the hills, and a throng of young warriors burst out from among the huts and came, tossing up their weapons as they ran, to close around the New Spears and swing back with them, shouting and chanting, towards the village.

How often Drem had seen this triumphal return of the New Spears that was the start of the Beltane Festival. How often he had looked forward to the fierce and shining day when he would be one of those for whom the Clan roared in their rejoicing. Then had come last year; last year that was not good to think about; and now, after all, against all seeming possibility the fierce and shining day had come, and he was returning out of the Sunset like a warrior from victory. And he cried out inside himself, 'It is real, it is true! I am a warrior like my brothers,' and could not quite believe it.

Afterwards, that sunset time, the final ceremonies of his initiation remained with Drem only as a blur, shining but without form; but out of it stood up small, clear-edged memories. He remembered the heat of the Council Fire on his cheek as he stood beside it to receive his weapons. He remembered the Grandfather towering over him as he towered over most people when he cared to stand erect, setting the great new war spear in his hand with a grumbling, 'There, take it. Did I not always say that the boy would make a warrior?' and a golden glare under his eyebrows for anyone who dared to contradict him. He remembered Talore's swift, dark smile lifting his lip over the strong dog-teeth as he raised the ancient bronze and bull's-hide shield. 'Small fierce cub, was it well that

I found you under the oak tree, seven summers ago?' And the proud smart of the shoulder harness as the heavy shield dragged its straps down on the lately healed wolf scars and the sore new lines of tattooing. He remembered the flash of his spear blade as he tossed it up in salute to the setting sun, and brought it crashing across his shield. He remembered Whitethroat's growling song of gladness at finding him again, and the taste of the piece of rib that he and Vortrix shared between them, sitting shoulder to shoulder, when the ceremonies were over, and the cooking pits had been opened, and the feasting began.

But Drem was to remember the day of his Warrior Scarlet for another thing; a thing that he did not as yet dream of, as the dusk deepened into the dark, and the Council Fire sank to red embers.

Save for the Council Fire, all the fires in the village had been quenched before the feasting started, and when that too had sunk, and the last red embers been scattered and stamped out under the heels of the young warriors, the village was a village without fire, dark save for the glow of a great, broom-yellow moon just shaking clear of the Chalk.

With the dying of the last fire, the Feast of New Spears was over, and the Feast of Beltane was begun; and it was time to raise the New Fire, the Living Fire. A strangeness came over the village, as it came every year between the fires; and it was in silence and a breath-caught expectancy and something very like fear that presently they laid aside their weapons and Clan and Half People together wound their way out of the village and up the Hill of Gathering, driving with them a young red bull garlanded for sacrifice with vervain and green broom and whitethorn blossom.

They thronged the crest of the hill, a crowd of shadows touched by the silver of the moon, no sound among them save the wind hushing through the furze and whitethorn bushes;

and in their midst the twin stacks of the Beltane fires, dark on one side, brushed on the other with that same silver of the moon, waiting as the whole night waited, for the Wonder.

Now the red bull who must die for the rest of the herd had played his part, and certain of the warriors were laying aside their cloaks and stepping forward to the trailing raw-hide ropes of the fire drill that stood reared beside the stacks.

On and on, as the moon rose higher into the glimmering, wind-streaked sky, they worked the fire drill, one team of nine taking over as another tired, while Midir, with the blood of the red bull on his breast and forehead, stood by to add his magic to their labour. Team followed team, while the whole aware-ness of the watching crowd, blent into one spearhead of intense concentration, was fixed upon the dark point where the sharp-ened spindle whirled in its socket, every soul waiting, waiting for the Wonder, half fearful, as they were half fearful every year, that this year the Wonder would not come.

Always the New Spears and the youngest warriors tried to hang back till towards the end, each eager to be in the team that actually woke the spark; and several teams had followed each other, when Drem, standing by among his own year, felt Vor-trix's hand on his shoulder. 'See, they are beginning to tire,' Vortrix said, 'and it is in my mind that the fire is not far off. Our turn now, my brother. Urian – Maelgan –'

They stepped forward, the rest of last year's warriors with them, and three of the New Spears, to make up the team; each taking up his stand beside one of the toiling men. The hide ropes changed hands, the old team fell back, and Drem and Vortrix, facing each other through the dark framework, with the rest ranged behind them, took up the swift, rhythmic pull and release, pull and release, the long step forward and the long swing back, that set the fire drill spinning. The hide rope thrummed under Drem's hand, the whirring squeal of the drill was in his ears, and the sense of being one with his own kind again, joined with his Spear Brothers in this, that was the very life and death of the Clan, rose hot in his breast until he felt it pressing out against the smarting patterns of his new manhood. He had tried so hard, down there through the ceremonies by the Council Fire, to believe in what was happening, and somehow never quite succeeded. And now suddenly it was all real and came piercing home to him, and he could have wept, as he had wept when Vortrix first told him that he was to be let into his own world after all.

In the same instant he caught the smell of charring, and from the sharp nose of the spindle a thread of smoke wisped up into the moonlight.

His eyes flew to meet those of his blood brother, as Vortrix also looked up; and in the hushed moment the excitement and the triumph and the swift, awed delight leapt between them like a shout. They were together in this thing, and the Wonder was coming, and it was good – everything was good. Instinctively they quickened the rhythm of the pull, and the squeal of the drill grew higher and more urgent.

The thread of smoke had become a whisping frond, a feather; suddenly a spark flew out to fall upon the dry moss with which the socket was packed, cling there an instant like a red jewel, and go out. Another followed, and another; and a soft, long-drawn gasp of relief and exultation burst from the watching throng as a little clear tongue of flame sprang up, yellow as a broom flower in the moony darkness.

Old Midir stirred as one rousing quietly from a thousand-year sleep, and brought from within his bull's-hide robe a torch of plaited straw, and bent to dip it into the flame. Then, drawing himself erect, he began to whirl it in the air until it burst into swooping circles of fire, as though a bird of flame flew about and about his head. And his deep throbbing cry rang out over the Hill of Gathering. 'Fire is come again! Behold, O ye people, O all ye people, there is fire again in the world of man!'

This year also, the Wonder had come! Roar on roar of fierce rejoicing beat up from the crowd, and as the old priest went from one stack to the other, kindling them from the torch in his hand, they broke into the chant of the Reborn Fire. 'We were in darkness and fire came again to us, the Red Fire, the Red Flower, the Flower of the Sun . . .' The little fork-tongued flames ran crackling through the brushwood and laid hold of the bigger branches, flaring up to light the eager, crowding faces of Golden and Dark People, and the Half People between, to flicker in men's eyes and jink on copper arm-ring and bronze, leaf-bladed spear, and kindle the eyes of the hounds to green lamps against the moon-watered dark.

Higher and higher leapt the flames, sending their fierce and fitful glare far out over the Hill of Gathering, warming the threshold of the great, quiet mound where the nameless champion slept with his copper sword beside him. And with the flames, the crowd's excitement mounted too. The young warriors sprang forward and began to whirl and stamp in the fierce glare between the fires, to the rhythm that the girls clapped for them, until with a lowing and a trampling out of the darkness, the first of the driven herds came pelting up. And then a yet wilder turmoil broke out, a chaos of gaunt, up-tossed heads, horns flashing in the firelight, an uproar of shouting and bellowing, barking and bleating, as the terrified sheep and cattle were driven through between the fires by their yelling and laughing herdsmen, that they might be protected and made fruitful for the year to come. Lastly the half wild pony herds were driven through, the mares with their foals running at heel, in a flood of streaming manes and trampling hooves; and the tumult was ripped across by their terrified neighing.

The uproar was sinking a little, by and by, when Drem, re-

turning from helping to gather in some of the ponies, caught sight of little dark Erp on the edge of the fire glow, with the dog Asal beside him. 'Erp!' he called. 'Erp!' and turned in his tracks, threading his way towards him through the shifting throng of men and beasts.

The boy stood to wait his coming, but did not look round. And when they stood side by side, he asked: 'Well then, what is it that you want with me?'

Drem looked at him, half puzzled, half already beginning to understand, while Asal and Whitethroat sniffed muzzles in the way of old friends. 'You have the dog, then,' he said at last. It was not what he had meant to say.

'Aye, I have the dog.'

Drem waited a moment, then, as it seemed the other had nothing more to say: 'Let you tell me of Doli.'

'Doli is gone back to the Dark. There is no more to tell.'

Another pause, full of the shouts of men and the lowing of scattered cattle – a fine job it would be to get them rounded up again. Drem looked down, a frown between his coppery brows, at the boy beside him. But Erp's face was shut fast in the fire-light, his own gaze caught between the pricked ears of his dog.

'At least let you tell me where they have laid him,' Drem said.

The little dark shepherd looked up then, looked him full in

the face for almost the first time in their lives, then let his gaze slide downwards. 'What is it to the Golden People where Tah-Nu's children lay their dead?' He whistled Asal to heel, and turned away about the business of the sheep.

Drem made a swift movement as though to catch him, then checked. What was the use? He shrugged and swung on his heel – to find himself face to face with Luga standing close by and looking on. 'Even the great Drem One-arm cannot hunt in two worlds at once,' Luga said.

'If Luga viper-tongue does not have a care, he will not hunt long in any world!' Drem retorted furiously, and thrust past him with his nose in the air, and went shouldering back to the fire.

The flames were sinking, and the warriors and their women who wished for sons in the coming year had for the most part already leapt hand in hand through the fire; and now some of the young warriors who had no wives as yet had begun to take the girls of their choice out of the Women's side – girls with star-wort and the magic vervain in their hair – to leap with them for the same purpose. Just as Drem reached the forefront of the crowd again, Vortrix had pulled out from among her own kind a tall, laughing girl with bright hair round her head. They cleared the fire easily, the girl shrilling like a curlew, and scattered a few hot embers on the edge as they landed. And

Drem, watching, thought that little Eyes-and-Ears had spoken the truth; she was indeed fair, the girl that Vortrix had under his cloak.

And now, before the fire sank too low, it was time to be taking home the New Fire to rekindle the dark hearths for another year; and in ones and twos the youngest grown men in every household began to come forward to take their fire; those whose homes were in the village merely dipping a branch into the flames and running with it streaming out in rags of smoking brightness behind, while those whose homes were the outland farms and the herdsmen's and shepherds' bothies among the Chalk took carefully chosen embers and stowed them in firepots. It dawned on Drem, watching, that it was no longer for Drustic to carry home the New Fire, but for himself.

He went in search of the Grandfather to tell him.

He found the Grandfather sitting defiantly on a pile of cut turfs, with a horn of heather beer on his knee, with Drem's mother and Cordaella hovering over him, and Drustic standing by at a safe distance. 'You should come home now,' Drem's mother was saying. 'It grows late, and so much heather beer is not good for your belly. You will be ill, and then I must tend you.'

The Grandfather was scowling at all of them under his thick, grey-gold brows. 'I am old, and it is not good for my belly that I do not have what I wish! What I wish is to be left in peace to enjoy myself, on this, the night that the youngest son of my youngest son becomes a man. The Fire will burn for a long while yet. Woman, I shall remain here so long as I choose, and *when* I choose, then Drustic shall bring me home. Let Drem go now and carry home the New Fire, that the hearth may be bright when I choose to come!'

And so in a little, Drem was loping back along the moonlit flanks of the Chalk, with the red seeds of the New Fire glowing in the fire-pot his mother had given him, under his wolfskin.

The steading lay quiet in the moonlight as he came up the driftway between the little irregular barley plots, pausing once to blow gently on the glowing embers in his fire-pot. As he came through the gate gap in the steading hedge, he saw Blai in the house-place doorway, sitting sideways against the rowan wood doorpost, with her head drooping as though she were very tired. He had forgotten that she must be at home; he had not missed the sight of her among the other girls about the Beltane fires. The wind fell away between one long, soft gust and another, and in the moment's stillness the shadows and the moonlight were sharply pied as a magpie's feathers; the shadows of the birch tree lay all across the threshold, across Blai's skirt and her hands that lay palm upward, empty, in her lap.

Whitethroat padded ahead, across the moon-washed garth, and thrust his muzzle against her neck, and she started and looked up, then rose to her feet. She had taken off the woollen net that usually bound her hair, and it hung about her neck and shoulders like black smoke. There were no flowers in it, no star-wort nor magic vervain. 'Drem,' she said, a little questioningly.

'I have brought the New Fire,' Drem said.

'Where are the others?'

'The Grandfather would not come away yet. They will be here in a while; but I have come now, to bring the New Fire.'

Not really aware that he did so, he held out the fire-pot towards her in a gesture of sharing. They stood with it between them, their heads bent to peer into it, like a pair of children holding a miracle cupped between their hands. The red seeds of the fire glowed in the darkness of the pot; Drem blew on them gently and the seeds brightened, casting a faint glow around them.

'Come, let us wake the fire on the hearth,' said Blai.

It was very dark in the house-place, with the moonlight shut out, a waiting darkness. They had to grope their way to the hearth. Kneeling beside it, Drem blew on the spark until it grew strong, and Blai dipped in a dry twig, and as they watched, suddenly there was a slender bud of flame at the tip of the twig. Then she kindled a piece of dry birch bark on the hearth, and then another and another, and dropped in the twig as the flame reached her fingers.

Drem blew on the little tender new flames, on the birch bark whose crumbling edges were suddenly strung with red jewels; then sat back on his heels, as the fire quickened and spread, watching the pale, eager tongues and petals of flame spring up out of the dark.

'It is like a flower,' Blai said very softly, feeding it with bigger and bigger bits of wood. 'A flower of the Sun.'

And they looked at each other, in the first firelight, both aware of having been joined in something potent and lovely.

'Blai,' Drem said after a while. 'Blai, why were you here?'

'I – saw you come back with the New Spears.' Blai set a piece of wild pear branch with infinite care in the midst of the fire. 'And then I came away. I had things to do.'

'What things could you do, without fire to see by?'

'The moon is very bright,' Blai said.

There was a small silence. The new flames fluttered on the hearth, and a long sigh of wind came over the shoulder of the Chalk and brushed across the thatch, and Whitethroat, who had settled himself beside the hearth, stretched out and began to lick his paws. At last Drem said: 'You were not doing anything when I came.' And then, as she still remained silent – 'Blai, why *did* you come away?'

She looked up then, but the stillness in her never stirred. 'What place have I yonder with the Women's side? I have no place among the maidens of the Tribe. I am not one with them, I am not one with the Half People either. It is better that I come away . . .'

It was as though her words called to something in Drem; something that called back in recognition and greeting. Suddenly he was aware of her as he had been only once before, but more strongly and clearly now, out of a new compassion, a new power of seeing that had grown in him through his outcast year: Blai, who was not quite a handmaid nor yet quite a daughter in his home, who had no dowry of cattle nor any beauty to take its place and make her desirable in the eyes of some young warrior. For a moment it was only compassion, and then quite suddenly and simply he understood that he and Blai belonged together, like to like; that no other girl could ever come as near to him as Blai could do, because she knew the things that he knew.

'They were still leaping through the flames when I came away,' he said; and then, as she did not answer, 'Vortrix leapt through with Rhun the daughter of Gwythno of the Singing Spear, when the flames still burned high, and neither of them was scorched. That means many sons for them by and by.'

Blai was watching him, but still she did not answer.

He drew his legs under him and made to rise. 'This fire is well enough now; if we bank it up, no harm will come to it. Blai, it may be that there will still be some fire left up yonder, if we go back now – if we run very quickly.'

Blai sat and looked at him, her face whiter and narrower than ever, in the black smoke of her hair. 'You are kind,' she said wonderingly. 'You did not use to be kind.'

He had sprung up, and taken a long pace towards the doorway, followed as ever by Whitethroat; but he turned, and stood looking at her across the hearth that was alive with fire again. He was understanding more things now. He was understanding

231

why Blai had not looked at him these past moons; that it was not that she hadn't looked at him since he began to get well, but that she hadn't looked at him except when he was sick since last sheep shearing. He remembered with sharp-edged clearness that small bitter scene at sheep shearing, and the white blind look on her face; the look that he had seen there once before – when the bronze-smith came with his magic dagger.

He thought he had left it too late. And as always with him, he met fear with anger. 'I am not kind!' He flung the word away as though it were a wasp that had settled on him, and swung round to the doorway; then checked again to look back at her. 'Well, are you coming, or is it that I must go back alone? There are other girls on the Hill of Gathering tonight.'

There was a sudden white flash of anger in Blai, answering his own as the fire in the grey dagger answered to the flint. 'Then let you take one of them to leap through the fire with you, my young Golden Lord!'

But Drem's anger had escaped him. He shook his head. 'I do not wish for any of them, Blai.'

She looked at him in silence, a long, clear look; and for a moment he was still afraid that he was too late. Then she smiled, and still without a word, began to tend the fire, so that it could be safely left. When that was done, she sprang up and came to Drem where he waited in the doorway; and he caught her hand in his sound one, and they ducked out into the moonlight and the blustering spring wind, and ran laughing, with Whitethroat at their heels, back towards the Beltane fires.

ABOUT THE AUTHOR

Rosemary Sutcliff was born in Surrey, the daughter of a naval officer. She was very ill as a small child, and as a result she had to spend several years on her back and was read to a great deal by her mother; from the age of five onwards she was enjoying the books of such authors as Dickens, Thackeray and Trollope, together with *Beowulf* and Greek and Roman legends.

She did not learn to read herself until she was nine, when she found that normal children's books were insipid reading. The family moved to a house in the Royal Dockyard at Chatham, and she was sent to a little dame school under the kindly eighty-six-year-old Miss Amelia Peck.

Apart from her own private and voracious reading, Rosemary Sutcliff made little progress with formal studies and left school at fourteen to attend the Art School in Bideford. Here she specialized in miniature painting and early in the 1940s exhibited her first miniature in the Royal Academy. She was elected a member of the Royal Society of Miniature Painters just after the war. In 1950 her first children's book, *The Queen Elizabeth Story*, was published, and from then on she devoted her time and talents to writing the children's historical novels which have placed her name high in the field of contemporary children's literature. Many of her books are set in Roman Britain, a period which particularly interests her. One of them, *The Lantern Bearers*, was awarded the 1959 Carnegie Medal.

Miss Sutcliff received the O.B.E. in the 1975 Birthday Honours List. She lives in a cottage in a Sussex village, and her pets include several dogs, pigeons and tortoises.

also by Rosemary Sutcliff

TRISTAN AND ISEULT

When the sailing weather came after the winter storms, Tristan, son of Rivalin King of Lothian, set out for Cornwall with his friends, little knowing what strange love and sorrow and tests of loyalty would be his in Cornwall, the land where he won Iseult of Ireland's love for himself, yet brought her back to be his uncle's Queen, weaving a story that would be sung and told throughout Europe for centuries to come.

This retelling of the old Celtic story is one of Rosemary Sutcliff's most memorable books, and one that pleases on many levels.

THE HIGH DEEDS OF FINN MAC COOL

In the proud and far back days, when Ireland was called Erin, there was a band of heroic warriors called the Fianna. Theirs was the task of guarding the shores of their country and controlling the blood feuds of the five kingdoms into which Erin was divided, and their most glorious time was when their leader was a hero named Finn Mac Cool.

DRAGON SLAYER
The Story of Beowulf

Lion-hearted Beowulf, the hero who had the strength of thirty men in his arms, sailed away over the whale road in his war-boat, his fast floater, to rid the Danes of their deadly scourge, the prowling monster who struck terror into the bravest warriors of Denmark as they waited night after night in King Hrothgar's court. Great glory came to Beowulf before he died, the renown from his three great battles, with Grendel and his fearful mother, and with the dragon who guarded the brilliant treasure-hoard hidden away in the earth.

This retelling of the Anglo-Saxon epic *Beowulf* is a story to feed the imagination powerfully, and fill the mind with a trembling awe.

... and some other Puffins

THE IRON LILY
Barbara Willard

'A year from now I'll be the Robber Queen!' cried Lilias on the day she fled from the home where she had suddenly learned she had no true place. Fifteen years old, her mother just dead of the plague, she was quite alone in the world, and on that day she started to grow up.

Lilias never became the Robber Queen but she worked and fought her way up until she was master of her own iron foundry in the Sussex Weald, and herself as strong as the metal she forged.

The fourth of the Mantlemass stories, set in sixteenth century England.

AN EDINBURGH REEL
Iona McGregor

It was six years since Christine Murray had seen her father go away, so proud in his tartan, and so sure that only a short campaign was needed to put a Stuart on the throne once more. But now she didn't even recognize the small, hesitant man, so downcast over his prince's defeat. And perhaps he was disappointed in her too – six years of poverty had changed her as well.

But Christine was too busy to spend time repining over lost property and the Jacobite cause – it was her father who refused to settle down, and he put both their lives in danger by his longing to regain the lost lands and his obsessive hatred of the unknown man who betrayed him after Culloden.

A splendid lively story set in the bustling overcrowded Edinburgh of the mid-eighteenth century.

VIKING'S DAWN
THE ROAD TO MIKLAGARD
VIKING'S SUNSET

Henry Treece

Jointly described as A Viking Saga, the three books were designed by Henry Treece to be read as a complete epic. They follow the life cycle of Harald Sigurdson from the time when, as a young boy, he joins the crew of a Viking ship and comes marauding to our shores in search of treasure, until his last 'sunset' voyage when, pursuing marauders who have broken the peace of his own country, the Viking longboat loses course and is obliged to make an epic voyage which takes them finally to North America.

'Vikings,' says a character in one of these marvellously exciting books, 'are tied to salt water as a prisoner is tied with chains. There's no understanding them, they are either madmen or heroes.'

Compulsive and worthwhile reading for anyone over nine.

THE MARSH KING
C. Walter Hodges

Mr Hodges continues the magnificent story of King Alfred which he began in *The Namesake*. In their war camp at Exeter King Alfred and the leaders of his army held council as to how they should deal with the Danish leader Guthorm and his Vikings whom they had surrounded. And the king said, 'Let them go back to their fellows in the north. Let them say that we in Wessex can afford to be generous because we are a strong nation and cannot be conquered.'

So Guthorm and his Danes went free, only to return and strike again in mid-winter, with a treacherous plot to kill the king.

If you have enjoyed reading this book and would like to know about others which we publish, why not join the Puffin Club? You will be sent the club magazine, *Puffin Post*, four times a year and a smart badge and membership book. You will also be able to enter all the competitions. For details of cost and an application form, send a stamped addressed envelope to:

The Puffin Club Dept A
Penguin Books Limited
Bath Road
Harmondsworth
Middlesex